The Resilient

Out of the Forbidden

To Becky
Hope you enjoy

Adam K. Ogden

Adam K. Ogden

This book is a work of fiction. Names, characters, places, and events contained therein are a product of the author's imagination. Any similarities to any events, places, or persons, living or dead, is strictly coincidental.

Second Edition. This book has been modified from its originally published version for edits of typographical errors and clarity.

Published by Breakpoint Publishing, LLC

www.breakpointpublishing.com

Breakpoint Publishing and associated logos are trademarks of Breakpoint Publishing, LLC

Front Cover Design by Adam K. Ogden
© 2017 by Adam K. Ogden

www.adamkogden.com

ISBN-13: 978-1-7329216-0-3
ISBN-10: 1-7329216-0-1

Be careful who you trust, for wolves lie in sheep's clothing, and lions are but little lambs...

Adam K. Ogden

1

I T WAS COLD THAT NIGHT. The fire was no more than an ember, and the supply of firewood was growing slim. *More will need to be cut in the morning*, Michael thought.

He pulled his jacket a little tighter around him. His clothes were tattered and had almost worn thin from taking care of his quaint home. He took it as his responsibility to make sure the day to day things ran as they should. Not that the others were counting on him to do so, he just enjoyed the work.

Michael never considered himself much of a leader, but he was willing to take care of the others with him. There were eight of them together in a small three-room shack they called home. It had once been a grand house, but the years were against it and most of the rooms had collapsed. A lingering scar from such a terrible war. Michael and his wife, Rebecca, had naturally emerged as the caretakers of the band of refugees hidden away within its walls.

Michael always looked up to his wife. Although he was intelligent by others' standards, his wife always seemed to have wisdom and insight into every situation. She was also the best cook of anyone he knew. He considered himself lucky to be living through these times with someone who was once a professional chef. The thought of food and all the meals she had cooked took his focus off the fire and onto the growing rumble from his stomach.

"Dear? How's dinner coming?" he called out to the kitchen through the rubble of what once was the dining room. The cool draft seeping through the boards nipped against his face.

"It'll still be a little while, sweetie," she replied.

"What are we having?"

"The usual. Mexican beans and beetles."

"Sounds delicious, just in mine can you hold the beans and hold the beetles?"

The thought of such meal genuinely repulsed him, but in these times, there was no use in being picky. Food choices were limited to what could be grown or killed, and supply for both was dwindling down to almost nothing. When he was younger, he had never dreamed his life would turn out this way. He had always seen himself living the city life. He could still remember glimpses of it looking out through the window of his classroom. He had always been serious about his job. As a chemistry professor, it was his duty to help the bright minds grow so that they may do something that would change the world. In all honesty, he wanted to be one of those, but it never seemed that he had the opportunity.

Although it wasn't the life he had planned, he did feel like he had a better sense of accomplishment. It wasn't the accomplishment of a goal like he had dreamed, but a fulfillment of purpose, nevertheless. His focus was on his survival and the care-taking of the others. It had also brought him a lot closer to Rebecca.

Back then, he had spent so much time working, she had taken a backseat in his life. Now they were working together to take care of her mother and all their friends. He was no longer tied to the day to day grind of trying to push ahead. At this point, he was happy just to wake up to another day.

Even though his childhood dreams seemed to be farther out of reach, his newfound purpose had allowed him to still be thankful. He was thankful for Rebecca for staying with him after all these years. He was thankful for the children they had together, wherever they may be. He was thankful that he was still alive and even had a place to call home. Most of all, he was thankful God had always been with him and held him even through his darkest times.

Rebecca would be proud of him for thinking that way. She was always the spiritual one of them. She would spend hours every day praying for him and those in their care. Humble and selfless were the two best ways to describe her. Her prayers were directed toward lifting him up and helping them find the guidance they needed. Even when times were trying and tore at her, those times that would cause even an old-time pastor to lose his hope and faith, she would stand firm and trust God. Michael admired her for that. Her faith stood as a rock of encouragement to him.

Such faith was a rare gem in these days, and it helped Michael to always keep hope. That in itself was rare. Michael wanted to believe that there was something out there that had a hand on his life. That somehow, in the end, everything worked out. When the government had outlawed everything to do with religion, hope seemed to have died with it.

Despite the law of the land, Michael tried to hold onto his beliefs. He mostly did so because of Rebecca's insistence. Even so, his faith wasn't comparable to that of his wife's. Maybe the reason was, although he had seen the powers of good, he had also seen the power of evil. The power of everything his entire existence seemed to be against. The power that could control even his own hands once. He began to shudder and pushed such thoughts and memories away from his mind as far as he could.

"You okay, Mike?"

The sudden voice invaded his thoughts. He looked around and saw Wesley staring at him from the corner of the room. He considered Wesley to be one of the closest friends he had. He and his wife had been with Michael and Rebecca for almost six years. He once was a police officer before the war that changed the world. He always carried with him a sense of strength and determination. Although it had been years since he had given up his profession, he still looked as if he could take someone down if needed. His muscles stretched tight the fabric of his shirt as he leaned over the small table in front of him. Michael noticed that he and several others had huddled together and started up a card game.

"I can't say I'm looking forward to beans and beetles either, but that wife of yours is one heck of a cook. She fixed some delicious squirrel skins earlier," Wesley said. He placed one hand on his stomach, and his mouth moved as if he could still taste it.

"Oh no, it's not that. I was just thinking," Michael said.

"Well snap out of it. Come join us and play a little rummy. We've only got thirty-eight cards, so it's kind of a challenge. We'll even be nice and tell you a few of the ones that we're missing."

Michael thought about it but decided against it. "I think I'll go check on the ladies in the kitchen. I hate for

Becca and Allie to be all alone in there. Besides, I am hungry."

He stood up and shuffled through the small passageway in the rubble of what once was the elaborate dining room. In its day, the house was rather exquisite. It had a grand living room with a fireplace, a dining room that could seat twenty people, and several other rooms. The house had belonged to Michael's parents. It was the house he had grown up in. His parents spent a lot of time there, throwing parties for various guests. They were well known throughout their community. When he was younger, he always hated having so many people in and out of his house. He would have never thought that its remnant would become a shelter to so many.

As he went into the kitchen, the sight surprised him. Instead of seeing his wife and daughter finishing up dinner, he saw Allie cleaning up the soup which had spread across the floor in all directions. Rebecca was nowhere to be found.

"Allie, what happened? Where's your mother?"

"Mommy's fine. That new lady was asking her a bunch of questions. She got really mad and ran down the stairs," she said, pointing to the stairway leading into the bedroom.

To his six-year-old daughter, she may have seemed fine, but Michael was concerned. It was unlike Rebecca to get mad at anyone, much less mad enough to waste the food that was so scarce to come by.

Without a second wasted, he ran across the kitchen. The bedroom was connected to the kitchen but had been built much lower than the rest of the house. A small stairwell ran along the wall down to it. Michael stepped through the doorway and saw Rebecca crying on the makeshift bed. Before he could take another step or even call to her, the other woman, Amanda, was in his face.

She was much older than Michael and Rebecca. The brown in her short, curly hair had almost been replaced by white. She looked as if she could be as old as his mother. Amanda had come to them two days ago. She had told them that she was in need of a place to stay for a few days and then she would be moving on. Rebecca had decided to make it a rule that anyone who came to them would always be welcomed and treated with kindness. Michael was uneasy about letting strangers in, but Rebecca reminded him that they were all strangers once. She had such a heart for people, regardless of what may happen. Her insistence persuaded Michael, and so he let Amanda join them. At that moment, he regretted that decision.

"You killed my son!" Amanda screamed at him, loud enough he was sure that everyone could hear.

"What are you talking about? I barely know you," Michael said out of sheer confusion.

"You were the reason my son died. You killed him."

"Ma'am, I have no idea what you are talking about. I only met you days ago, when you came to us for refuge. I don't even know who your son is." He was sure he had never met this woman before in his life. He searched the lines of her face for any sign of familiarity but found none.

"I have searched this world over to try and find you. You will pay for what you did to him. Don't pretend to be so ignorant. You killed Cade."

At the mention of that name, the memories flooded over Michael. He did know Cade. He knew him well. His death, however, was a distant memory. He couldn't remember it vividly. It was as if his mind was clouded. Michael searched for answers and told Amanda the only thing that seemed logical.

"Ma'am, I didn't kill your son. It had to have been an accident."

"First you say you don't know him, now you're trying to cop out and say he died in an accident. I know what happened, and I know you are lying. You can't even keep your story straight."

Amanda's anger toward him was apparent. She was very defensive and seemed to have her mind made up on Michael's guilt without hearing anything he had to say.

Michael tried to get through to her regardless. He concentrated as hard as he could on the memory. He remembered Cade had sent for him. He was supposed to meet him somewhere. The train station.

"I didn't know who your son was until you told me his name, and I am telling the truth. He died at the train station. It was an accident." Michael tried to remain calm to help defuse the situation, but the memory of that day made it difficult. Even more so because of its haziness.

Cade had been Michael's closest friend. He was a biology professor at the same university Michael worked at. He also joined the war with him, fighting alongside him. In all that time, he and Michael had gotten very close. Although his memory of Cade's death was spotty at best, he was sure it was an accident. There was no way he could have killed his friend.

"No. I know the truth," Amanda scoffed. "I received a letter from Metro Underground Security detailing everything."

"I don't know what that letter said, but I worked with Cade and served with him. Why would I want to kill him? Besides, that day at the train station was the first time I had seen him since the war. He had wanted to tell me something. I can't remember what it was, but I do know that it wasn't long after he just collapsed onto the tracks."

As painful as it was to relive the horror of that moment, he had to try to ease the tension between them. He thought he was getting through to her. She had begun looking down while he was talking. As his own memory was working its way back, he began to feel a little more confident in himself. The supposed letter concerned him, though.

Amanda was digging through a surprisingly pristine purse as he attempted to talk to her. His hopes of ending the argument dissipated when her eyes locked onto his. Up sprung her hand, holding a letter with some photos.

"I have the proof," she exclaimed.

Michael grabbed the so-called "proof" from her hand and began to look at the pictures. They were fuzzy but were clearly taken the day Cade died. He saw himself walking up to Cade next to the track at the station. The next one showed him with his finger pointed at Cade in anger, while he made a questioning gesture. Then one photo where both of his hands were at Cade's collar, pulling him in toward him.

The fourth photo was the one she was considering proof. He saw Cade falling helplessly onto the tracks as the oncoming train approached inches away. He saw himself with both arms outstretched toward him. From looking at the photo, it appeared as if Michael had pushed Cade into the oncoming train.

He was in shock. He could see why Amanda made the assumptions she had. If only he could remember it in more detail. No matter how hard he tried, he couldn't seem to break through the fog. He began to read the letter in an attempt to jog his memory.

Ms. Amanda Simon,

My name is Ben Rogers. I work for the Metro Underground Station as captain of the security guard. I am writing this letter to you today with information about your son's death. We have been working closely with the Federal Police on the investigation. The day in question, I was monitoring the activity near the tracks. I witnessed two men arguing, one of which has been identified as your son, Cade Simon.

When I noticed the argument, I began to go toward them to resolve the issue. As I got close, the argument became very heated. Then the assailant pushed Mr. Simon in front of the oncoming train before fleeing the scene. The photos I have sent with this letter are stills from the security camera that filmed the incident.

We have recently identified the assailant as Michael Anderton, a known terrorist at large. Despite reports to the contrary, we have yet to apprehend him. He managed to evade us, and the man we arrested that day was simply part of an elaborate plan of Anderton's. We know that he has prior history with Mr. Simon. We believe this is the reason for the altercation. It is our hope that if he has contacted you, you will aid us in bringing justice to your son.

Thank you,

Ben Rogers
Captain, Metropolian Underground Station

After reading the letter and seeing the photos, Michael's head was spinning. He was being accused of murder, and now there was evidence and a witness set against him. He knew the truth, or at least he thought he did. What he didn't know was why a security guard captain would make such an accusation.

He didn't push Cade. He was sure of it. But the photos and the letter made him doubt himself. He was certain that he didn't remember pushing him into the train, but he also couldn't remember how he fell. That part was still blank to him. His head kept spinning, and he began to feel dizzy. He pushed past Amanda and went down the stairs next to his wife. Rebecca looked up at him. Her eyes were red and swollen from crying.

"I know you, Michael. I've known you for a long time, before any of this even started. Before the suffering. Before the war. I've known you. I can't believe any of this. When she came to me trying to get me to incriminate you, I fought her. I fought her with all that I had. Then she showed me the letter and the pictures. Now I don't know what I know. I didn't think you had even gone to see him that day. I've sat here and prayed continuously seeking an answer, but none has come."

Her words cut deep. Not only had Michael's own faith in himself been shaken, but also the faith of his wife. If she couldn't believe in him, then what hope was there for him? He couldn't even believe in himself.

He was beginning to settle in his mind to just accept the punishment. Perhaps Amanda did know the truth. She had physical proof, and he couldn't even rely on his own memory of the incident. He feared what that meant for him. If she turned him over to the Federal Police, with the heinous crime of murder, they would sentence him to death. To even think that he had murdered his best friend in cold blood, though, was death itself. As he began to speak, to admit his guilt to the accusations, Rebecca spoke up again.

"I may not have an answer yet, but when I do, we'll make sense of this. I know how close you and Cade were, so I know there has to be a better explanation. I may not understand what's going on, but I believe this will work out. God knows the truth as to what happened that day, and that is good enough for me."

There was the Rebecca he knew. There was her surety. Her faith. Amanda couldn't shake it, even with physical evidence. Rebecca knew the truth, regardless of what anyone tried to say. Even if it were her own hopes that were saying it.

"Thanks for still trusting me," Michael said.

"Michael," she said. "I know this may be painful, but could you tell us what you remember about that day?"

Amanda scorned the idea. Her mind was made up. There was no use trying to change it, but Michael obliged to Rebecca's request, if nothing else, for his own peace of mind. He closed his eyes to concentrate. He was determined. He wanted to remember. Of all the horrible things he had done, he couldn't believe he had murdered Cade. He was sure he didn't, but he couldn't remember.

He remembered going to the train station. He remembered greeting Cade at the platform. He remembered him dying. Everything in between and everything after was blank. He cleared his mind and thought about what the letter had said. The pictures he had seen entered his mind. Then there was the answer as the images flooded in.

15

2

"HEY, MIKE," Cade mumbled as Michael approached. His nervousness was apparent. He was twitching, wringing his hands, and glancing in every direction. Michael had grown accustomed to his tension. He had been that way since the war. He was one of the unlucky few who never seemed to be able to return home from it. Michael had hoped this time it would have been different. He was hoping to see his old friend again. It was the first time he had seen him since the end of the war. Although Michael had gotten used to it, Cade's diligence to find him and his behavior made him feel uneasy.

"I'm so glad Trent gave you my message. There's something you've got to know, and it won't be easy to believe…" Cade took a breath, running both hands through his hair. He leaned in close and began whispering. "Everything you know, everything you believe…it's all a lie. None of it is real."

There it was—the same paranoid story he had heard a thousand times. Cade was no better now than he had been. Anger shot through Michael. Both hands snatched Cade's shirt. He didn't mean to be so angry at his friend, but there seemed to be no other way to get through to him. Michael was frustrated. He wanted nothing more than to have his friend back. He wanted to help him break through the paranoia he carried with him. It was that paranoia that had caused them to drift apart. Michael thought that he would be better over time. That he would be cured. He was obviously wrong.

"You need to snap out of it, Cade. There is no conspiracy. There is no big puppeteer in the sky pulling at the strings. Whatever the heck you believe is going on isn't being caused by anyone. That's not real. That's the only thing not real. I know the war was hard on you. I know we did things…terrible things, and maybe this is just your way of dealing with it. When Trent told me that you had spent the last few months in a hospital, I had hoped your stay had changed things. I had hoped they made you better."

"Hospital?" Cade snapped. "That was no hospital. That was a science experiment. I can prove it."

Michael threw Cade back and shoved his finger in his face.

"You need to get your head on straight. There are still people who care about you. Listen, I'm sorry you feel that way about it. I'm sure after these last two years, it may seem like it was far worse than it was. I'm sorry, too, that I haven't been able to see you in all this time. If I had known, I would have been there."

"Mike, listen to me. I'm telling you the truth. Come with me and let me show you."

Michael hesitated.

"Why can't you believe me?"

"Because the last time I saw you, you were on a self-destructive rampage. You were going on and on about how someone was using the war for their own personal gain. How everything that happened was being controlled by someone higher up. But the truth is, there is no conspiracy. What happened during the war happened because there was no choice. It was the only way to survive. You let the enemy into your head, and apparently, they've never left."

"Mike, I need you to trust me. I'm not crazy and I never was. Just get on the train with me. I can prove it to you."

"No, Cade. I don't have time to chase your wild fantasies. I've tried to go on living after the war. Me and Becca have a baby on the way."

"Mike, please. Just come with me. You, Rebecca...everybody... are all in danger. What we did is coming back to haunt..."

His words were cut off by a sound—a small gentle sound as if an insect had caught a gust of wind. There it was, the source of it. A tiny dart, no more than a half an inch long, was lodged in the side of Cade's neck. Its effects were almost immediately noticeable. His eyes rolled back, and his mouth drooped.

"Cade? What about what we did?"

Cade stumbled backward. One step. Two steps. He couldn't catch his balance. The train was approaching faster than usual. The whistle blew. Cade collapsed at the edge of the platform toward the tracks. Glass sprayed into the train as his lifeless body bounced upward against the sloped front of it and into the window.

"Cade!" Michael screamed at the top of his lungs.

He was running. He was reaching for his friend, trying to get there in time. He was too late.

Michael collapsed to his knees, sobbing. Cade was his closest friend. Closer than even his own brother had ever been. He couldn't believe he was gone. Michael's greatest hope was that one day he would get to come home from the war. One day get to be the Cade he had known.

To make it worse, Cade possibly had information about something important, and Michael was too stubborn to listen. Michael sat there trying to grasp the situation. Did Cade know something or was it all a part of his paranoia? Was he even that paranoid? He saw the dart with his own eyes. There had to be some kind of explanation. He couldn't fathom the thought of someone being deliberately out to attack Cade. The most probable solution was that some kind of insect coincidentally landed on him right before he fell. Even that didn't explain his collapse.

Michael glanced back over his shoulder. If someone had attacked his friend, he wanted to know who. There was no one there. They were alone on the platform. He went over every scenario in his mind, trying to find an answer to what had happened. Michael had always feared that what they had done in the war would come back to haunt them. The memory still haunted his dreams.

The more he thought about it, the more he wanted to believe Cade. He seemed so sure of what he was saying. He didn't speak like he was crazy, but more so of a man determined to be heard. Michael wished he would have given him a chance. Whatever it was that he had wanted him to see was somewhere along the way of the train. If he would have let Cade speak, he would have known what was coming and understood what he meant by everything being a lie.

Before he could think about it further, sirens resonated through the air. The sirens were so loud, they felt as if they were coming from his own mind. Their screams rang out louder than his thoughts. The sirens forced him up from the floor. As he stood, he noticed he was no longer alone on the platform. He was unaware that such a large crowd had formed around him, many out of curiosity as to what had happened. Some were throwing out accusations that Michael had pushed him. He saw station security taking statements from different witnesses. Some were trying to clear out people for the medical staff attending to passengers on the train. He saw Cade being closed up in a black bag. The horrid sight made his whole body shudder. Except for the few instigators dealing their accusations toward him, no one seemed to acknowledge his presence. Then he felt the hand on his shoulder.

"Sir, I'm Captain Rogers of Metro Underground Security. If you would, follow me to my office. I think it would be much better for you in there."

Michael turned his head back and noticed the short, balding gentleman behind him. He was wearing the standard green uniform of Metro Security, with his captain's pin proudly displayed on it. Michael nodded at the request and followed him through the crowd to a small office on the other side of the station. They sat down across from each other at a small table the captain had for a desk.

"Make yourself comfortable, son," the captain said. "If there's anything I can get for you—water, food, anything—just let me know. Despite what a lot of the hoodlums out there are saying about you, I know you didn't push that man. I saw him fall with my own eyes. Everyone's so riddled with fear these days, they're quick to blame anybody. I would just like to take a few minutes of your time to find out the truth about what happened."

Michael was still in shock after witnessing what happened to Cade, but he was relieved when the captain said he knew he didn't push him. He was glad that security guards didn't take heed to the accusations of the bystanders. Though he didn't have to try to talk his way to innocence, he wasn't sure how he was supposed to answer the captain's questions. What was he supposed to say? Should he tell him about the dart that may or may not have been there? Was he even sure what happened?

"Um, sir...I mean, Captain...I," Michael stammered.

"Please, call me Bill. Captain sounds too official in times like this. Just relax and tell me what happened."

"Well, Captain...Bill, sir, my friend Cade, the man who...well..." Michael took a deep breath, trying to collect his thoughts. He tried to form a sentence the best he could with the facts he was sure of. "Cade wanted to meet with me to tell me something. Before he could, he fainted and fell in front of the train."

"So, he just fainted?" Bill puzzled, writing something down in his notebook. "So, no groaning, no signs of a heart attack or a stroke, nothing? Just fainted?"

"Yes, sir. To the best of my knowledge."

It truly was the best of his knowledge. He wasn't sure what he had seen. It had looked like a dart, but he wasn't certain. None of the medical staff had mentioned it, though, when they tended to Cade's body. Michael convinced himself that he was only imagining it. He must have found himself so encapsulated by Cade's story, his mind made it real to help him believe his friend.

"So, it had nothing to do with the little argument you two were having right before?"

Although the captain said he knew Michael didn't push him, the question still made him feel uncomfortable. He didn't want to try to explain Cade's paranoia and what they were arguing about.

"The argument is a long story, but it was really about two old friends who had drifted apart over the years," Michael said. "We were about to board the train together. There was something he wanted to show me. It had something to do with whatever he had to say."

"You know, son, after talking to you, you seem like a pretty nice fellow. I know this has to be hard for you. My theory is that the argument caused him to overexert himself enough that he had a heart attack and collapsed. That's what I'm putting in my report at least. I'm sure the medical examiner will have the same conclusion."

Michael squirmed at the idea that it may have actually been his fault. Bill seemed to have noticed and continued on.

"But don't think it's your fault. I'm not trying to blame you for any of this. I'm just thinking out loud. The problem is, Federal Police called and they're stepping in to investigate. I'll give them the tape, and you just tell them what you told me. Everything should be fine."

Before Michael could ask any questions, Bill walked out of the room. He could see through the frosted glass window three figures meet him outside. They spent several minutes discussing something. The accident and his role in it, Michael assumed. He hoped Bill had shared his theory with them. While Michael wasn't fond of the idea that his anger could have contributed to Cade's death, it was the only answer that made sense to him. To ease his guilt, he reminded himself there was no way he could have known Cade had heart problems. He had always been in good physical shape. The heart attack also didn't explain the appearance of the black dart-like object.

Michael looked back at the window and saw two of the men walk away with Bill. The other one turned and came through the door. He wore the standard black tactical uniform of the Federal Police. His shoulders were well decorated, letting Michael know he was a high-ranking officer and the man in charge of the investigation.

"Mr. Anderton, it seems we may have a problem," the officer said in a dry, creaky voice. The mere sound of it irked Michael. It was as if the man wrote every word he said with his nails on an antique chalkboard.

"Yes sir, we do have a problem. My best friend just died," Michael said, sounding snider than he had intended. For some reason, the arrogance the officer portrayed on his face unnerved him. He didn't have the same warm and comforting personality as Bill did.

"Yes, about this friend, what can you tell me about him?"

"His name is Cade. He was my best friend. We used to work together, and then during the war, we even served together."

"So, you two were very close."

"Yes, sir. Until recent years. Cade had difficulty after the war. He suffered from post-traumatic stress and has been hospitalized for the last couple of months. He was just recently released."

"You're saying this man, Cade Simon, told you he was released from the hospital?"

"Not explicitly, but I assumed."

"Mr. Anderton, the truth is, your friend escaped. Violently. Two nurses and a security guard were shot. So, my real question for you is not what happened to cause today's accident, but how were you involved in his escape?"

"Involved? Escape?" Michael's blood boiled. Why didn't Cade mention any of this to him? Was he really on the run and trying to use Michael's friendship as a means to escape? Michael doubted it. He seemed genuine in what he had told him, regardless of how illogical it seemed.

"Listen, I don't know what you are talking about, but I haven't seen Cade in two years. More importantly, I know him. He may have had his problems, but I know he couldn't have done what you are accusing him of."

"You are very right, Mr. Anderton. He couldn't have done it. He had to have had help. You were a skilled sniper when you served, were you not?"

"Listen, you cannot pin this on me. I served my country proudly, and when the job ended, I haven't picked up a firearm since."

"Regardless of what you say, Mr. Anderton, we know the truth. You helped your friend escape. You told him to meet you here. It's a public place where you can avoid suspicion. From there you were to board the train together, heading south to sneak into the Forbidden Zone, the most war ravished area of the country. You have a childhood home there. We know that's where you've been since you defected from the armed forces. It was the grand escape plan. You knew no one would think to look for him in such a deserted place because no one has yet come looking for you. The plan was quite brilliant, but at the last minute, you had a change of heart. You did not want to live your life as a fugitive. Defecting from the armed forces is a serious crime but aiding and abetting a known murderer is much worse. You secretly wanted to one day get to rejoin the rest of society, so you pushed him into the train. You tried to erase your wrongdoings by making it appear as an accident. But it's too late for you, Mr. Anderton. You're in too deep, and it's time for you to reap the consequences of your actions."

Before Michael could even think about the accusations, much less speak up to defend himself against them, two guards were behind him. They slammed his face down onto the table and cuffed his hands behind him. He was then gagged, and a black bag was put over his head. They pulled him to his feet and forced him out of the office toward the public area of the train station.

Through the hood, he could make out lights from the various camera crews that had come to film the incident. He could hear crowds cheering at his arrest. Michael knew he was innocent, yet the crowds seemed to mock him and ridicule him as if he was a captured terrorist. He winced at some of their words. Not only did he lose his best friend, but he was also humiliated and belittled on television. His only solace was that at least they gave him the dignity of hiding his face.

The officers pushed their way through the people to some type of vehicle. Blinded by the hood, Michael was unable to tell what type, but the cheap, uncomfortable seats seemed suited just for prisoners. When they had arrived at wherever it was that they had taken him, they led him up to a room. There, they chained him to a chair bolted to the floor.

Once the hood was removed, he could see that it was a very dark room with only a single light. To his right, he could make out the face of the arrogant officer he met at the train station. In front of him sat another man, but the light was too dim to see any details. His silhouette cast in such a soft glow seemed menacing.

The man leaned forward to reveal himself to be an older, slightly overweight man with a very stern gaze. The man had the look of a politician. He even wore the purple velvet robes of one. A small, black onyx ring adorned his little finger. The same ring that was worn by the arrogant officer. Michael could only assume that it was something worn by the elites of the Federal Police.

"Hello, Mr. Anderton. My name is Richard Myers, secretary of security of our great nation."

So, the man is a politician, Michael thought. The Office of the Secretary of Security was a high office to have. His job was to oversee the Federal Police as well as maintain certain levels of security within the country's borders. The position was created during the war to deal with the re-occurring terror attacks and to promote peace in the country once again. He and his army of Federal Police were key in securing victory against the terrorist groups whose sole purpose seemed to be harbingers of death.

"You've already met Colonel Hempton," he said, referring to the arrogant officer. "We've brought you here today on grave charges. Multiple accounts of murder, aiding a fugitive, and terrorism."

"Terrorism?" Michael exclaimed. It seemed the longer the day went, the more charges were being brought against him. What started out as trying to help a friend, had led him to several charges that carry out a death sentence.

"Yes, terrorism. It has come to our attention that your partner had planted multiple explosive devices at a medical research facility."

"Sir, I can explain. Talk to Captain Rogers at the train station. He's the head of security there. He will tell you that I've had nothing to do with any of this. I went to the train station simply to meet with an old friend."

"We have spoken with Captain Rogers and viewed the security tapes. It seems they agree with what I have said. However, there is a bright side in this, Mr. Anderton. You see, my superiors want this problem handled. You took care of one half of the problem by eliminating Cade Simon. We took care of the other half by broadcasting your arrest over national television. The entire afternoon news has been filled with headlines of how one deranged terrorist turned on his partner right before their escape. That terrorist was then immediately apprehended by the Federal Police. You see how it all works out? The terrorists have been either captured or killed, there were no other casualties, and the Federal Police prove that we are protecting our citizens. Everyone is happy with your arrest. Now, that arrest should then be followed by an execution after this interview, but that's your bright side. You are too valuable of an asset for that to happen. We are in need of you, Mr. Anderton. Therefore, we have selected another criminal to take the fall for you."

Michael didn't know what he meant by being "in need" of him. After the war, he had been living a quiet life. He had left everything behind and was just surviving in the Forbidden Zone. That was his only true crime, other than leaving the army. He wouldn't have done that if they hadn't forced him to do such an appalling thing. Somehow, that had to be connected. Cade tried to warn him that it was coming back to haunt him. But still, he didn't know why they needed him. He had never been a part of the Federal Police and was sure he had never had any contact with any politicians. Before he could ask any questions, Secretary Myers continued.

"Yes, those are all the reasons why this is good for all of us. The best part for you is that by tomorrow, you won't remember any of it."

Michael felt a sharp pain on the inner side of his elbow, where one of the officers had inserted a syringe. Heat began to fill his arm as if the officer was injecting him with liquid fire. As it spread throughout him, his eyes began to fade until all he could see was darkness. Soon, his whole body burned, and he couldn't remember why. All he could remember was being at the train station with Cade, and then, there was nothing.

3

ICHAEL SCREAMED. The pain was so intense, it felt as if his head had been split in half. He had never experienced pain so strongly. He was sure he was dying.

"Michael, are you alright?" Rebecca cried.

Hearing his wife's voice helped to ease the agony. He tried to focus on her more than how he felt. He could feel her arms wrapped around him. He could hear her crying. He opened his eyes slightly and noticed Rebecca's cheeks were swollen. Tears were streaming down her face. She looked as if she had been crying for hours. Then he remembered. Amanda had accused him of murder, and Rebecca was trying to defend him. She was upset over Amanda's confrontation with him and the accusations she hurled against him. Accusations he couldn't defend himself from. That had upset her the most. Now, he had made it worse by scaring her.

Behind her, Amanda still stood with her arms folded. The same look of anger radiated from her face. He was in agony, and yet, she was unrelenting. He was sure he could get through to her. He was finally able to remember what had happened, although he wasn't sure any of it made sense. What made him believe in it was how real it felt. Michael found himself so involved, it was as if it were still happening. No other memory had ever felt so vivid. It was as if he was reliving it all over again in great detail. For a moment, he was encapsulated in his memory rather than what was going on around him. He had no idea how much time had passed. Then he realized he was no longer standing but lying down on the floor.

"What happened?" Michael asked, still shaken.

Although the pain in his head was subsiding, it was still sharp enough to make him feel weak. He felt as if his brain was in overload. It was working so hard to regain his memory, pushing back the dark clouds of his mind, that now it wanted to shut down. He wanted to sleep. To continue to lie on the floor and let himself recover.

Though his brain ached, he knew he couldn't. He wanted to share his memories with Amanda and Rebecca before they faded again. At that moment, he could remember everything, so he pulled himself up to look at Rebecca and collect his thoughts.

"You started to tell us about what happened to Cade, then you passed out and fell on the floor. We didn't know what happened. After a few minutes, you let out this awful scream. I'm just thankful you're okay," Rebecca sobbed. Michael felt her warm embrace around him. The gentle kiss on his forehead as she brushed back his hair.

I'm just thankful for you, he thought, looking into her soft brown eyes.

"All that happened is he's trying to get out of admitting the truth," Amanda sneered.

Michael's scream had alerted the others to something going on. Wesley, Allie, and the others were huddled at the entrance to the bedroom to check on Michael. Wesley rushed down to help Rebecca with him.

"What's going on down here?" Trent asked sternly. He was the only member of Michael's unit that he still had any contact with. He was a soldier before the war started. He was proud of his time serving. So much so, that he continued to wear the remnants of his uniform. He was the one Cade had trusted to deliver the message to Michael. Trent had searched him out in the Forbidden Zone and volunteered to stay with Rebecca when Michael left to see Cade.

"Michael was just about to admit his guilt in the murder of my son, Cade," Amanda said. "That is before he decided to put on this little show to stall for time."

"I was unaware Cade had been killed," Trent admitted.

"I have proof that he was murdered." Amanda shook the letter in her hand. She then proceeded to pass it toward Trent so that he could read it as well.

"Let me see that," Michael said, struggling to stand again. Amanda shook her head and handed it to Trent. He began to read it aloud to everyone.

"Ms. Amanda Simon, my name is Ben Rogers. I work for the Metro Underground Station as captain of the security guard..."

"That's wrong," Michael interjected. "The captain's name wasn't Ben. It was Bill, and he was my friend. He was the nicest officer on the scene that day. He told me he thought it was a heart attack."

"Oh, so now you remember," Amanda retorted.

"Yes...no...maybe..." Michael stumbled. "I remembered going to the train station to meet Cade right after he got out of the hospital. We argued and then he fell into the train. Then the Federal Police stepped in and arrested me.

They accused me of murder and attempting to commit terrorism with Cade."

Michael's words made everyone anxious. The tension was very high in the room. Everyone there had some reason or another to be leery of the Federal Police. Being in the Forbidden Zone was against the law, but nothing they had done was anywhere near comparable to his claims of murder and terrorism. They were just the outcasts of society. Those that didn't fit the ideal model of a citizen. In a country that was built on the acceptance of everyone, several people still found themselves left out. Those that didn't belong often found themselves captured by the Federal Police. That was why they chose the life of hiding.

"That is ridiculous," Amanda said. "If your story was true, you would have been dead six years ago. Besides, my son was not a terrorist, so the only part of that story I believe is the part where you admit to being a murderer."

Michael was tired of arguing, so he decided to tell the whole story the best he could remember it. He started with meeting Cade and his strange behavior. He told them about meeting with the captain and then the Federal Police. He told them about the arrest and the dark room with the secretary of security. He could see the whole day in his mind as clear as if it were in front of him. He told them all the details he could remember. All except the details he was unsure of. As he told the story, he began to listen to himself. Even if they thought he sounded absurd, it was so engraved in his mind, it was as if it had happened yesterday. He knew his memory was correct. For once, he was sure of it. His only hope was that the others would believe it too.

Everyone looked as if they were still trying to take it all in. There was murmuring among them. Wesley and his wife, Joanna, discussed what it meant for their own safety if Michael had been captured by the Federal Police. She found it unlikely someone accused of terrorism would be set free, even in the barren wasteland of the Forbidden Zone. She was convinced that the Federal Police were still looking for him. She feared what would happen when they succeeded in finding him. Wesley tried to reassure her by telling her that the officer had mentioned Michael living in the Forbidden Zone. If they knew that, then they should know of their hideout as well. Such reassurance did not go over well, as she began to cry hysterically.

Amanda, Rebecca, and Rebecca's mother, Nelda, sounded as if they were still discussing Michael's guilt or innocence through it all. Steadfast, Rebecca remained on Michael's side, in spite of the things he told her he had been accused of. She remembered him leaving to go meet with Cade that day after Trent had come to deliver his message. She didn't think he had ever made it, though. They had found him days later in the woods, in a daze. They all suspected it was caused by a car accident. Michael had tried to drive there in Trent's car, but the roads in the Forbidden Zone were more nonexistent than traversable.

Allie, being so young, seemed more preoccupied thinking about nothing being real. She was born not long after Cade's death. Michael had already lived in the Forbidden Zone a couple years then. She knew nothing of the Federal Police or life outside of their three-room home. Her innocence and naivety were often refreshing.

Trent had the most serious look of them all. He wasn't speaking, but rather seemed as if he was trying to piece it all together. His eyes kept moving about as if he were solving a puzzle in his mind.

"What did he mean by an asset?" Trent questioned. Of all the things that could have been asked, Michael wondered why that. Maybe he believed him. If that was so, then he supposed that would be the only logical question to ask. It was also one of the main questions he didn't have an answer to.

"I'm not sure," Michael admitted. "It seemed as if he was calling me an asset to the government."

"Sweetie, I've known you since we were kids," Rebecca said. "The closest I've seen you come to anything government related is the stamp on Amanda's letter."

"Very funny, Becca, but what if something happened while we were apart during the war?"

"You never talk about the war, but if something had happened, wouldn't you know about it?"

Michael shrugged. Something had happened. Something he had never shared with anyone. But he couldn't figure out its importance. Even so, he couldn't shake the feeling that he was missing something. There had to have been a reason for them to call him that. Maybe they had him confused with someone else; another Michael Anderton perhaps.

"This is ridiculous," Amanda scoffed. "I can't believe you're all buying into this crap. Can you not tell a made-up story when you hear one?"

"Actually Amanda, you're right. I find this whole thing to be ridiculous," Wesley said. "We've lived here with Michael for almost six years. Considering my former job, I know murderers when I see one, and Michael has never shown any sign of being one. Rough around the edges maybe, but he's never been anything other than kind and compassionate to anyone. So why don't we all calm down and take a second to think this through? If Michael is telling the truth, then we've got more important things to have to deal with."

Amanda snorted and walked toward the living room. Michael was glad she had left him alone, even if only for a little while. Although she had left, the tension remained in the room. Everyone was concerned for their own safety. Michael tried to reassure them that even if the story was true, it happened over six years ago. That fact provided little solace as the Federal Police were known to be relentless in completing their missions. Michael didn't even know if they were actively looking for him. They had caught him. He was chained to a table. If they had wanted something from him, they would have gotten it then. The more logic he applied to his story, the more he was able to ease the tension among them.

The late hour was also beginning to take its toll on the group. Curiosity and worry began to subside in favor of sleep, or at least the attempt of it. Everyone dispersed between the bedroom and the living room. They each settled into their typical sleeping places, but sleep wasn't coming easy for them that night. Each of them was worried. They wondered if Michael's story was true, what that meant for them. Was he really a fugitive? Were the Federal Police looking for him? What would happen if they found him? Would they arrest them all for just being there with him?

Michael only had one question. What was so important about him that they let him go?

4

THE NEXT MORNING was peaceful, even after the restless night. Rebecca could be heard in the kitchen making breakfast. The house was silent otherwise. Glimmers of sun shone through the cracks in the walls, yet no one seemed disturbed by them. Michael moved out of its rays and noticed a strange look on Rebecca's face as she walked past the bedroom doorway.

"Becca…" Michael began.

With all that had happened the night before, he wanted to be sure to tread with caution. The last thing he wanted to do was to upset her more. He debated on just letting her work through it on her own. Cooking was her hobby and the thing she would do if she needed to clear her head. It was normally her time of peace, but peace wasn't the expression on her face.

"I'm fine, sweetie. I was thinking about what you told us last night," Rebecca said. "I know Cade was quirky and rambled on about his conspiracy theories, but do you think he was capable of doing what they said he did?"

Michael wasn't sure. He had known Cade's fun and good-natured side, but he had also seen what he could do when he was focused on a mission. During the war, Rebecca had been taken by the terrorists. They had come to their house and tore through it, taking everything of value and kidnapping her. Cade was the reason Michael found her. Amidst his paranoia, he was able to track down a lead to a prisoner camp in the Forbidden Zone. He tore through the camp and helped rescue Rebecca. For that, Michael owed him a lifetime of gratitude. He couldn't believe that Cade would join a terrorist group after that.

"I don't know. But if it hadn't been for him, I may never have found you," Michael said.

Before they could discuss it further, rustling began throughout the house. The others had awoken. Allie came sprinting into the kitchen, grasping her mother tightly. Her bright eyes looked up at Michael as she gave him a playful "good morning." Michael smiled at her and tried to match her enthusiasm.

At six years old, she didn't understand the fear that coursed through the others. She didn't know the danger and the weight that Michael's story carried. While everyone was always leery of the Federal Police finding them, they never thought that they could be searching for them. They thought they had slipped through the cracks unnoticed. Allie knew nothing of it. Her world was full of laughter and joy. The only thing she knew was to hide if she heard something fly over, but even that was rare.

Rebecca and Michael decided they would finish their conversation later when it was just them. Michael took the opportunity to begin his daily chores in an attempt to return to more normalcy. He walked through the rubble to the living room to get Wesley and Trent to help him gather firewood. As he approached the doorway, he could hear low whispers. Wesley and his wife were discussing something that they didn't want to be overheard. The sound of his movement made them momentarily pause, but before he could take another step, they began talking again.

"So, what do we do if the Federal Police come here?" Joanna asked.

"We're not criminals. The only real law we're breaking is being here," Wesley reassured her. "We'll just talk to them and give them what they want, even if that means Michael."

Though they were whispering, Michael still was able to hear them. Their words cut him deep. There was his friend willing to give him up at a moment's notice just to protect himself and Joanna. Michael couldn't blame him, though. He was sure he would do the same thing if it came to protecting Rebecca or Allie. It had been hard on him enough when Rebecca had been kidnapped, he couldn't imagine losing her again. At that thought, he realized Wesley wouldn't have to give him up. He was willing to sacrifice himself to save them both. His two sons had already disappeared from his life. He couldn't stand to lose Rebecca and Allie.

"It won't come to that," Michael said, interrupting them as he walked into the room. Wesley looked sheepish at the thought of him listening to their conversation. "If the Federal Police come, I'll turn myself over to them to protect the rest of you."

Michael sounded nobler than he actually felt about it. In truth, he was terrified of what would happen if they came. The fact remained, though, that he would do whatever it took to protect his family.

"It wouldn't make any difference," Trent said flatly. "If the Federal Police come here, they'll arrest us all. We're no different than Michael. In the eyes of the Federal Police, anyone who is found in the Forbidden Zone is a potential threat. By technicality, we would all be considered terrorists by them."

Joanna shrilled out of both anguish and fear. She had never wanted to leave the city. She was happy there. It wasn't her decision to leave the luxurious life she had known. She was once the nation's leading fashion designer, owning her own production company. She had control of the fashion world.

Everyone on every corner wore her designs. They combined elements of both older fashion popular before the war and the beautiful elegance of the dignified elite of the present. She had spent years working on the perfect design. It was her life's work, and the people loved it. Those with power did not. The aristocrats pressured the government to squash her company. They felt as though she was blurring the lines between the upper and lower classes. Their status was no more elevated than the commoner, and so, they fought back.

The government caved. They reprimanded her with a heavy fine and threatened to shut her business down if she didn't comply. She was so disgusted, she didn't give them the option. She walked away from it all, not realizing her actions would lead her on a path to the place she now called home.

"Way to go, Trent. Why don't you learn to lighten up every once in a while?" Wesley menaced.

"Why don't we all just let it go for a little while," Michael said. "Trent, you and Wesley come help me collect some more firewood for tonight. We could use the break from the stress we're all feeling. Besides, if we don't collect any wood, you can forget about the Federal Police coming. These ladies would kill us for letting them get cold."

He wanted to offer something to keep everyone's mind off the thing they feared. For the eight years he had lived there, he had never considered the Federal Police finding him. They were in isolation, surrounded by wilderness and ruin. Nobody had been looking for them. Nobody even knew they were alive. Life was a lot simpler then.

Michael walked to the door with Trent and Wesley behind him. Outside the shack was a small grove of saplings Nelda tended to. She loved gardening and thought it would be beneficial to continue to try to replenish the trees as they were cut down. She was already outside that morning, surrounding the trees with mulch to help keep them warm.

"Good morning, gentlemen," she said, smiling at them. She was covered in dirt and leaves. It was evident she was enjoying her work. If the events of the night before had any effect on her, she didn't show it.

"Hey, Ms. Nelda, we've come to take all your trees," Wesley joked, waving around the saw he had picked up from near the shack.

"If you take so much as one limb from one of my trees, I'll take a limb from you."

"Don't worry, Ms. Nelda. We'll be far away from any of your trees," Trent said, already walking ahead. The other two men hurried to follow him.

The deeper they walked through the grove, the shorter the trees became. It seemed as if Nelda planted new ones each time they went out to cut them down. It was only a short span of clearing before reaching the edge of the woods.

Michael and Wesley spread out to find the best trees for firewood. Trent, however, called them back and told them to keep moving forward. Michael thought that was unusual. They typically went with the easy route and collected the nearest ones they could, so that they wouldn't have as far to carry it back. Trent seemed determined. Michael assumed he must have already found a good tree or perhaps something of greater interest up ahead. Maybe he had found signs of a deer. He knew they had no way to kill it with them, but the thought of even seeing one was worth it to him. Deer had seemed to have died out around three years ago. Michael missed the rich, bold taste of venison. More so, now that he remembered they had left before breakfast.

Trent kept going. They walked for what seemed like miles. There was no stopping. No time for breaks. Wherever Trent was heading, he was determined to get there, and soon.

"Hey man, unless you hid a big juicy steak out here, I think one of these hundreds of trees we've just passed will be fine," Wesley said to Trent. It was obvious he was thinking of food as well.

"Just a little farther," Trent said as he kept walking.

Wesley sighed as he readjusted the saw on his shoulder. It seemed as if he were carrying a lead weight more than a saw. At least since he was carrying it, he didn't have to worry about carrying wood back all the way. That job would rest with Michael and Trent, though he would probably be too tired to operate it once they got there.

Moments later, they came to the edge of the woods. Just beyond the trees was a vast stretch of open grasslands. In the middle rose three walls of an old chemical plant that had been destroyed in the war.

"That's where we're going," Trent said.

"What happened to collecting firewood? And why did I have to carry this saw the entire way?" Wesley asked.

"We will, but there's something we need to do first."

40

They walked slowly through the grass. Although it was still early March, they were careful walking in places they couldn't see. Michael was glad for Trent's detour. He had kept quiet during the walk. He was enjoying nature; the breeze blowing through the withered grass. Yesterday's stress seemed to have melted away. This was why he enjoyed his life now. He could never have just enjoyed such things had he stayed in the city. There, he would have been constantly busy. Constantly trying to live up to the expectations of him. Here, he was free. He was free to just walk through the grass. Free to explore his curiosity.

Trent led the way, squeezing through the broken chain link fence, up to the fallen wall, and over the rubble. Whatever it was he was looking for must have been inside the facility. Michael had visited the place before, many years ago, looking for food and any supplies he could gather. He knew there was nothing of importance there, so he couldn't understand why Trent felt the need to bring them to it. He continued to follow, simply because of Trent's determination to get there.

"They're not here…" Trent mumbled to himself as he stood at the center of the factory.

"Who's not here?" Michael pressed, startled by his comment. He trusted Trent and knew he would never lead them into any danger. He had always been loyal to Michael since the war. Something about it still made him feel uneasy. He was sure they were the only people for miles. He brushed it off, considering nothing had been normal since Amanda made her accusations.

"Huh? Oh, there was a rabbit near the house yesterday. I followed it to a family of them in here. This time I came prepared," Trent said, brandishing a small pistol he pulled out of his pocket.

"How long have you had that?" Wesley asked.

"Remember, we all have our reasons for being here," Trent said as he ran off to check under some rubble.

"Does that strike you as odd?" Michael asked, also surprised by Trent.

"Mike, everything lately has been odd," Wesley said. "I mean, you tell us you're a fugitive from the Feds for murder and terrorism. Trent's running around with a gun. And Amanda…Where did she come from? We all thought she was just another refugee who stumbled upon our shack, but if she knew you…If she searched you out…how did she find us?"

Michael's eyes widened. Wesley may have been on to something. Perhaps they weren't as safe as they had thought. What if the Federal Police didn't know exactly where they were? What if they had used Amanda to flush him out? They did know they were hiding in the Forbidden Zone. They could be at the shack already. They could be waiting for them to return.

Michael's heart began pounding in his chest. He felt as if it were about to explode. He had to get back. He had to protect Rebecca.

"We have to go. Now!" Michael screamed, turning to run before he could even finish speaking.

"What? Why?" Trent asked, still fishing in the rubble.

"We just have to. Now go!"

Gunshot filled his ears. The ringing deafened out all other sounds of the factory. He had felt the presence of the bullet flying by. He turned to see smoke rising from the barrel of Trent's gun.

"I got one," Trent yelled as he rushed over to collect his catch. Michael saw the twitching white feet of a small rabbit out of the corner of his eye.

"We don't have time for this," Michael yelled over the ringing still in his ears. He left without giving Trent another chance to refuse. He had to get back, even if the others weren't coming.

Michael ran, no longer cautious of the tall grass. His adrenaline coursed through him. He felt as though even if he were to spook something, he could outrun it. He had more important things to do. Protecting his family was all he could think about. That was his mission. There was nothing that was going to stand in his way. He had to get back before it was too late.

He was through the woods before he realized Wesley and Trent were right behind him, following him step for step. At the edge of the grove was where he also realized there was a smell in the air. A heavy, pungent smell filled his nostrils. Smoke. The sky above was blackened by it.

I'm too late, he thought, but his feet never stopped moving.

Dodging and weaving through branches of the taller trees, he didn't let anything slow him down. If there was even a glimmer of hope of saving them, he wasn't going to stop short of reaching them.

The heat could be felt against his face. He was close. The entirety of the shack had been replaced by a glowing ball of fire. Flames lapped upwards, sending out sparks as the boards were engulfed in them. There was no sign of people. No sign of what started the fire. Nothing. Michael searched the ground diligently for any sign of Rebecca or Allie but found none.

"No. No. No!" Wesley screamed as he ran past Michael. Just at the edge of the fire, almost consumed by it, Michael saw her. Joanna was lying face down in the grass, with her arms and legs spread out. Michael and Wesley ran to save her. She must have been trying to stop the fire. The heat must have gotten to her.

Wesley ran to try to resuscitate her. To bring her back. He pulled her back from the fire, rolled her over, and fell to his knees, weeping. There she lied. Her eyes gazed lifelessly up at the dim sky. The tell-tale sign between them. She had been murdered.

5

"WHO COULD HAVE DONE THIS?" Wesley cried in agony. Streams of grief rolled down his face onto Joanna's stiffening body. The truth was, he already knew who it could be. His fears had been realized. During the run back to the shack, all he could think about was Joanna. In front of him, Michael had run. He ran as if he knew it was happening. Maybe he did. Wesley's anger grew against his friend. Michael was the one who told them to leave the shack. He had insisted on collecting firewood. All the men had left because of him.

Wesley felt stupid. He should never have left them alone. The women had no one there to protect them. It was all Michael's fault. He led the Federal Police to their home. His secrets had caught up with him. Wesley didn't know the Federal Police were looking for Michael. Had he known, he wouldn't have stayed in the house with him for so long.

He should have left. He should have gone to find his own way like he wanted to from the beginning. He was the officer. He had better training than the professor. He knew tactics and skills to protect his family. Why didn't he listen to his own instincts? If he had, his wife would still be alive. Where was Michael's wife in all this? His family seemed to have conveniently disappeared without a trace. Could it have been a plan all along? Was he trying to have Joanna killed? And what about Trent? He was leading them so far from the shack. Where they were, there was no way to know what was going on at home. No way to hear the gunshot. No way to protect his family.

Wesley lost control of his anger. His blood burned in his veins. He would get his vengeance. He found himself on his feet, leaving Joanna's body to lie in the dirt. There was nothing he could do for her anymore. Nothing, except get his revenge.

He picked up a smoldering board. The end was glowing red hot. The heat singed the palms of his hands. He didn't care. Michael had betrayed them. Wesley's trust and loyalty had been repaid with cruelty and injustice. Michael had to feel what he felt. He had to feel the world slip away from him. To feel nothing but the crushing weight of losing everything.

Wesley swung the board with all his might. There was no friendship left in him, only hate. The board sliced through the air. The embers crackled as the wind caused them to glow brighter. There it was, the satisfying thud, as the wood connected with bone. Charred board splintered, sending wood and sparks showering around them. Michael's face bore the scars of the impact. Wesley had caught him underneath his left eye, burning him when it hit. Michael collapsed.

Wesley stood over him, watching him, with the board still in his hand. Michael didn't fight back. He didn't get up. He didn't move. Short bursts of shallow breath were the only indications of life from him. Wesley's anger subsided as waves of guilt flooded over him. What had he done? In his anger, he had struck down his friend. He struck down the only other person left he truly cared about. The board fell to the ground. Wesley planted his knees into the dirt beside him.

Trent ran over at the sight of the commotion. The unexpected event led him to do the only thing he could—help Michael. Without even acknowledging Wesley's presence, he stooped down and began tending to him. He stretched him out and began to check his breathing. It was beginning to regulate. When he concluded Michael's life was not in danger, he began looking at the wound. The burn was substantial, but the bruising and swelling were the worst part of the injury.

Wesley was relieved. It seemed Michael would be okay. Okay in body at least. In his mind, Wesley was sure he burned with the same feelings of betrayal he himself had felt moments ago. He knew his friend would never be able to forgive him. Michael's face would bear the scars of his anger. It would serve as a constant reminder that he couldn't be trusted. That was how Wesley felt at least.

Michael's eyes opened slowly. He was groggy but frantically tried to wake up. When he saw Wesley standing near him, he pulled back but then gave him a look of confusion. His hands drifted up to his cheek. He winced at the slightest touch of his fingertips. Swelling had already overtaken the left side of his face. His jaw was unable to move. He tried to speak, but all that came was unintelligible mumbles.

Wesley knew what he was trying to say. He knew he was blaming him, cursing him with his breath. With his head hung in shame, he stood up and walked away from Michael. He knew that's what he wanted.

"No…" The small, almost inaudible words emanated from the space between Michael's swollen lips. "I'm sor-sorry."

Wesley stood in shock. In his anger, he had blamed Michael for what had happened to Joanna and their home. Hearing Michael's weak, gentle apology made the crushing weight of Wesley's guilt even heavier. How could Michael even want to look at him, when he didn't want to look at himself? Michael's friendship was stronger than his. He apologized to him, even after Wesley viciously attacked him. The truth was, it was never Michael's fault to begin with. He had no right to blame him for what happened to Joanna. He was only trying to do what was best to survive, the same as everyone else who had sought shelter in their shack.

"No, I'm sorry my friend," Wesley said, unable to look him in the eye.

"I'm sorry to break up this sappy bonding moment, but we need to get back to the old chemical plant. This smoke will likely draw attention," Trent said, already trying to pick up Michael from the ground. Michael gripped his shoulder hard and shook his head no. His gaze was on the burning embers. The fiery blaze had begun to shrink down, revealing the rubble and ashes.

"Search…" Michael mumbled, pointing to the debris.

"We have no time to search. We have to get back now."

"Search…" Michael repeated, stumbling toward where he had been pointing.

***

A sound broke through the silence. A low rumble boomed as if a thousand wings were beating at once.

Shadows were cast along the ground around them. Rising from the trees, three black helicopters emerged from the sun's glowing rays. Michael's suspicions were right. The Federal Police had come. They torched his home and killed his family. They had let him go, why did they come looking for him? Why now?

He turned back and saw Wesley and Trent staring at the helicopters in horror. They knew as well as he did, it wouldn't be long before they reached the same fate as Joanna. If the Federal Police were hunting them, they were as good as dead. Now was not the time to worry about that. He had more important things to do. He had to find Rebecca and Allie. With his strength regaining, he ran back to the remains of the shack. Each step made his face ache, but he didn't let it stop him. He had a mission.

He first went to where they had found Joanna. Hoping for any sign of a clue, he drew closer to the rubble. The smoldering embers were still red hot. The heat took his breath away, but he pressed on.

Nothing.

Nothing was there except for odds and ends of charred boards and household items. He studied the debris harder. He broke off a limb from one of the more mature saplings that had grown near the shack. Using it as a poker, he stirred the ashes, trying to look underneath. Flames burst up with every move he made. Although he wanted answers, each time his search found him nothing, he was relieved. The more he searched, the more he found hope. Finding nothing meant that there was a possibility his family was still alive. Perhaps they escaped before the Federal Police attacked them.

"Rebecca...Nelda...Allie...Amanda."

Wesley and Trent were calling for them. With Michael unable to speak, he was grateful his friends were helping him look for the others. As they shouted, Michael kept digging.

Minutes turned into hours. The flames had almost burned themselves out. Michael's search had led him to nothing. With the fire and heat dissipating, he moved his search deeper inward. Near the middle of the ashes was a large oddly shaped heap. Michael walked to it with his stick still in hand. He poked at it gently, knocking pieces of debris down the pile. Then he saw something.

A hand protruded from the side of the pile. Michael's heart sank. Panic and worry spread over him like wildfire. Could it be Rebecca or Nelda? It was too big to be Allie's. For that, he was thankful. He kept digging. The body was lying face down. Not that it mattered, it was too blackened and shriveled to be recognizable anyway. Underneath the body, lying unscathed by the flames, Michael found Rebecca's bible. It had to be Rebecca. She would never have let it get far away. It was too valuable to her. Michael was crushed. He had thought he had lost her before. This time he had proof. He had seen it with his own eyes.

"We've given up the search," Trent said, walking up behind him. "Most likely anyone that wasn't killed was captured."

Michael turned around and showed Trent and Wesley the bible and then the body. They both understood what he was trying to say. They each offered their condolences to him. Their words fell on deaf ears. Michael clutched the bible next to his chest and walked into the grove of trees. He found a soft spot in the mulch and curled up underneath a tree.

"We should head back to the facility," Trent suggested. "There is food and shelter there. We don't want to be left out here in this cold tonight."

"You can go. I'm staying here with Michael," Wesley said, finding his own pile of mulch to lie on. "It's the least I can do with all that's happened today."

"Suit yourself," Trent said as he walked away in the direction of the chemical plant.

As the night approached, the silence of it amplified Michael's grief. He tossed in the mulch, trying to sleep. Sleep was all he wanted to do. He would have slept the rest of his life away if he could. It was the only thing that could ease the pain of losing Rebecca. But his dreams became haunting nightmares. When he closed his eyes, he could see Rebecca's face staring back at him. He could feel her arms wrapped around him. But as quickly as her warmth spread over him, it vanished. It was replaced by the cold loneliness that consumed him.

This was the second time he had lost her. The second time he felt as if his world had ended. The first time, he went to war to find her. He could satisfy his want for revenge with every mission he had. He also had Cade and his unit to rely on. They were his support, and he felt their friendship. All he felt now was numb.

He had lost his love, his daughter had been taken from him, and his closest friend had attacked him. He wanted to sleep. To push those thoughts far away from his mind. To live in the world of his choosing, where his family was still around him. Where his sons were still with him, being brothers to Allie. He and Rebecca watching over them. The cold truth was that it would never be. His sons never knew of Allie. They left too long ago. Now she too was gone from his life. The pain in his heart made sleep impossible. His eyes opened wide, peering at the night sky through the trees.

He clutched Rebecca's bible tightly in his arms. It was the last token he had of her. Holding on to it, he promised her that wherever Allie may be, he would find her. He would get her back, no matter what it took.

Michael rose to his feet. There was no use trying to sleep. It was too cold, and his face and heart hurt too much. He would make his time useful. He would spend every second he had searching for Allie.

"Where are you going?" Wesley asked.

"Wherever I have to," Michael said, the cold air reducing the swelling enough that he could speak. He didn't want to tell Wesley what his thoughts were. Although he understood why he had attacked him, he didn't want to risk it happening again. His trust in him had been shaken.

"You're going to find them, aren't you?" Wesley asked, already on his feet. "I'm coming too. Rebecca wasn't the only one they killed."

"No. I've seen what you can do," Michael scolded, pointing to his face.

"I was angry, Mike. They killed Joanna. I just…I lost it. I took my anger out on you, and I'm sorry."

Michael could feel Wesley's sincerity, but he couldn't let it go that easily. He walked away without saying a word. Being left with no other choice, Wesley followed him. Secretly, Michael was glad he did. He didn't know where he was going to go or where to begin to look for Allie.

"Trent is at the chemical plant. We should go meet up with him. We could use his help," Wesley suggested.

"No, leave him. This doesn't concern him. He's safer where he is," Michael said.

"That's true. It's probably a good thing I have this then," Wesley told him, showing him Trent's gun.

"How did you end up with it?"

"I used to be a cop, remember? I'm pretty good at disarming people. Even without them knowing."

Michael was unsure how to feel about Wesley having the gun. For one, if they were caught with it, they'd be shot on sight. Not only that, Wesley had already attacked him with a burning board. He didn't want to give him the chance to shoot him also.

"Let me have that," Michael said, reaching for the gun.

"Uh, no. Which one of us is the trained policeman?"

"Which of us was a sniper who just so happened to grow up in these woods? Where do you think I learned how to shoot in the first place?" Michael asked, snatching the weapon away. "For this to even be useful, we need to conserve bullets. Doing so means we need someone who knows the area and can be effective in it."

Wesley protested, but let Michael keep it.

"You do realize we're two men, who are about to pick a fight with the country's homeland army, right?" Wesley asked. "Even with it, we're outmatched and outnumbered more times than I can even imagine. I hate to admit it, but I think our best option would be to surrender."

As much as Michael wanted to find Allie, he knew that surrendering would be their best choice if the Federal Police came after them. After the incident with Cade, he was sure he was on every billboard in every city listed as a terrorist at large. Even if they managed to keep a low profile, should someone recognize them, the Federal Police would be called immediately. To make it worse, it was the Federal Police that they had to go up against. Even so, he knew he couldn't give up. He couldn't let the men who murdered his wife in cold blood go unpunished. And they took Allie.

"I can't surrender," Michael said. "Not after what they did to Becca. I have to get Allie back."

"I know how you feel. Joanna was all that I had left. And I've been there since Allie was an infant. I think I've had as much of a hand in raising her as anyone else in the house." Wesley paused. "I'm her Uncle Wesley. I can't leave her in their hands, and I know you'll do anything to protect her. So, let's do it."

Wesley walked toward the woods, disappearing behind the trees. Michael rushed to him to catch up. They kept walking for miles. Michael didn't say a word along the way. He was strangely silent even for him. He was nervous about where they were heading and about what was waiting for them.

Wesley had made a good suggestion as to where to begin their search. He had pointed out that the type of helicopters they had left in would only be able to travel a short range. That meant that there was a Federal Police base somewhere in the area. Michael had assumed being deep in the Forbidden Zone, there was at least several hundred miles between him and the Federal Police. He would never have guessed there would be a base nearby.

Three days they had walked through wilderness and ruin, never saying more than what needed to be said. The most they had spoken to each other was during arguments over direction. Neither of them were the best navigators and were only assuming the helicopters had made a direct approach to their base. Michael's silence was out of fear. He was afraid that they had made a wrong turn. Afraid that they were simply lost and never would be able to find Allie. He was afraid he wouldn't be able to save her if they did.

It wasn't long before they came to an impasse. They stood at the edge of the Great River, the largest river in the country. With its strong currents and immense width, swimming and rafting were impossible. Concrete pillars emerged from the water, but the bridge that once crossed it had most likely been destroyed in the war. There was no way around and no way across. Their journey was hopeless.

Michael charged for the water, leaving all sense of reason behind. He had to save Allie. His adrenaline told him he could swim it if he had to.

"Michael, stop," Wesley shouted, trying to catch up to him.

Before he had the chance, an old man tackled Michael and knocked him to the ground.

"You wouldn't want to be trying that, sonny. I've seen that ol' girl take many o' men to a watery grave," the old man said, lifting himself up from the ground with ease. To be an old man, he was in surprisingly fit condition.

"Who are you?" Wesley demanded.

"I reckon I should be asking you that, seeing as you two are trespassing and all. This here's my property." The old man pointed back over the tall grass to an old house with a large barn beside it. The red paint of it had flaked so much, it was beginning to look gray.

"We didn't mean to," Michael said. "We just need to get across the river."

"Why?"

"I have no choice."

"There's always a choice if you're thinking o' killing yourself."

"That's not it at all." Michael debated how much to tell the old stranger, but he had to keep going. He wasn't seeking suicide, he was doing what he had to for Allie.

"Well, tell me what ails you, my boy."

"I have to save my daughter. She's just a child," Michael yelled without thinking. "They have her."

"I reckon you mean them Fed cops, eh? Lot of those sniffing around the other side o' that river. They came for me and Murdock once." The old man nodded toward a picture of a German shepherd mounted on a tombstone. A neatly folded red handkerchief adorned its top. "Yep, ol' Murdock gave his life protecting this place, but they ain't come back since. Tell you what, my friend, you tell me your name, and I'll tell you how to get across that there river."

"Jimmy...Riverfield..." Michael lied. He wasn't sure if he could trust the old man. His real name was wanted by the Federal Police. He didn't want to spook him if he did, in fact, have a way across.

"Well Jimmy, name's Bud Henry. You've got that look in your eye like you're about to do something crazy. Crazier than just trying to swim the mighty missy."

"I have to get her back," Michael said, hanging his head down. "Whatever it takes."

"Oh boy, my kind o' fellow. Someone actually man 'nough to stand up to them Fed bullies. Come with me. Now what I'm about to show you is a secret, okay? You see, I built her myself."

The old man walked over to the large wooden barn. As he swung the door open, Michael could see a boat made of mismatched salvaged parts with plastic barrels under the bottom to keep it afloat. The driving engine was a paddle wheel system. Michael severely doubted its ability to float, much less cross the Great River. There was no stopping the old man, however. He was already pulling on the cart underneath it, steering it to the water's edge.

"Now since there's a kid involved, I'll let you borrow her. She may not look like much, but she'll get you there. Once you get over there, best watch your backs. Them Fed cops you're looking for are about nine or ten miles northwest. Their 'copters are always buzzing in and out o' there."

"Sir, is there any way we can repay you for your generosity?" Wesley asked.

"I ain't givin' this boat away for free, sonny. You've got to promise me if you're taking her, you go take care of them hoodlums. You ain't the only one who's lost somebody to them. Murdock was all I had left, and they got him too. But shoot, anyone crazy 'nough to try to swim the mighty missy is crazy 'nough to go toe to toe with them yahoos. Sure be nice if they'd get their nose out o' my backyard. Now, if you need some assistance, once you get there look under your seats. You may find some tools to help. Hope you find your little one."

With that, Michael and Wesley boarded the boat as Bud rolled them down the landing ramp and into the water. To Michael's surprise, the boat was buoyant and stable. At twelve-foot long and almost as wide, steering became an issue, especially against the strong currents. It was almost nightfall when they reached the other side. Fighting to steer and paddle the boat made them exhausted, but they had no time to rest. The darkness of night would make a good cover should the base be guarded by scouting patrol.

They tied the boat off to a nearby tree, pulling it tight against the shore under some brush to camouflage it. The last thing they needed was for someone to spot the boat and put the base on alert. In a deserted area, a mysterious boat would concern anyone. Before abandoning it, they followed Bud's advice to look under the seat. Inside the storage container beneath it, they found some rope, a few canteens of water, two long barrel rifles, and a box of bullets.

Whoever that guy was, Michael thought, *he was preparing for this day.*

Michael calculated that if they kept a steady walking pace, they could reach the base within a couple hours or so. The problem with his math, however, was that his legs were too tired to keep up such a pace. They had already been walking for almost four days and then paddled a boat across the Great River. It didn't matter. He had no time. He had to get to Allie. Michael knew the odds were against him. He knew that even if they did reach the base, it would have been days since she was taken. She had probably already been moved if she was ever at this one to begin with. Regardless, he had to try. If nothing else, he may be able to find some clue to where she was. He couldn't give up. He forced his feet to keep moving. Forced them to step one in front of the other. He had to keep going. He promised Rebecca to save Allie.

Dawn was swiftly approaching. Wesley had collapsed under the trunk of an old, fallen tree. Michael wanted to keep going but he could no longer will his legs to move. He pulled out one of the canteens he had gotten from the boat. The water rushed over his parched lips. It was refreshing. The taste of cool, clean water was almost foreign to him. It had been years since he had tasted pure, fresh water. Neither the collected rainwater nor what they dipped from the creek was ever that clean.

Michael pondered over their journey. They had left with nothing but the clothes on their backs and a pistol Wesley took from Trent. It seemed impossible to him that they were almost to the end of it. Somehow, they managed to survive the cold nights without blankets or shelter. They managed to survive with almost no food or water to eat or drink. Michael was amazed. It was only by sheer determination they had come this far. Now they were only a few mere minutes away from reaching Allie. If she was in that federal compound, no matter how exhausted he felt, Michael was going to find a way to reach her.

6

THE COMPOUND WAS MASSIVE, much larger than either of them had expected. It was as if this one facility was used to monitor and patrol the entire western part of the Forbidden Zone. Tall fences bordered its perimeter. Barbed wire spiraled around its top. Guardsmen stood atop towers spaced every thirty feet. A series of large concrete buildings lined its interior. Dozens of black helicopters were parked in rows, while some were constantly coming and going.

Each helicopter that arrived carried with it either an army of Federal Police or a cluster of prisoners. The prisoners that arrived all looked the same. They each wore a solid white jumpsuit with a black hood covering their faces. Chains were linking them together, bound at their wrists and feet. Although they were all dressed the same, it was clear it was a mixture of men, women, and children.

Michael shuddered. Seeing the prisoners made him think about such a thing happening to Allie. Had they bound her and led her away into the compound like cows being led to slaughter? She was an innocent child. She had no part in any of this.

"What's our plan?" Wesley asked, staring down into the valley at the Federal Police base.

The more Michael continued to look at the compound, the more the anger raged within him. He would not stand by as the innocent were punished the same as the guilty. What right did they have to target his family, simply because they chose to live outside of the oppression?

"I don't have a plan, but I'm taking action," he said through gritted teeth. His grip tightened around his rifle. Without hesitation, he pulled the stock to his shoulder and focused one of the officers in his sights. Before he could pull the trigger, the gun was snatched to the side.

"That's a terrible plan," Wesley said, still holding on to the barrel of the rifle. "If you shoot one, you better shoot them all at once, because as soon as you do, they'll know we're here. They'll swarm this hilltop and we'll lose all chance of saving anyone."

Michael sighed through his anger. He couldn't argue with him. The sound of the shot alone would trigger the alarms. He didn't feel like he had much of a choice, though. The compound was too massive and too well secured to get into, much less search. The only way he could get in was with an army of his own to surround the compound. There was an idea.

"Okay, Wesley, I think I may have a better plan. It's a long shot and will use up a significant amount of ammo, but I think it'll work."

"If you have any plan, let me hear it. I've been looking it over and I haven't found a weakness yet."

"We attack it like an army," Michael said as if it made complete sense.

"Um, I think the walk may have made you delirious. We don't have an army. We have you and me. They... They have an army."

"All we have to do is make them think that we do. Take both rifles and go to the main entrance. Fire as many shots as you can, as quickly as you can. That will draw their attention, so I can move in from the rear. When they get too close, run to meet me on the other side."

"I don't like it."

"It'll work. Trust me."

Michael and Wesley both knew the plan was risky, but they couldn't find a better option. Time was against them in finding Allie, and the morning light would eliminate their cover. As they each got into position, Michael's heart started pounding. Planning was never one of Michael's strongest traits. During the war, that was always Trent's job, and at that moment, he wished they had brought him with them. The last time he had led a group with his own plan was the day in his life he regretted the most.

Terror seized him. What if he had to make that decision again? Could he do it? He had always told Cade that it had to be done and that there was no choice. Similar logic was used here. Michael's decision had cost Cade his sanity. He couldn't bear to do the same to Wesley. Michael froze in his steps, unable to move. He couldn't stop thinking about what had happened.

Gunfire invaded his thoughts. Wesley was already firing off his first set of rounds, and Michael was still fifty yards out of position. With no way to communicate with each other on opposite sides of the compound, they were relying on strict timing. Michael's hesitation had cost him that. The plan had only begun and was already falling apart.

Michael ran to the rear gate. It was the only gate in the compound that was continuously left open for the easy passage of vehicles in and out. His plan was working.

Several of the guards at the gate were running toward the front of the compound, leaving only one to close it.

Michael pulled the pistol he had been carrying from his waistband. He sprinted as fast as he could to get to the entrance. He only had a few moments to enter in unde-tected. Their window of time was small between the guards in the towers losing focus due to the gunshots and more guards arriving to barricade the gates. That window was closing quickly.

One guard stood at the entryway, pulling the gate closed. He was engrossed by the gunfire echoing through the compound and the orders barking through his radio. Michael rushed him and subdued him quietly. Now, nothing stood between Michael and the doorway to the compound.

Michael moved the guard's body out of the main lights and into the shadows. He tried to be as quick and stealthy as possible to avoid the attention from the guards at the watchtowers. His hope was that their attention would still be elsewhere as well. He then stripped the un-conscious guard and took his uniform and radio.

As he did, one of the guards came over the radio ask-ing about the rear gate. Michael pulled his cap down low over his eyes and stepped back into the light. Giving the thumbs-up signal to the nearest watchtower, he walked to the end of the gate and pushed it almost closed. He couldn't afford to push it completely and take the chance of it locking, effectively trapping him inside. His actions seemed to appease the other guards and no more mention of it was made. He took that as a sign that it was clear for him to enter the compound.

Michael opened the door and was immediately taken back. The smell was so pungent that had his stomach not have been empty, he would have spilled its contents on the floor. It was the smell of death and rot. Michael thought he must have entered the morgue until he heard the cries of those living within.

The room wasn't a morgue but a prison with large, overpopulated cages. Those locked in it were treated and behaved like animals. They were thrashing and gnawing at each other; fighting over crumbs of food scattered across the floor of their cages. There was nothing humane there. Those that were living were doing so among the dead. Most appeared as if they would soon join them. Their bodies weren't much more than a skeleton. They were so frail that a child could knock them over. The sight chilled Michael's bones. The two guards standing watch at the opposite end of the building seemed unaffected. They stood there watching these people suffer, with their masks pulled tight against their faces to cut down the smell.

Slowly, Michael tread through the alleyway between the cages. He could only imagine the horror Allie witnessed when they brought her here. He had to save her. He looked through every face in every cage he saw, but no sign of her. These people looked as if they had been there for years. He assumed the new arrivals must have been in a different section of the compound. His best chance of finding her was to ask someone more familiar with the place. The problem was, his disguise was only believable at a distance. He couldn't ask one of the guardsmen for fear of them recognizing him. He thought of asking one of the prisoners, but they were all too afraid and huddled in the corner when he approached. In spite of his persistence, his questions fell on deaf ears as each of them ignored him. Each of them, except one. This one young girl, slightly older than Allie, was very intrigued by him.

"You don't act like the other guards," she said to him.

Her words were weak, and she acted as if it took all her energy to muster them. Her condition was the same as everyone else Michael had encountered. She was frail and thin. Her white jumper had turned to brownish gray. Michael's heart hurt at the sight of her, thinking Allie could end up like her if he couldn't get to her.

"Have you seen any other young girls your age lately?" Michael asked.

"Lots of girls come, but very few stay. Neither are very lucky," the little girl said.

"I'm looking for a girl who's probably just a little younger than you. She has blond hair and green eyes. Her name is Allie."

"Oh, Allie-Cat. She was nice." The girl smiled at her own memory.

"Was?"

"Yeah. She's gone now. We only got to be friends a little while."

"Where did she go?"

"She came with another lady. They threw them in here with us. She was so scared. I tried to help her be happy. The other lady wasn't being very nice. She yelled a lot. I was glad when they took her away. But then the mean guards came and got Allie-Cat too," the little girl said as she pouted her lips. "They told her it was time she got to see the city."

Michael pressed his forehead against the side of the cage. He didn't know how to take the little girl's story. Part of him was relieved that Allie may still be alive, but if she was in the city, he may never find her. Of all the cities in the country, Michael knew exactly which one she meant—Metropolian. Metropolian was hundreds of square miles and was the heart of the nation, more so than even the new capitol building in Imperia. Decades ago, during the time civil unrest had reached a pinnacle, Metropolian offered promises of peace and prosperity. Most of the country's population migrated there. It was also the headquarters of the Federal Police. It had been six years since Michael had been there, and now this little girl was telling him he had to go back.

He wasn't sure if he should believe the girl's story. For all he knew, she could be referring to a different girl if several had come and gone from there. The girl seemed so sure, though, and he didn't have time to search the entire compound if her story was true. Michael made the difficult decision to trust the girl. He thanked her and quickly walked back toward the exit. He needed to regroup with Wesley so that they could find a way into the city without wasting any more time.

He opened the door he came in from, only to see the outside was crawling with Federal Police. The gate had been securely closed, and a group of officers huddled near it. Through the spaces between them, he saw the guard he attacked lying on the ground at their feet. He had been discovered. Michael's heart began racing. If they found the guard, then that meant they were also onto him.

Michael retreated back into the building and ducked behind a set of cages. He didn't know what to do. He had spent too long checking cages and now they were onto him. He thought he had time. He never heard any announcements over the radio. He reached back to grab it and noticed the radio he had in his pocket was missing. Someone had stolen it as he was wandering through the cages. Fortunately, he had left his gun and Rebecca's bible tucked against him, or else he may have lost those too. Now was not the time to be concerned with material objects, though. He had to save his life.

Frantically, Michael searched the room for another exit. There were only two doors in the room—the one he came in and the one guarded by the two officers. He sized up the situation. How could he have been so stupid? He knew the Federal Police would barricade the gates at the first sign of trouble. His plan had failed because he had forgotten to plan an escape route. His only choice it seemed was to fight his way out.

He checked his pistol. Five rounds were left in the clip. At least two would be needed just to walk through the door. If anyone heard the shots, even a fully loaded gun wouldn't help him. He was backed into a corner. He had no choice. Going through two guards would be much more efficient than through an army.

"Hey, Friedman, you okay down there?"

Michael peered through the cages, looking for who it was calling and who they were calling to. One of the guards at the door had begun walking down the steps toward him. He was only forty feet away and coming closer. Michael's plan was ruined. If he shot this guard, the other one would radio for help, and there was already one more person in the room—Friedman, the man the guard was calling for.

Michael held his gun tight. He was preparing for the worst. Then it occurred to him. There was no one guarding the door he came in from. Why would two guards be at the door leading deeper into the compound, and no one at the one leading outside? Friedman was the missing guard. Michael looked at the name tag on his uniform. His suspicions were correct. Friedman must have stepped outside to close the gate, and when Michael entered back in, they must have thought he was resuming his post.

"I'm fine," Michael replied back in a gruff voice to appease the guard.

"You don't sound fine. You haven't caught what your partner has, have you?" the guard asked.

There was Michael's escape. If he could pretend to be sick, they may let him pass through.

"I think I might. I'm going to go find a toilet," Michael said, emerging from behind the cages with his face buried in his elbow.

"Man, if I was in here without a mask on I'd be sick too."

The guard reached behind Michael to a metal box on the wall. He pulled out a mask like the one he was wearing and offered it to him. Michael gladly accepted it since it gave him a better way to hide his face. He slipped the straps over his head, making sure the guard didn't notice that he wasn't actually Friedman. With the mask hiding his face, he nodded at the guard and began walking toward the door to the rest of the compound. The other guard examined him as he approached the door. Michael grabbed his stomach and shook his head. Before the guard had a chance to complain about him leaving, the door flew open. Four new guards and a high-ranking officer walked in.

"Gentleman, I'm here to inform you of the situation," the high-ranking officer said. "It seems after the attack at the main gate, an impostor has slipped in among us through the rear gate. We're still trying to identify the guard that was attacked, so at this point, he could be anyone. We're relieving all teams in the vicinity until everyone is properly identified. Please follow me."

"Sir, if I may, Friedman here may need to make a little pit stop," the guard said, placing a hand on Michael's shoulder. He was still hunched over, holding his stomach.

"Negative. Until this impostor is caught, we are on full lockdown, and everyone in this area must be accounted for."

"Okay, Captain, but if he blows chunks on my shoes, our team is going to lose another member."

"One day, Tobias, your mouth will find you on the other side of those cages," the captain snapped. "He is in your care, and I expect to see you both in interrogation in ten minutes."

As soon as the captain turned to leave, Michael and the other two guards were right on his heels. They were walking through a short dimly lit hallway. A small two-inch window ran the length of the hallway at eye level. Through the window, Michael saw other groups of guards replacing the ones outside. They were lining them up, shining flashlights in their faces, and checking IDs. Michael watched them searching relentlessly. He was amazed that he was lucky enough to slip through.

The room on the other side of the hallway was drastically different than the one he had left. It was very state-of-the-art and seemed to glow from the bright lights. Large screens coordinated the movements of everything. From the dispersing of prisoners to the flight patterns of the helicopters, any needed information was displayed on them. Even with the early morning hour, the area was filled with people. Prisoners were corralled into chutes awaiting instructions on where to be taken next. Some were arriving through a door on the side, still chained together as Michael had seen them before. Others were leaving in the same fashion.

The guard the captain called Tobias, separated himself from the captain and the other guard. Michael followed close behind, trying to act as if he knew where the restroom was. They walked to a small corridor with a door on the side, halfway down.

"While you hit the head, I'm going to go see what's going on around here," Tobias said as Michael walked to the door.

After a few minutes of waiting, Michael peeked out and saw that Tobias was nowhere to be seen. He strolled to the end of the corridor. The coast was clear. Although the captain had said that the facility was on lockdown, everything was business as usual, or so it seemed to Michael. Prisoners and guards were all being loaded onto helicopters. Guards were leading other guards to what Michael assumed to be the interrogation room. Men in lab coats with clipboards meandered through the commotion to some of the screens on the wall.

Michael walked to the screens to try to find a way out. His hope was that he may be able to leave with the prisoners. That would give him a chance to reach the city much faster if he could find a flight there. Trying to comprehend the information was a challenge. Everything was written in shorthand, and the screens were constantly changing. To make matters worse, it had been so long since Michael had looked at such a bright screen, it made his eyes water.

"Excuse me, sir. Prisoners being moved to holding," an officer shouted at Michael. He glanced at the officer and nodded his head.

As he stepped out of the way, he saw his first glimpse of hope. Amanda was being brought out of a room on the side. Michael saw her just before they hooded her. He fought his way through the crowds of people. Gently pushing on people in front of him, he cut through the lines of prisoners. He had to get to where she was. Allie had to be somewhere close. The guards shackled her and linked her to another line of prisoners. They were being led to the exit gate. Michael hurried and joined the Federal Police officers that were loading up to leave with them. He walked casually alongside them, trying hard not to draw attention to himself.

"You're one too heavy," the pilot told them as they approached the helicopter. Immediately, the other officers looked to Michael for an answer.

"Room for one more?" Michael asked timidly.

"Not without orders. We received notice of an impostor on base, and you're wearing a mask."

Michael hung his head. This was it. He had reached the end of his journey. As soon as they saw his face, they'd know he was the impostor. They would arrest him or, most likely, kill him. He had failed in his efforts to save Allie. He had broken the promise he made to his dead wife. He would soon be joining her. Michael surrendered. He lifted the mask and revealed his face to the Federal Police.

To his surprise, the guards looked at him with blank faces, waiting for an explanation. They didn't recognize him. Michael scrambled to find words that could save him. He may have one more chance to save his life and Allie's.

"I- I forgot I still had it on. I've been in the holding area since I've been here."

Michael chuckled to himself over the truth of his statement. His answer seemed to appease the other officers, but the pilot was unrelenting.

"Still, without orders, I can't let you board."

"Please, sir, my flight doesn't leave out until tomorrow and I'm just trying to get to Metropolian. I just want to see my daughter," Michael said, lowering his face. He was never a good liar, so he opted to share the truth. He hoped that he wouldn't regret doing so. In reality, he wasn't sure if this helicopter was even going to Metropolian. It was merely a hope he carried.

"No," the pilot said sternly. "Not without orders. This is my aircraft. No one boards it unless I say so. I will not be the pilot that allows an impostor to escape."

"Just let him go, Vasher. Friedman's good. He just doesn't want to admit he was puking his guts up earlier."

Michael glanced around and noticed it was Tobias. Even without a mask on, he recognized him. Michael was confused. He knew the guard could see his face. There was no way he could possibly look that much like Friedman, even under the twilight sky. He didn't question it. At the moment, the guard was helping him, and he didn't want to take the chance of messing that up. He gave the pilot a sheepish smile as he walked past him to board the helicopter.

The officers sat on either end of the prisoners. Tobias sat on the opposite end from Michael. He had nestled into his seat and leaned his head against the window, preparing for a nap. Michael watched him carefully. He didn't know why this one guard was risking himself to help him. He seemed no different than the others. But, then again, the others weren't hassling him either. He was sure his face was plastered everywhere listing him as a wanted fugitive. Only the pilot gave him any grief. Michael assumed he was merely vying for a promotion. He carried himself with such authority, he seemed out of place as just a pilot.

Michael turned to collect his thoughts, gazing out of the window. Then he understood why the other guards weren't after him. In the window, he saw his reflection. It was the first time he had seen his own face in quite some time. Even he barely recognized the person staring back at him. His beard had grown out, covering his face in stubble. He had lost weight from his time spent living off the land. His eyes were sunken in from exhaustion and dehydration. The left side of his face had been disfigured from the burning board Wesley attacked him with. Wesley.

In his search for an escape and his fight to stay close to Amanda, Michael had forgotten about Wesley. They were supposed to have met at the rear of the compound. He hoped that he had escaped. Hoped that he had given up on his return and found his own way to safety. He could only hope because the only other option would mean he had been captured.

7

WESLEY SAT IN A COLD DARK ROOM. A single light shone above him. He was afraid. Terror crept up his spine like a serpent lurking for its prey.

He had always felt uneasy about Michael's plan. He felt as if they were going up against a well-armed giant with only a slingshot. He had kept quiet about his concerns because none of his ideas seemed any better. He should have listened to his instincts. If he would have, he wouldn't be stuck here, chained to a chair.

They had come on him so fast. Seven shots he fired. Three before they fired back. A barrage of bullets surrounded him. One clipped him in the shoulder, knocking him to the ground. Heat and pain flooded the right side of his body. Footsteps were fast approaching. The sounds of leaves and twigs rustling amplified the sound. In Wesley's mind, he pictured at least a hundred armed guards running toward him. It was too late to run. Too late to fight back. His only chance was to hide.

He curled himself up beneath an old fallen log, squeezing into its hollowed-out crevice. Footsteps surrounded him. Trees splintered as bullets shredded limb and bark. Sweat and blood pooled under him, but he couldn't let himself move.

He tried to calm his shivering. The footsteps faded. He was safe for the moment. Still, he dared not move. For all he knew, they were surrounding him. Waiting for him to appear. He wouldn't give them the satisfaction. He would wait them out.

It felt as if hours had passed, although Wesley knew it was more like minutes. He listened closely. All was silent. The shouting and gunfire had faded into the distance. They were chasing ghosts. Gently, he crawled out of his hiding space. There was nothing around him. Nothing but trees and grass. Michael's plan was working. Wesley hoped that he was having luck as well.

With the coast clear, he followed through with Michael's plan. He scurried toward the rear side of the compound. His shoulder ached, but he was managing. That wasn't the first time he had been shot. In his policeman days, he had taken a bullet to the thigh and then had to continue running on it. He may have been younger then, but this wound was not as serious. He applied pressure to it with his hand and kept going.

Wesley approached the rear gate, staying hidden in the trees. Guards had already arrived to fortify it. He hoped that Michael had a better escape route in mind. Then he noticed something that horrified him. The guards were lifting a man onto a stretcher. The man was naked, and they were putting Michael's clothes into an evidence bag. His face was covered in blood, and he wasn't moving.

Michael, Wesley thought.

He had to save him. He charged through the trees, rifle in hand. He lifted it up to fire a shot, but the sudden impact of the stock of the rifle digging deep into his wound caused him to flinch, loosening his grip. Before he could regain control of the weapon, the guards were on him. One tackled him, knocking him to the ground. The commotion tipped the stretcher, causing the man's body to fall at their feet. Wesley looked up and saw several Federal Police officers huddled around him. Their guns trained on him.

He panicked. There was nothing he could do to help neither himself nor Michael. He peered through the gaps between them and saw a door swing open. More guards stepped through. At the sight of more guards approaching, Wesley lost all hope. He quit struggling against them as they bound his hands together and put a black hood over his head. The world went dark.

When the hood was removed, he was in this room, alone. His shoulder still ached, worse from all the commotion. He noticed a brown circular stain on his new white jumpsuit. He knew that they had bandaged him, but he must have still been bleeding through. He tried to readjust to find a more comfortable position but being chained to the chair made it impossible.

Wesley glanced around the room. There was nothing. Nothing but darkness surrounding the dim bulb that hung above him. He was afraid of what they were going to do to him. He assumed they were going to kill him. Death seemed more humane than leaving him in the solitude of that room. No one had come to talk to him. No one had come to offer him anything. There were no questions. There were no answers. There were no people. There was only him with his own thoughts and fears, trapped inside this room.

"What do you want from me?" Wesley yelled, rattling the chains against the chair.

It was the question that burned in his mind. The question he couldn't understand. Why would they capture him and leave him alone in that room? If they wanted information, why were they not asking questions? If they wanted to kill him, why leave him trapped? He had nothing for them. He had lived off the grid for the last several years. There was nothing he could tell them that would prove to be valuable. There was nothing left of anything he knew.

Visions of his life filled the darkness around him. He kept thinking of Joanna. They, like Michael and Rebecca, had been together most of their lives. He was the reason she had left the city. With the stress the government put on her with the rejection of her design, Wesley thought it would be a nice change of pace. He saw it as an opportunity to relax and rejuvenate themselves. They had found themselves a small cottage in the mountains overlooking a beautiful valley. It was a picture-perfect scene. They had friendly neighbors who lived far enough away that he and his wife had all the privacy they could want.

It was just the way Wesley had envisioned it would be when he offered for them to move there. Little did he know that a law would be passed later that year, stating that the border of the Forbidden Zone would be moved to include their little haven. Those that they found living there would be deemed a threat to national security. The Federal Police came then too.

While Wesley and Joanna were away, they burned their cottage to the ground. Everything he and Joanna ever owned had gone up in smoke that day. Joanna was heartbroken, and Wesley was angered at the way things were handled. No one had warned them that it was coming. No one had given them the chance to come back. They fled down the mountains. They traveled farther and farther south, never staying in one place very long. That was until they came across an old broken-down shack near the woods.

They had snuck inside for shelter one night. It appeared to be vacant. Most of the rooms had fallen down. In the dim moonlight, they found a soft place to rest. When the face of an older lady emerged from the darkness, they were terrified. More so, when the deep, booming voice of a man echoed through the room.

That was the first time he had ever met Michael. Wesley would never have guessed after breaking into his house, he and Michael would become such good friends.

As Wesley sat there, staring into the darkness, he saw Michael and Rebecca welcoming him into their home. He saw Nelda tending to her plants. He saw Joanna standing in front of him. Her arms were open, inviting him in. He wanted to go. He wanted to leave this place and run to her. He missed her.

The visions changed with his thoughts. In an instant, she was no longer standing there but lying on the ground staring at the sky. Blood pooled under her head. He wasn't there to protect her, just like he couldn't protect Michael. Even with all the lives he had saved over the years, he couldn't save those that mattered to him the most.

Breathing penetrated his thoughts. His anger with himself and with the Federal Police had caused him to hyperventilate. His heart thundered in his ears like a caravan of horses. He closed his eyes, trying to focus on anything positive that he could. He had to control his breathing. There was no use. He had to escape that room. He had to be free. He pulled at the chains on his arms with all his strength. He gave himself two options, either breaking the chains or breaking his arms. Whichever the case, he was going to get free.

His mind was determined, but his body couldn't hold out. He collapsed back into his chair, exhausted. He was upset. He had let down everyone he had ever cared about. He hung his head down, weeping.

"Mr. Steele, we expected more from you. We never thought you'd give up so easily, after all the tenacity you showed in your little raid on our prisoner compound."

Wesley looked around the room. There was still no one there. No one was with him in that room but the darkness. Then a hand was placed on his left shoulder, causing him to jar to the side. The sudden movement intensified the pain in his wound. The silhouette of a man walked around him. He took a seat in front of him just outside of the light.

"Listen, I don't know who you are, but I demand to know what you want from me," Wesley yelled at the man.

"Mr. Steele, please. You are hardly in any position to be making demands."

The man was right, and Wesley knew it. He had deliberately attacked the Federal Police, a crime as punishable as treason. Attacking them was no different than a direct assault on the potentate. He was lucky to still be alive, even if he was imprisoned in a small room.

"Mr. Steele, if it were up to me, we wouldn't be having this conversation. If it were up to me, I wouldn't be sitting here watching you squirm in your shackles. Watching the sweat roll down your face in fear. Oh, if it were up to me, you'd be long dead, and I could be free from looking at your undeserving existence. But it's not up to me. No. You have information we need."

"You want information, get a phonebook."

"The last person that smarted off to me got a bullet between the eyes. Which reminds me, how's your wife?"

Wesley lunged at the man with all his might, but the short chains snapped him back into his chair. He tried a second time before letting out a scream at the top of his lungs.

"I promise you, before you see the last of me, I will kill you," Wesley snapped through gritted teeth.

"And I promise you, Mr. Steele, before you ever get to be free from this room, you will tell me all that I want to know. Where is Michael Anderton?"

Wesley's eyes widened. Was this officer playing games with him or was Michael still alive? He was sure they had captured them together. Was that really Michael he had seen on the gurney? Wesley's head was spinning. He was searching for the truth through all the head games being played by the Federal Police. It was likely that they had set him up by posing someone as Michael. They used him as a trap to lure Wesley into their grasp. But how did they get Michael's clothes? How did they know where to find him?

"He's dead," Wesley exclaimed. It was the only solution that made sense to him. The only way things added up to what he knew.

"No, Mr. Steele, he is not dead. Where is he?"

A sudden jolt of electricity surged through Wesley's body. Someone else was behind him. They had hit him with an electric baton. All his muscles constricted. It made his whole body hurt and made breathing difficult. Wesley was determined to stick with his story. They may have believed it to have been a lie, but for all he knew, it was the truth.

"Don't come at me with that thing again," Wesley snarled, peering over his shoulder to try to get a glimpse of the person behind him. "Listen, you need to get your facts together. He's dead. Killed by your people. I saw it with my own eyes."

Another jolt of electricity. Wesley slumped in his chair. He didn't have the strength left to put up a fight with the officer but was still unwilling to change his story. He told the truth that he knew. There was nothing more he could say. He honestly didn't know where Michael was or whether he was alive or dead.

"You seem to think you have a choice in the matter, Mr. Steele. Do you think that lying to me is going to save anyone? No. The only chance you have to save even your own pathetic life is by telling me the truth. Trust me, very soon you'll be begging to tell me where he is."

Wesley glared at the man's silhouette. He was helpless to move but that didn't stop his anger. He would find a way to get free. He would find a way to stop whatever plan this man was devising. There was no way he would give in to the demands of someone so bent on causing death and destruction. He would rather die than help them find Michael if he was still alive. Fortunately, for his sake, he didn't know where Michael was, so there was no way he could help them. Regardless, the only thing Wesley was willing to do for them was to get his revenge. This dark figure in front of him was the cause of Joanna's death. He was the reason his love was taken from him, along with everything else in his life. There was nothing left for him to live for other than avenging his wife.

"Very soon, you'll be dead," Wesley spat at the man.

"Such temper from such a powerless man. Guard, tend to his shackles and then leave him to think about his answers a little more," the figure said to the guard with the electric baton.

"Right away, Colonel Hempton."

Hempton. That name sounded so familiar. Realization swept over Wesley like a crashing wave. This was the man Michael had been captured by after Cade's death. This was probably the same room they kept him in. Michael's story had become much more vivid to him. If only he had mentioned how he had escaped from this place. That would have been a big help to him now.

Wesley assessed the situation. His arms and legs were each chained to the metal chair he sat on. The chair was securely bolted to the floor. His arms were limited to a reach of only a few inches. A single bulb shone overhead, producing light in a two-foot circle covering himself and part of the table in front of him. There were no other sources of light, no shadows, and no reflections. The edges of the room were pure blackness. Colonel Hempton and the other guard had disappeared from the room, but no door was ever opened that Wesley knew of. For all he knew, they could still be in the room, lurking in the shadows.

He had to risk it. He had nothing to lose. If he was discovered making an escape, the worst they could do would be to kill him, but if he stayed he was as good as dead. His first mission was to find a way out of the shackles that kept him bound to the chair. With such limited mobility, he had very few options.

When he was younger, he used to be fascinated by watching illusionists escape from things. He would watch them lift their arms and shake them, only to have the chains fall off from them. If only it were so simple in real life. In reality, he didn't need magic or trickery to escape. The object of his salvation was literally under his nose. A tiny paper clip had been left at the edge of the table by mistake, almost invisible in the dim light. With his time spent on the police force, he learned how to pick a set of handcuffs easily, especially since his partner always seemed to lose the keys.

It wasn't but a few minutes, and Wesley was free from the cold grips of the metal chair. He surveyed the room carefully, waiting for someone to emerge from the shadows at any moment. When no one came, he eased himself out of the glow of the soft light. His hope was that he could conceal himself as the guards had done earlier. He kept moving farther back to try to press up against the wall. He wasn't sure what waited for him on the other side of it, but if he could feel against it, he could find an exit somewhere along it. The problem was, he couldn't find the wall. He turned around and kept walking farther and farther into the darkness, but there was only emptiness in front of him. Wesley looked back only to discover the light that had shone above him had been switched off. He was completely surrounded by darkness.

A panic arose within Wesley. If they had turned off the light, they must know that he had escaped from the chair. He started running toward what he assumed was the edge with his arms held straight out in front of him. To his dismay, they never made an impact with anything. The sheer blackness made him dizzy. He stumbled and fell. There was nothing around him but floor and space and darkness.

Wesley's mind boggled. He had been under the assumption the room was the size of any normal interrogation room. Now it seemed the room grew with every step he took. He couldn't understand it. The unknown wreaked havoc on his mind. He felt as if he could go insane in that room. This was a room of nothing. The deafening silence of it only amplified the thunderous beating of his heart. Each pulse made his head throb more.

Wesley fell to his knees. He tried to assess the situation. This was a room, and therefore it had its limits. He just needed to find them. His will to escape surged through him. He had to get free. He had a score to settle with Hempton. He had a hand in killing Joanna. Wesley was sure of it. He began creating a picture of the room in his mind. He was unsure of how far he had walked, so he couldn't pinpoint exactly where he should be in the room. He could be a mere foot away from a wall or walking farther from one. He decided his best bet would be to return to the table and regroup.

He started walking in the direction he had come from. If he could find the table, he would have a reference point to find one of the other sides. Finding it in such a place was a challenge. With no way to see the table, his only hope was to bump into it. He walked slightly bent over with his hands low. This caused him to stumble occasionally in expectation to find the table, but it never came. He continued to walk and walk, and still, there was nothing. Disheartened, he attempted to run, only to lose his balance and topple over. His situation seemed hopeless. He was trapped in a void.

He felt a growing sense of paranoia as the solitude overtook him. The endless darkness. The deafening silence. Time passed by slowly, but in that room, time was meaningless. Five minutes or five hours may have passed; Wesley couldn't tell the difference. Exhaustion and hunger began to take their toll on him as well. It had been days since he had had a decent meal, and it seemed to have been that long since he had food at all. His body felt numb. He had done nothing but walk for so long, when he stopped, his muscles would quiver. But they were too weak to try to keep on. He collapsed to the floor.

He was imprisoned in an endless room, and yet claustrophobia began to set in. The darkness around him began to take on weight. He could feel the darkness pressing on him. He struggled to breathe. His shoulder began to ache again, shooting pain through the right side of his body. All he could feel was pain and numbness as the darkness around him felt as if it was crushing him. He curled himself up on the floor, desperate for any relief.

The silence was broken.

There were voices. Voices were all around him. What were they saying? Wesley couldn't tell. They were mumbled, barely audible above the pounding of his heart. He listened more keenly, determined to make out the words. One of them mentioned Joanna, he was sure of it. Why were they talking of Joanna? He was sure of her death. He had held her lifeless body in his arms. It was the last time he would ever get to hold her. He remembered looking into her blank eyes as they stared at the sky. Her dark brown hair matted with blood. He had never been a religious person, unlike Michael and Rebecca, but in that moment, he had hoped they were right. He longed to see Joanna again soon. He felt as if he was about to join her.

8

THE HELICOPTER FLEW LOW. They were close to the fence line of the Forbidden Zone. Miles of war-torn lands had passed by. Craters dotted the landscape, separated only by the remnants of buildings and the vast abandoned farmlands. Michael found it hard to believe that this area had once had a thriving civilization of its own. Although he had lived in the Forbidden Zone for years, this was the first time he had seen it from the air. The barren wasteland he considered home looked nothing like he had imagined it would. His home was secluded in a grove of trees. It hadn't seen as much of the war as many places. If it weren't for the attack on the chemical plant nearby, his home would have probably never collapsed.

The rest of the Forbidden Zone was a different story. Evidence of explosions was everywhere. Vegetation was still slow to return even after all these years. Entire cities had been reduced to mounds of concrete and dirt. Michael couldn't imagine the devastation it would cause if someone tried to level Metropolian the same way these cities had been. These cities were a fraction of its size and still their destruction left a footprint for miles.

Michael tried not to think of the lives that were involved in the attacks. He tried not to think of the war at all. Just seeing the results of it brought back painful memories. He understood why the government had sanctioned the area as forbidden. There were so many memories of a time better left forgotten strewn about among the earth.

Michael missed his simple life. He had hidden himself away from the war, the Federal Police, and all the Federation. He had made peace with himself living on his own, providing shelter for those that needed it. He felt as if helping others not only gave him a purpose, but also an opportunity for redemption. As he flew over the Forbidden Zone, he realized that peace was a lie. He hadn't made peace with himself. He simply hid from his past. He had run away and went into hiding. There was no honor in him. He was a coward.

"Friedman."

The voice broke into Michael's thoughts. His eyes snapped away from the window and onto the source of the voice. It was Tobias on the other side of the helicopter, giving him a concerned look. Michael assumed his thoughts had betrayed him. That he was wearing his disdain for the war on his face. Tobias had most likely noticed his hands were clenched so tight his knuckles were white. Michael chastised himself for not being more alert and collected amidst so many Federal Policemen. As he looked, he noticed Tobias wasn't the only one looking apprehensive. The others were as well. Each of them had their rifles gripped tightly in their hands.

This is it, Michael thought. *I've been discovered.*

The officers weren't looking at him, however. They were staring out the open doorway on the side of the helicopter. Michael glanced back through the window and noticed they weren't flying over the fence of the Forbidden Zone, but rather alongside it.

The helicopter was flying even lower than before, and Michael had a close view of the thirty-foot-tall fence. The chain link ran from the ground to the top of the fence, with electric lines running every few feet for those that were tempted to climb it. Barbed wire swirled the top. The fence was truly designed to keep people from entering the Forbidden Zone. Michael wondered how anyone had ever found their way into the Forbidden Zone. People like Amanda, Wesley, and Joanna. They talked about their days outside of the zone but had somehow managed to find a way in, even with the efforts to keep people out. Perhaps they were like him and entered in before construction was completed. The fence seemed to tower even taller in the early morning light than it had the last time he saw it.

It wasn't long until the helicopter touched down next to what once was a small village. They were about forty yards away from the few remaining buildings. Michael strained his eyes and saw a face peering at them through a hole in the wall of a building. Within seconds of landing, there was a sound against the outside of the helicopter. It was a peppering sound that grew more and more intense. They were being fired on. The pilot quickly lifted back into the air and flew just out of range of the bullets. The officers linked themselves to ropes within the helicopter and began repelling down.

"Stay here and keep an eye on our guests," Tobias said to Michael, motioning to the prisoners on board the aircraft. With that, he repelled down to join the other officers.

Michael leaned closer to the window to watch the action unfold. The face he had seen had disappeared from inside the building, but twenty or so more had taken his place. The buildings were crawling with well-armed people. Some were aiming rifles through the holes in the walls. Some were perched on top. The Federal Police inched closer, spreading out to try to encircle the area. Chaos ensued.

The ones in the village had been prepared for this day. They were well armed and used the ruins as a bunker. The assault rifles of the Federal Police couldn't penetrate the thick concrete walls. They were undeterred. Using the tall grass as cover, they made an approach. Michael had always viewed the Federal Police as a group that was well armed and well trained. He saw them as a group to be feared, but these people were holding their own trying to protect themselves.

The fighting continued. But the losses weighed heavily against the Federal Police. They were outnumbered against a well-defended enemy. They were retreating. For the first time, Michael saw the Federal Police bleed. At that moment, he knew there was hope for him to save Allie. If these people could hold their own against them, then so could he. It wasn't but a moment later when that glimmer of hope vanished like a vapor in the wind.

Three large helicopters appeared over the horizon. As they approached, Michael could tell they were built for war. The helicopter he was in paled in comparison to their size. His was strictly for prisoner transport. These were for destruction. They were very wide and appeared to have wings. Under each wing was a set of missiles. A machine gun was mounted on its nose. The officers on the ground weren't retreating. They were simply making room for the heavy artillery. Within moments, a barrage of bullets flew toward the ruins. Explosions of missiles turned the concrete bunker to ash and dust. The thunderous roar shook Michael's helicopter.

Michael watched in awe and horror. He hadn't seen so much brutality since the war. The war was supposed to have ended years ago. These were supposed to be times of peace. Michael had been out of touch with what was going on in the rest of the world for so long, he was astounded by what he saw. First, they had come and killed his family. Then they locked hundreds of sick and dying people in cages and destroyed an entire village. The war was far from over.

Michael's anger and hatred for the Federal Police grew. Were these people they were attacking actually terrorists, or were they like him and his family, simply trying to protect their homes? How many innocent people had the Federal Police killed and captured? Trent knew what he was saying about them. These people had no compassion. They didn't listen to reason. Their mission was death and destruction.

Michael looked down at the uniform he was wearing. For years he avoided the Federal Police, despising the fact that they were the reason he couldn't return home. Now he was among them, sitting comfortably in a helicopter watching the death of countless innocents. He looked up at the prisoners in front of him. They were shaking in their seats. They had heard the gunshots and felt the explosions the same as Michael had. They were fortunate the black hoods kept them from witnessing it as well.

Without thinking, Michael stood up with the pistol in his hand. He couldn't sit idly by and let these people fall victim to the same fate as the village and his family. He would find a way to get to Allie but not like this. He couldn't allow others to die while he did nothing. He crawled his way to the cockpit. He pressed his pistol to the back of the pilot's head, just below his helmet. He wanted him to feel the barrel on his skin.

"Set us down. Now!" he barked. The pilot went to draw his weapon. Michael pressed the barrel deeper into his skin.

"If you kill me, we're all dead," the pilot said.

"I'm not going to kill you, but I'm not going to let you kill anyone else either."

"That's not your decision to make," the pilot snapped, pulling the joystick to the side and pressing hard on the pedal.

The helicopter went into a tailspin. Michael grabbed for anything he could to hold on to. He threw his arm around the pilot's neck. The pilot tried to reverse the spin, but the momentum was too great. The helicopter stalled. They were in a tin can free falling to the ground. The pilot pulled Michael's arm from around his neck, trying desperately to regain control. Michael gripped the seat tightly, closing his eyes and bracing for impact. There was a thud. Dirt filled the air in the helicopter.

The taste of mud and iron filled his mouth. His lip was bleeding, but he was alive. Michael opened his eyes and saw Tobias standing over him.

"What was the plan here, Michael?" Tobias asked angrily. "Crash this helicopter and then what? Take on those three AF-15s with a pistol?" He waved the gun in Michael's face, before tucking it into his waistband.

"I-I don't..." Michael stumbled.

Two more officers boarded the damaged helicopter behind Tobias. Michael was amazed that it was still intact and standing upright.

"What happened here?" one of the officers asked.

"The percussive blasts from the attack caused her to spin," the pilot said. "Luckily, I got her to land in one piece."

"Nice landing, Vasher, but a good pilot would have never lost it in the first place."

The two officers had begun checking on the prisoners. Three had been shot during the initial assault on the aircraft. Stray bullets had found their way in through the open sides. The rest of the prisoners seemed fine except for being rattled from the commotion. Tobias continued to stay close to Michael, tending to his few wounds from the crash.

"How many did we get?" Vasher inquired.

"A few," replied Tobias, pointing out the window to the officers dragging along some captives.

"And the leader?"

Tobias gave him a quick thumbs-up, before retaking his seat on the helicopter. Within moments, Vasher had the blades whirring. Despite the heavy damage sustained during the fall, the helicopter was still flyable. He never once mentioned Michael's attempted attack. He had taken the blame for no apparent reason. Michael had a terrible feeling in his gut. So far along the way, he felt like he had had the most fortunate luck, but this didn't feel like luck. This felt like someone deliberately wanted him alive and on that aircraft. Why else would his actions have been completely ignored?

Michael sat in silence for the rest of the flight. He couldn't take his eyes off the officers around him. Adrenaline and determination had gotten him through the compound and onto that flight, but all that was gone. All he felt now was uneasy. There was more going on around him than he had realized. He had been brash and careless, and now he felt as if he had walked into a trap.

His gaze shifted to each of them, waiting for one to make a move. His mind raced, trying to formulate a plan, or at least figure theirs out. None of it made sense, but then nothing had since Amanda accused him of killing his best friend. He was a nobody, living in isolation in the Forbidden Zone, yet everyone seemed to place great importance on his life. He couldn't understand it.

The bright lights of Metropolian took his concern off the officers. They were landing at another Federal Police facility at the edge of the city. The jagged skyline spread as wide as he could see, sitting like a backdrop across an expanse from the compound.

Michael tried to come up with an escape route, but not knowing the situation made it difficult. He was sure the Federal Police would make their move once they were on the ground. Without knowing what it was, he found it hard to figure out a good defense. Trying to just run away would most likely get himself shot. His only option was to be patient and play along until the most opportune moment. His impatience was what had landed him there in the first place. He was determined this time to keep his emotions in check and to think each situation through before making any more actions hastily.

When the helicopter touched down, the officers began unshackling the prisoners from their seats. They linked them into a chain. The seven living prisoners plus the five they had picked up at the village formed a single file line that was being led into the facility. Michael tried to go with them. Amanda was part of that chain, assuming she was one of the ones still alive. It was impossible to tell with the hoods over their faces. She had to be alive. She was the only reason he had boarded that particular aircraft in the first place. As he tried to leave, Tobias stopped him.

Michael tried to push through, but his grip on him grew tighter. He glared at Michael intensely.

"We've got three bodies here. Help me carry them in," Tobias said to Michael. Before Michael had a chance to refuse, he heaved one onto his shoulder. He then took one up himself, leaving another guard to grab the last one. As they walked toward the compound, Tobias took the lead while the other officer took the rear. Michael was sandwiched between them.

"Take those three to holding," an officer said as they neared the compound.

Great, I'm going right back to where I started, Michael thought.

The inside of this facility's holding area was much nicer than the last he had seen. The dim lights were replaced with bright lights around every cage, the steel cage bars with clear glass, the dirty, grimy floors with white tile. The ones trapped within them didn't appear to be near death, but rather fat and gluttonous. They appeared as if they were enjoying their stay within the walls. The dead and the living were kept separate here. The dead had their own enclosed area. When Tobias opened it, Michael realized it was refrigerated. They laid the bodies in the room, and the guard that was with them turned and left. As Michael turned to do the same, Tobias stopped him again.

"I asked on the 'copter, and I'll ask you again. What's your plan here, Michael?"

Michael hadn't misheard him the first time. Tobias did know who he really was. A lump formed in his throat. He began to shake uncontrollably, either from nerves or the severe cold of the room.

"Do you even have a plan?" Tobias pressed.

Michael was frozen. He couldn't think his way out of his predicament. He never had a plan. He had acted on pure instinct to get him that far. He wished he had a plan. A plan would help him to escape.

"I have no plan," Michael admitted, hanging his head down in shame.

"Then you're very lucky to have come across me. It took a lot of quick thinking to keep you from getting caught or killed back at Camp Delta."

"What are you talking about?"

"You don't think blind luck saved you back there, do you? Who gave you the mask and the free pass to the can? Who dragged that woman friend of yours out unmasked just so you'd see her and follow her to the 'copter? All me. You're welcome."

Michael was dumbfounded. All this time he thought he had been succeeding on his own wit and luck, but he had merely been set up by Tobias every step of the way. To what end? It didn't matter. Tobias knew of Amanda, so he had to know of Allie as well.

"Where is my daughter?" Michael screamed, gripping Tobias' uniform and pulling him within inches of his gritted teeth.

"First of all, back off. I just saved your life. I don't know anything about a daughter. All I knew was that there was a connection between that woman and you, so I knew you would follow her to the helicopter."

"If you can't help me, then take me to her. She'll know where Allie is," Michael said, pushing Tobias back.

"Patience, friend. Vasher is out there helping to redirect the prisoners as we speak. You'll get a chance to talk to her. Just stick close to me and try not to show anyone your face. The guards from the 'copter were just grunts. As long as Vasher accepted you, you were good. Plus, this caveman look you've got going on helped too, but I can't say that'll work with everyone. I mean, I recognized you pretty quick."

Before Michael could ask any more questions, Tobias was out the door. Michael followed closely behind, keeping his head down. He tried not to make eye contact with anyone and chose instead to spend most of the walk staring at Tobias' heels.

They walked deep into the compound. With every step, Michael gained a sense of familiarity. Something about this place felt like somewhere he had been before. They passed by a locked steel door with a bright red light shining outside. Michael had a gut-wrenching feeling deep within him at the sight of it.

"What is this room?" he asked.

"That? That's Hempton's baby," Tobias said. "They call it the Void. It's the room of nothing, but it's filled with your deepest, darkest fears. An hour in there and Hempton can get information on your great aunt's shoe size. Three hours and you're being spoon fed the rest of your life, because your mind is broke. The most anyone can really stand in there is forty-five minutes, after that...I've seen that room drive many people insane. I wouldn't want to go in there."

The sound of the room. The name. Hempton. It was all too familiar. That must have been the room they took him to after Cade's death. He felt sorry for anyone who may have been in there. Michael's heart raced just from being near it again. He quickly turned and caught back up to Tobias. He wanted to get as far away from that room as he could. He only remembered being in there for a matter of minutes, but the pain that followed was engraved in his memory. He had to get out of there. He had to get away before they found him again. Before he had to endure the worst horrors of that room.

The next set of corridors brought relief. At the end of the hallway was the door to the outside. He was finally free of the compound. He found himself in the parking lot. Vasher was waiting for them, leaning against a vehicle.

"He's the one coming with us, huh? You're driving."

9

THE VOICES WERE CALLING to him. Beckoning him. He wanted to go with them. To the sound of home calling from the center of the darkest abyss. The sweet sound of the soft melody protruding from those lips. The lips that once gave him the most succulent kiss, now a rose dipped in poison. He missed her.

"Joanna," Wesley cried with his every being.

He could hear her voice. He could see her face. Taunting him. Haunting him. The shackles of darkness surrounded her. Swirling. Blurring the image of her beauty. Twisting it until all he could see was death. Wesley's heart ached. A thousand times he watched it. A thousand times he sat helplessly as the life ebbed from those deep brown eyes. Over and over he relived its horror.

The darkness took on shape. Molding into the shape of men. Black. The color of the uniforms of the Federal Police. The very evil that took his love away from him. They surrounded him in countless numbers. They were around him. They were above him. They were everywhere. The cold steel of their weapons pressed into him. They were waiting for the right moment to strike.

There it was. The sound of gunfire radiated throughout the room. Gone was the sweet melody. Replaced by the ringing of a thousand bullets piercing his skin. Pain overwhelmed him. A pain more intense than any he had ever felt. His heart ached for the death of Joanna. His body ached of the hot lead piercing through it. He waited for the sweet relief of death. It never came.

The pain eased as fast as it had gripped him. The army of Federal Police vanished in plumes of black smoke. He was alone. The voices that had become his companion fell silent. The ringing in his ears remained. The chiming of bells resounding through his mind grew louder with each passing moment. He tried to scream to break the monotony that threatened his sanity. He had no voice. His mouth was too parched to make a sound. He tried to stand. He was too weak. He was helpless.

The light above the table turned back on. The dim light was blinding to his eyes. He found himself lying within inches of the chair he had been chained to. His efforts had been in vain. He was no closer to escape than he had been when he started.

"How are you feeling, Mr. Steele," Hempton asked, emerging from the shadows. Hands appeared on Wesley's shoulders, pulling him back up into the chair.

Wesley tried to focus his eyes. Was this real? Reality was a concept that had been lost to him hours ago. Or was it days? It didn't matter. It was all the same. He glared at Hempton's face, trying to make sense of his surroundings. As he focused, it changed. It was Michael sitting in front of him. No, not Michael, but still familiar. The image blurred again. It was Trent. He was sure of it.

"What have they done to you, my friend?" Trent asked.

Wesley tried to speak, producing only an inaudible grunt. Trent handed him a glass of water. The cool refreshing liquid quenched his parched lips.

"All of this will be over soon. Just tell me what happened to Michael, so I can help him too," Trent said.

"Trent? Is that really you? Is this real?" Wesley asked.

"I know this is hard for you. I can only imagine what you must be going through. I'm here to save you, Wesley. I'm here to save you from the Federal Police. All they want to know is where you went after you left the shack."

"We went to save his daughter. We followed them to a Fed compound," Wesley managed. His voice was still weak.

"Them?"

"Them. The Federal Police."

"So, you and Michael managed to find and launch an attack on a Federal Police compound, without any knowledge of its existence? I know you're a talented man, but that seems a little far-fetched."

Wesley lifted his hands to his face to wipe his eyes. It was the first he had noticed they hadn't chained him back down. Not that it really mattered. He was too weak to resist. It took all the strength he could muster to wipe away the moisture from his eyes. He had to see Trent's face clearly. He couldn't understand why he was there. Why he was pressing him so hard about Michael. Why Trent was even with the Federal Police. Wesley's mind swirled. His head collapsed down, his chin connecting to his chest as he tried to regain some focus.

"We walked where the helicopters were flying, and then this old man by the river gave us directions and weapons. Michael was going to try to sneak in while I covered him. That's all I know. They caught me before I could meet up with him."

"Why didn't you tell me, Wesley? I could have spared us all this trouble."

"Michael didn't want to put you in danger. They took his family and killed my wife, but that didn't make it your responsibility."

"How many years was I with you? And yet you just leave me behind. I have a hard time believing it. And I still don't believe you and Michael broke into a Federal Police compound alone. Who was helping you?"

"I told you, Trent. Other than the old man that gave us the rifles, it was just us. Me and Michael. I shot a few rounds to give him some cover and then hid for my life. I charged for the guards when I saw a beaten man, I thought was Michael. Trent, I think they killed him."

"Thank you, Mr. Steele." The face morphed back into Hempton as it approached the light. "If only you would have been as forthright to begin with."

There was a pain on the inside of Wesley's arm. A pain that felt like fire burning through his veins. He collapsed onto the table.

***

When Wesley awoke, his head ached. It pulsed like a thundering stampede, only to be intensified when he opened his eyes. They were sensitive to the bright lights around him. The white tile beneath him radiated the light from above. The crystalline glass bars around him twinkled in the rays. He tried to lift himself up, but he was too weak.

"Look, Maud, the new guy's waking up."

Wesley looked up and saw a heavy-set, middle-aged man talking to a woman with a similar description. They were sitting on a small, clear bench next to one of the walls of glass bars.

"Where am I, and who are you?" Wesley managed to ask.

"Name's Fred Goodman, and this here is my wife, Maud," the man said, pointing to the woman beside him. "Right now, you're in holding, which means one of three things. You have something they want, you're someone they want, or you're like the rest of us and you're just a genuinely healthy individual. Since you can't seem to get off the floor, my money's on one of the first two."

Wesley struggled to pull himself up into a sitting position. His eyes slowly adjusted to the lights. He gazed around the cell and noticed it was full of people hugging the edges of it. Their white jumpsuits blended in so well with their surroundings, he hadn't noticed.

"All these people are in here just for being...healthy?" Wesley asked.

"Well in a sense," Fred said. "The unhealthy ones die off pretty quick. Hard for them to test their experiments if the person isn't up to it to begin with."

"What? Experiments?" Wesley asked in bewilderment. He had never heard of anyone using people for experiments. Especially experiments that could kill someone. "That's completely inhumane."

"Geez, friend. You've got a lot to learn about this place. Where'd they pull you from? An island in the backwoods of the Forbidden Zone? Anyway, picture it this way. You've got a place like Metropolian, a city full of millions of people. Let's say a dangerous virus broke out. How do you treat it? With drugs that have to be tested. What's the best way to test them?"

"With rats or…"

"Look at me. Do I look like a rat? What if the wonder drug worked on Mr. Nibbles and then still managed to kill me? It's more efficient to test direct. It lets them stop the outbreak faster."

"But still it's inhumane."

"Inhumane? Really? It's not like they're rounding up citizens off the street. When they got me, I was living in the landfill, hoping for a tiny scrap of food. Now, look at me. I get five full meals a day, a clean place to sleep, and where do you think I met Maud? I'm telling you, being here…best five years of my life."

"Five years?" Wesley screeched. He couldn't imagine being trapped there for five years. But then, had his life at the shack been any better? He had traded in collapsing wooden walls for those made of glass. The scarcity of food for the abundance. The company of his friends for the company of strangers. What of his freedom? Was he ever really free then?

Wesley pushed such thoughts from his mind. The effects of the dark room were still taking a toll on his mental state. He shook his head, trying to focus. He had to break free, if for no reason other than to finish Michael's mission to save Allie. He pictured her being probed by needles. Surely, they wouldn't do such things to a child. He didn't want to chance it. He had to save her. He couldn't let her get hurt.

He pulled himself to his feet. The pain in his head made him feel dizzy, but he was determined. He lunged for the glass bars, hoping his weight would shatter them. The collision made his head feel as if it were about to explode, and yet, the wall stood.

"What are you trying to do? Clean the glass?" Fred chuckled.

"I guess I thought I could break the bars," Wesley admitted. In retrospect, it was a terrible idea. He should have been smart enough to know they wouldn't keep prisoners detained in such a delicate cage.

"Bars? Those aren't bars. They're more like ribs attached to the inch-thick plate of glass behind it. Of course, none of it is real glass. It's some kind of dense clear stuff."

Wesley placed a hand between the bars. He had failed to notice there was a pane between them. The walls were solid.

"It's for looks mainly. And it also provides a good bit of soundproofing," Fred continued. "I've been through several of these compounds before ending up here. Let me tell you, this one is all about show. They've got to impress the big wigs of Imperia. Can't have cramped dingy cells and people screaming when they walk through. Speaking of which…"

Wesley turned to look in the direction of Fred's nod. Four men and two women were being escorted through the holding area. They were unmistakably different from the Federal Police. Each of the men wore bulky velvet robes over their silk suits. The reds, blues, and purples of their coats wildly contrasted the strict black and white of the compound. The women dressed just as vividly in their long gowns and flashy jewelry.

They walked up to Wesley's cell. One of the guards opened the cell door, and immediately, the politicians put napkins to their faces to mask the smell. Wesley was surprised they could smell anything. The scent of perfume was so piquant from among them that it burned the back of his throat. The guard walked up to Fred and chained his hands together.

"Woohoo, today I might get the good food," Fred said, just before they hooded him.

Wesley watched as Fred casually walked out with them. He seemed surprisingly happy to be called out of his cell. Wesley didn't understand it. He continued to watch as they closed his cell door and collected a few more prisoners from the adjacent cells, before leaving the holding area.

"What are they going to do with him?" Wesley asked Maud.

"There's no way to know for sure, dear," she said.

"Well, what do they normally do?"

"Honestly, I don't know. They take you to a room and strap you to a table. Then they put you to sleep, and you wake up back here. You have no memory of what happened so it's fairly easy, and they reward you. If you're called out, afterward they bring you a big meal."

Wesley didn't like the fact that they were unconscious during the experimentation but assumed it was better than the alternative. If he were called on, he wanted to know what they were going to do to him. Fred went back so calmly. He was more focused on the food afterward than what lay before him. This was a man who had been through it so many times, it was commonplace. Wesley knew he couldn't be that calm. They wouldn't get him without a fight. No amount of food was worth being a pin cushion to whatever chemical they wanted to run through him. To these people in their cages, it was a way of life, but to Wesley, it was no life at all. He would break free of their grasp.

Hours seemed to have passed by when they brought Fred back to his cell. He looked as if he was near death. Under the cuffs of his jumper, Wesley noticed his wrists were bright red and bruised. His eyes were bloodshot. He was unable to stand on his own, yet the guard tossed him into the cell. He landed on the hard tile with a thud, letting out a terrible groan.

"They must've got me good this time, Maud. I feel terrible," Fred sputtered as blood poured from his nose and mouth. His breathing was quick but shallow. He acted as if he was drowning, choking on the air as it entered his lungs. Wesley went to help him, but then he noticed the guard had him. In his concern for Fred, he didn't realize the guard was chaining him.

Instinct took over. Wesley threw his arms over the guard, pulling the chain tight against his neck. The guard gargled and within minutes his eyes rolled back. More guards were coming. There was nowhere to hide in a glass cell. Wesley charged for the door, tackling one of the guards as he tried to enter. Another guard tried to pin him down while he was on the floor. Wesley began thrashing and kicking until he was on his feet. Electricity hit him from behind, seizing his muscles. A guard behind him had a wand with electric probes at the end. Wesley tried to kick it away but three more hit him on all sides. His muscles began twitching. No longer could he control his arms or legs. He was helpless to defend against them.

They dragged him through the holding area. The prisoners looked on in shock. They couldn't believe someone had been either brave or foolish enough to try to resist the Federal Police. Wesley had become an example of why no one tried. They were relentless in completing their missions.

They took him to a cold and sterile room. The politicians stood behind a glass window just to the left of the doorway, observing the process. A metal table stood in the center, angled toward the door. Wesley was tossed against it. Metal shackles were rolled over his wrists, legs, chest, and waist, making it impossible for him to move. It was just as Maud had described it. He wondered how anyone could get as used to it as they had. He closed his eyes. Unable to move against the restraints, he waited for them to put him to sleep. His only consolation was that he would soon awaken back in his cell.

"Inmate number Z4-5874. Name, Wesley James Steele. Identity confirmed through fingerprint and DNA testing. Captured in Sector Eleven of the Forbidden Zone."

Wesley opened his eyes. A man was standing over him, reading through information on a clipboard. Two others were gathering things on a metal cart, while one was keying information into a computer. They were all dressed in hazmat suits, which terrified Wesley. What kind of experiment could they be running on him to need such equipment? He had seen Fred and knew the outcome wasn't going to be pleasant.

"Give him the full panel," the man with the clipboard ordered.

Immediately, the other two began pulling up the sleeves of Wesley's jumpsuit. Hoses with needles attached were pressed into the tops of his hands and the creases of his elbows. Electric probes were attached to his forehead and neck. Chemicals were pumped into one arm as blood was drawn from the other.

The chemical was cold and felt like knives running through his veins. Just before Wesley thought he would freeze to death, a new chemical was pushed through with sensations of the opposite extreme. This time it felt as though it were boiling water. The sudden change threw his body into shock. He began convulsing. Those around him didn't care, all the while he felt as though his organs were melting.

"Tests are coming back negative. Low-level pathogens mostly. Most have been eradicated. Nothing airborne, and scanners show no radiation," the woman at the computer told the others.

"Good," the man said, removing his hazmat suit. "You people. There is a reason it's called the Forbidden Zone. The guards think their little masks will protect them. If they only knew what kind of diseases you people can be carriers of. At least this one's healthy. Let's try rerunning our last test on a fresh specimen. Z5-6832 has been here so long, it is likely the cause for the results to be inconclusive."

"Sir? Are you sure?" the woman asked. "Records show his file has been flagged by Hempton himself."

"We're so close to a breakthrough. Having an untainted specimen may be just what we need to finally succeed. If I'm right, Hempton will commend us." The man dropped his voice to just barely audible. "Besides, the senators are here. That means our funding is here. This is the time we need to have it working."

"I hope you're right," the woman sighed as she began keying the orders into her computer.

The two others rolled the metal cart closer to Wesley. Several canisters and colored tiles were on it. One of them checked the hoses still attached to his arm. The other began pouring one of the canisters into the machine they were attached to at the other end. The man in charge grabbed the colored tiles and began cycling through them.

The man nodded to the one operating the machine. A low hum emanated from it as it began pumping the chemical through it. Wesley knew the instant it reached him. Liquid fire coursed through his veins, hotter than the boiling chemical they had just run through him. His body began to shake, and he felt as if he was choking. Little droplets of blood sprayed from his mouth as he coughed.

He managed to take a breath just as the symptoms were subsiding.

"Before we begin, Mr. Steele, I want you to look at these and tell me what colors you see," the man said.

Begin? Wesley thought. He had already been put through the wringer. He felt as if he had been both frozen and boiled alive at the same time, and yet they hadn't even begun. Where was the promise of being able to sleep through the agony? This was torture. He had no choice. If he wanted to get through it, he had to go along with it.

"Red, blue, yellow, green, and purple," he said.

The man nodded, and the machine was switched on again. Wesley was relieved it had no effect. Maybe this wouldn't be as bad as he had thought. He still didn't like the fact that foreign chemicals were being put into his body, but there was no use in trying to resist. Unable to move on the table, he was at their mercy. They were monitoring him closely, noting even the smallest twitch of an eye. If he were to somehow get free, they would run something else through him to sedate him.

"The five colors, can you tell them to me again?"

"Red, blue, yellow, green, and purple."

"Thank you, Mr. Steele. Administer compound number two."

The second canister was poured into the machine. When the process began, this chemical wasn't as easy to endure. It burned throughout his body. Wesley gritted his teeth. His lungs restricted making it more difficult to breathe. He could feel his heart fluttering with the combination of chemicals that had run through him.

"The colors?"

"Red, blue, yellow, green, and purple. Why do you keep asking me about colors, and why are you running that crap through me?"

gone

The man shook his head and the third canister was poured into the machine. This chemical burned like fire, just as the first had. This one was different. The heat before had come and went. This lingered, seeming to intensify until it engulfed his whole body. His dark skin took on a reddish hue. He lost all control of his breathing. Blood spewed from his lips. His body shook uncontrollably. He felt as if he was dying. He arched his body, pulling as hard as he could on the restraints. The corners dug into his skin. He pulled harder. He had to get free. He wouldn't allow them to kill him. He let out a scream gargled in blood. He could finally breathe. He slumped back against the table.

"The colors, Mr. Steele?" the man asked with frustration in his voice.

"Red, blue, yellow…black and orange! I don't know. What do you want from me?" Wesley cried. Blood dripped from the corners of his mouth. The front of his jumper was completely red.

"Run the next compound."

"Sir, he won't survive another round," the woman monitoring the computer told him.

"We will run every compound until one works."

"It's no use. And if Hempton finds out we killed him, it'll be our heads next."

The man threw his clipboard, breaking one of the monitors near Wesley. Glass sprayed across him. The man hastily snatched a syringe off the cart and jabbed it into Wesley's neck. Wesley's world grew dark.

10

"HE LOOKS TERRIBLE," a woman's voice said, disrupting the ringing echoes in Wesley's ear. He had only thought what they had done to him in the silent room was horrendous. It seemed like they were not only trying to break his mind but his body as well. He felt as though his inner organs had been turned to mush.

"Turkey leg?"

Wesley opened his eyes and saw Fred and Maud standing over him. Fred was thrusting a half-eaten turkey leg up to Wesley's face. In his other hand, he had a plate of food three inches thick. It was full of food Wesley hadn't seen in a decade. Turkey, ham, green beans, and corn, among other things, adorned his plate. Wesley had lived so long on rodents and the remaining wild game, he had forgotten what farm raised food tasted like.

He looked at the turkey leg Fred had outstretched toward him. He was so focused on the food, for a moment, he had forgotten how bad he felt. His stomach began to rumble. He couldn't remember the last time he ate. He lifted his head slightly off the floor. Fred handed the

111

drumstick down to his mouth. Wesley latched on, ignoring all manners and decency.

"He's going to get it all over his nice clean jumpsuit," Maud said.

Wesley stopped eating and looked down at his chest. The bloodstains were gone. They had changed his clothes before bringing him back to the others. He wiped his face only to find nothing but turkey.

"He'll be alright, Maud. He just needs to eat to get his strength back. You know them tests take a lot out of you," Fred said, handing Wesley more food.

"Takes a lot out of you is right. How do you survive doing that so much?" Wesley asked, refusing the offer for more. While he was hungry, he was still recovering from what they had done to him. Just the small portion he had managed to shovel down was already beginning to make him feel nauseated.

"What do you mean? You just lay down and take you a good nap while they try out whatever drug it is they're testing."

"I don't remember sleeping."

"Does anyone ever remember sleeping?"

"No, I mean, I remember them standing over me, asking about…colors…"

"That's funny. I had the same dream while I was back there."

"It wasn't a dream. They injected me with something. It almost killed me."

All the prisoners in the cell looked apprehensive. Was he the only one to have ever been treated that way, or could they all simply not remember? They all began talking among themselves. Fred sat smiling like it was all a big joke.

"I've been through the routine countless times in five years. If they were doing something that severe, don't you think I would know about it?" he asked as he bent down and began looking Wesley over. He looked at his eyes, his hands, and even opened his mouth.

"How does he look?" Maud asked.

"Eyes are a little bloodshot, but he looks the same as he did when he left."

Wesley remembered the sores on Fred's wrists and looked at his own. Beneath the cuff of his jumpsuit was a wide strip of red. A mark he bore from his attempt to free himself from the restraints when he was gasping for life. They weren't as noticeable on his dark skin as they were on Fred, but they were there, nevertheless. He showed the mark to Fred, who compared it to his own. He had never thought that they could be bringing him to the brink of death each time they called him.

"If this is what the Federal Police do to you while you're asleep, do you really want to let them continue?" Wesley asked, trying to pick himself up off the floor.

"What choice do we have?" one of them asked.

"Really? We saw what happens if you stand up against them. I don't want to be electrocuted," another one shouted.

Fred helped lift Wesley up into a standing position. Wesley threw his arm around him for support as he surveyed the room. There were ten of them in the cell together. Through the glass walls, he counted the guards. He quickly began to come up with a plan.

"There are only four guards in here. Two at either door. So long as more don't come to collect any prisoners, we have them outnumbered. We can overpower them."

"That's a terrible plan," Fred said. "First off, hello, door's locked. We're stuck in here. Secondly, they're trained in combat. And most important of all, then what? Let's say we manage to take out these four, there's probably a hundred or so here. Face it, new guy, this is your life now. Besides, our fearless leader can't even stand on his own." Fred let go of Wesley who began to wobble.

Fred would have been right had Wesley not have already begun planning further ahead. He had scoped out the things they needed for their escape. He did wish he was a little stronger. In spite of his best efforts, he couldn't shake the damage the chemicals had done to him. He would make his plan work regardless.

"We can do this. We don't try to beat them. We join them. Once we subdue the guards, four of you will take their uniforms. The rest of us will form a prison chain using the chains and hoods on the far wall. With the sound-proofing of the cells, we shouldn't have to worry about alerting the rest of the compound. We just have to wait until they bring our food."

Considering the number of meals they fed the prisoners, the wait was only a few hours. Wesley spent his time pacing the cell, trying to regain his strength. It would take them all for the plan to succeed. He saw the food carts being brought in. Most guards tended to avoid the holding area, leaving the distribution duties to the ones that were already in there. Three of them would be preoccupied handing out food, leaving only one to stand watch. The guards relied too heavily on fear for their security, which Wesley planned to exploit to their advantage.

"Food," Fred exclaimed as soon as the cell door opened.

He charged for the cart, knocking it and the officer to the floor. The others surrounded him, while Wesley quietly put the guard to sleep. The commotion caught the attention of the guard standing watch. He was coming toward them. The other two were still preoccupied with their duties. Everything was going to plan. In mere moments, the large crowd had overtaken another guard. Only two more stood in their way.

The prisoners split into two groups. Wesley wanted to attack the remaining two simultaneously to avoid the risk of one of them calling for backup. Wesley and Fred each took charge of a team. They kept watch of each other through the glass cages. Fred's team attacked and incapacitated their guard with relative ease. It was up to Wesley to do the same and the first part of their mission for freedom would be complete. Wesley was within inches, preparing his attack. Just one more step. His legs gave out beneath him, causing him to fall harmlessly against the guard's back.

Wesley felt an elbow crash against the side of his face. The others of his team tried to jump in and take his place, but not before the guard let out a yell. It was loud enough, given their proximity to the door, anyone standing outside of it would have heard. They had to act fast. Fred's team had already begun putting on their uniforms. With Wesley's condition, he didn't want to risk having another episode and collapsing in a guard's uniform. No one would look twice at a fallen prisoner. He felt an arm lift him up. Fred had managed to squeeze into a guard's uniform and began carrying him on his shoulder to the door. The door sprang open, and two more guards ran through.

"What's going on in here?" a guard shouted.

Wesley looked back over his shoulder. To his surprise, everyone had fallen in line. Behind him stood a chain of prisoners surrounded by three guards. He was the only one out of position.

"Prisoner here tried to start a riot," Fred said, referring to Wesley who was slung over his shoulder. "We rounded up the whole cell of them. See if we can teach these boys some manners. Cover us for a minute."

Fred boldly strode up to the door with Wesley still over his shoulder. The others followed closely behind. Fred was acting very nonchalant about the situation, but Wesley could see the sweat dripping on his forehead. He himself fought off his own nervousness. Any sign of apprehension would have given them away. They couldn't afford to fail. The guards were watching them keenly.

"We'll take the prisoners. You can return to your post," the captain of the guards said, cutting Fred and the others off.

"Fat chance. This one here insulted me. I'm going to take him out back and rearrange his face for him. Might make him look a little better," Fred chuckled. Wesley was not amused. This was not the time for jokes. The guards were not thrilled by his antics either. The captain clenched his sidearm in its holster, standing tall in Fred's face.

"I gave you an order, officer. You will follow it, or you will find your place among this scum."

The guards were unrelenting. Without Fred and the others posing as guards, they wouldn't be allowed to move freely through the compound. Wesley scrambled to alter his plan. There had to be a way to convince the guards to let them through. Wesley looked up to study the officers carefully. To his horror, one of them had begun walking away. The others were trying to stall him, but it was to no avail. He kept pushing his way through despite their diligence.

Orders came through the captain's radio. The compound almost instantaneously went on high alert. Red lights began flashing as sirens began to blare. The wandering guard had also found the real guards unconscious on the floor, tucked away next to the glass wall. Everything was falling apart.

The captain, with his hand already on his gun, began to draw. Wesley mustered all the strength he had within him and grabbed the captain's arm. The gun fired wildly to the side, narrowly missing Fred. The bullet struck the wall of the cell and ricocheted into the leg of one of the prisoners. The prisoner fell to the floor writhing in pain.

Hysteria erupted. The prisoners began trying to flee for their lives. The chain connecting them caused them to stumble and fall. Those posing as guards trampled over them, trying to escape. The real guard raced back toward the group. More guards came flooding in through the doors on either end. They were trapped. Electric batons prodded at the prisoners fighting against their chains. Screams of agony and fear filled the air. Those that were still in their cells watched on in horror as the escapees were overwhelmed.

Wesley tried to pry the gun from the captain's hand. He had to do something to protect the others. It was his fault they were in that situation. It was his plan that went awry. More gunshots. They connected with the control panel, releasing the lock on the prison cell behind them.

The guards swarmed Wesley, knocking him off Fred's shoulder. Fred was holding his own one-handedly, but his attention was diverted to trying to catch Wesley. Both of them fell to the floor. Wesley felt a hand pulling at his ankle. He spun his body around to see who was pulling on him. In the chaos, Maud found her way to them. Although she was still chained to the other prisoners, she had fought her way close to Fred. The chain pulled tight, dragging her back into the fray. She disappeared amidst the legs of the guards surrounding them.

Fred must have been watching her also, because as soon as she disappeared, Wesley felt a heavy hand pressing down onto his back. Fred was trying to crawl over him to get to Maud. He began twitching and collapsed on top of him. The guards had struck him with their electric batons. Wesley was pinned, unable to move. He fixed his eyes on the prisoners in the open cell.

"Help us," he cried with great difficulty. Fred's body weight was pressing on his lungs, making it hard to breathe.

The prisoners were afraid. They huddled together in the far corner of the cell. No one wanted to get involved, especially after seeing the onslaught that ensued when Wesley had tried. Fear had gripped them tightly. They were slaves to it. It was the same fear the guards had always used to their advantage.

If only they would help, it might save us all, Wesley thought.

One boy stood out among the rest. While the prisoners cowered, he glared at the guards. It was as if he was waiting for the most opportune moment to strike. This boy was only a teenager, but he carried himself with such fierce determination. He seemed to stand a foot taller than the other prisoners cowering in the cell. He wasn't afraid. This was someone Wesley desperately needed on his side, but it was too late. There was nothing a boy could do against such a mass of guards. They had the upper hand.

The guards had won the battle. Wesley was pinned down underneath the weight of an unconscious Fred. The other prisoners had succumbed to the inevitable as they were carried away back to their cell. Two guards stood watch at the open cell door with electric batons in hand. Technicians were approaching to begin work on the control panel.

The captain and another guard were discussing the fate of Fred and Wesley as the ringleaders of the incursion. The guard tried to lift Fred but was unable to alone. The others had left out after fulfilling their duties, leaving only the captain and the two at the door to offer assistance. The captain reluctantly walked over and began lifting up Fred's upper body.

"I'm not about to carry this sack of potatoes halfway through this holding area," the captain scoffed, disgruntled by having to do a lower rank's work. "Just set him down in this cell, I'll take care of the paperwork."

They dragged Fred into the broken cell and dropped him on the floor.

"Don't run off," the guard smirked at Fred's unconscious body as he walked through the open door.

They were coming back for Wesley. All he could do was lie on the floor and watch and wait. The struggle to escape had zapped all the strength he had in his body. He should have waited. He did exactly what he always condemned Michael for. He acted too hastily, and it cost not only him but those he was in a cell with. Wesley tried to convince himself he had no choice. Between the eternal darkness of that room and the mixture of chemicals, they were going to kill him. Another round of either would surely finish him.

Wesley felt their hands gripping his arms, lifting him. The weight of his body pulling against his shoulder shot pain through him. The acute intensity of his unhealed wound contrasted sharply to the dull ache he felt throughout his body. This was it. This was how he was going to die. He should never have attempted escaping. He knew he was in no condition, but the choice had been made. Here he was a broken shell of the man he once was.

"Mr. Steele…"

Wesley's eyes darted up at the sound of that familiar voice. His pity party had to wait. His mortal enemy was staring him in the face. No matter how bad he felt, he would not show weakness to Hempton. He forced himself to stand on his own, shrugging off the hands of the guards. His knees were shaky, his muscles quivered, but he was not going to be moved.

"Is this how you reward my generosity?" Hempton asked, waving his hand at the carnage.

"Ah yes, the generosity of the devil," Wesley said.

"Careful, Mr. Steele. Right now, I'm the only thing standing between you and a fate worse than death. This is my facility. Nothing happens here without my approval. For instance, beginning immediately a three-day fast for every inmate in this area. We'll see how long you can maintain your strength."

Wesley gritted his teeth. He could feel the eyes of the inmates glaring at him. It was because of him that no one would get to eat for the next three days. As soon as the other cells found out, the whole compound would be against him. He buried his fear and his hurt. He couldn't let Hempton see that he was affected.

"As for you personally, Mr. Steele, I think maybe a little more time in the Void is what you need."

11

THERE IT WAS. The cold shiver running down his spine. The eternal darkness. The deafening silence. The Void.

Time once again stood still. This time, though, things were different. Wesley wasn't afraid. He was angry. He was angry that everything he loved had been stripped away from him. That he got himself trapped in this room again. He was angry at the world for allowing the Federal Police to even come to be. That the government could be so power hungry that people could be merely pawns to them. He was angry that Hempton was still alive. He was angry that he missed a spot the last time he shaved, and now part of his stubble was longer than the rest. He was angry.

His anger rejuvenated what the chemicals had stolen from him. As his hate-fueled rage surged within him, he no longer cared what his body felt like. No matter what they put him through, he wouldn't be held back by it. He forced his body to bend itself to his will.

As the darkness would twist and take shape, Wesley would wildly throw a fist at the emptiness. Crashing into the floor, he'd pull himself up and swing again. His frustration came through his flailing fists as they connected with air. The lack of satisfaction of hitting anything only made him more furious. Wesley yelled. He stomped the floor and pounded it with his fists. In his mind, all he could see was Hempton's face. All he wanted was to tear it apart piece by piece, but the darkness kept shifting. Remolding itself into a renewed image of his anger.

Wesley collapsed to the floor from pure exhaustion. Pain no longer mattered to him. He had grown numb to it. His muscles just would no longer respond. As he laid there, the light shone above the table. Above the illuminated face of his enemy. Hempton.

Wesley sprang to his feet, using every ounce of willpower that he had left in him. In one fell swoop, he smashed Hempton's face into the table. Blood smeared its surface. He did it again. And again. And again. He would have his revenge. He would not rest until he had relieved Hempton of his right to live. For once he was in control. Hempton was powerless against him. His face would no longer bear such arrogance as it was dented by the table.

Alas, Wesley laid prostrate on the floor. His arms and legs unable to move. Hempton's face glared at him unscathed. It was only in his mind that Wesley had that power.

"I'm going to kill you," Wesley said, drawing out every breath in his body.

The light turned off.

***

Minutes. Hours. Days. The whole concept of time had become lost to him. What actually is time? You can't see it. You can't touch it. Yet, in all the world it drives us along.

Is it a link in a chain that slowly passes by? A tiny stone in a longer road? Where does it lead?

Wesley's mind drifted aimlessly from random question to random question. What is his meaning? What is his purpose? Is it revenge? Is it justice? Does it matter? If Hempton dies, does that bring back Joanna? Is he forever stuck in his loneliness? In his guilt for not being there?

"Mr. Steele, how are we feeling?" Hempton asked.

Wesley responded with incoherent babble. His mind was roaming free. His body was merely a vessel, for Wesley was absent behind his eyes.

***

"The colors, Mr. Steele. What are the colors?"

Wesley's head snapped back against the cold metal table. His stomach rolled. His head felt as if it were about to explode. He felt as if he was dying. He wanted to. Anything to cease the never-ending torment. He no longer knew what was real or what was in his head. Was he dreaming? Was he still trapped in the Void and just reliving the memory of the lab, or had they taken him back to it? Wesley didn't even know the colors anymore. His eyes hurt too much to open them. His mind hurt too much to think. He felt sick.

Vomit sprayed across the floor onto the physician's shoe. Wesley hung his head over the edge of the table. Through slits between his eyelids, he saw what he had feared. They had brought him back into the lab.

"It's no use, sir. His mind still hasn't recovered from the Void," the woman said, looking back from her computer.

"I know. It'll make him more susceptible. We just have to push harder."

123

The physician held Wesley's face in his hand, forcibly holding open his eyes. The light was blinding.

"I can't see," Wesley tried to say, but even to his own ears, the words were foreign. Before he could think or even attempt to blink, color panels were being shoved into his face. He knew he would have to answer questions about them again. He tried to focus his eyes. The harder he tried, the more his mind hurt. His eyes would just roll back into his head.

"Let's try this again. The colors?"

Again, Wesley tried to speak but was unable. It was as if the link between his mind and his mouth had been severed. All he could manage were grunts and moans. In his frustration, the physician held up a chart with different options of color groups on it. He instructed Wesley to point to the ones they had shown him.

Wesley smiled. The greens reminded him of the luscious green grass of home. The blues of the clear sky hanging up above it. He could feel the breeze on his face as it gently whisked through the tall blades adorned in their purple flowers. The yellow sunbeam breaking over the horizon, shining on him. Mixed with the red, it shown like fire. Fire. The shack. Joanna. The thought snapped him back to reality. He wasn't in the blackness of the Void. These colors were real and vivid even to his hazy eyes.

With all his strength, he pointed to them. Red, blue, yellow, green, and purple. The same colors they had gone through before. The physician's face flooded with anger. Even with his absent state of mind, Wesley was sure he had it right. He knew his colors. He couldn't grasp the reason for the doctor's frustration.

The pain of a thousand needles rushed through Wesley's body. It was as if liquid fire had been poured into his veins. His body constricted. He couldn't breathe. Every muscle within him felt like it was ripping itself apart. In the distance, he could hear the sound of sirens and alarms singing their dissonant alerts. Then there was only silence. Darkness. Nothing.

***

"What do you think they did to him?"

The voice sounded familiar, but Wesley couldn't place it. He tried to open his eyes, but as he tried, they would roll back in his head. It was no use. He gave up trying. He listened closer. It was all he could do. He had to know where he was. He had to know if he was still trapped in their experiments. The familiarity of the voice gave him solace. Fred.

He finally placed it. Who was he talking to?

"They broke him," another voice said. "Too long in the Void will do that to you."

The voice was unfamiliar. It was young, but not youthful. It was as if a man had grown and seen the world in only a decade's worth of time. Wesley remembered the boy standing in the cell during his attempted escape. The intensity in the boy's eyes. That had to be him.

"I've heard of that place. Do you think he'll be okay?" Fred asked.

"It's hard to tell," the boy said. "The Void is a room that strips you of all your senses. You can't see, hear, feel…Nothing. Your brain doesn't know how to handle it, so it just shuts down and creates its own world."

"I'm not dead?" Wesley asked. His voice was dry and scratchy. For the first time in what seemed like forever, he understood his own words. Such a small accomplishment brought him joy amidst his misery.

The boy looked at Wesley wide-eyed. Fred scooped him up and held him in a seated position.

"I'm not sure how. I've never seen anyone stay in the Void that long and not go completely insane," the boy said in bewilderment.

"Hempton. He has to be stopped," Wesley said, still trying to collect his strength.

"Listen, bub. This is your life now. You have to get over it. Last time you tried something, look what happened. And now they've taken Maud…" Fred's voice trailed off.

"We'll get her back, Fred. I promise," Wesley assured him.

"Can you stand?" the boy asked. Wesley tried to lift himself up but fell back to the floor. "That's to be expected. Your body is most likely in shock. You need to eat something."

"What's he supposed to eat? We're still in a fast, remember?" Fred said.

The boy reached inside his jumpsuit and came up holding several granola type bars.

"The others may go for the good tasting food, but this is where it's at. They're full of all the nutrients you need to get your strength back. I hid a few of these back in case I ever needed them."

"You've been holding out on us?" Fred asked almost immediately. "We are how many hours into this three-day fast, and you're holding out on us?"

Wesley took a large bite of the bar as Fred and the boy bickered. The taste caused him to smack his lips. It was true that "good tasting" was not the way to describe them. Dirt was a more accurate description. Still, he kept eating.

"Planning an escape when the guards brought around the food carts was good thinking," the boy said, letting

Fred eat one of his granola bars also. "Good thinking, but still foolish. It took too long. I'm sure you had every camera watching you almost from the time you started. A better plan would be during shift change. At midnight, all guards are relieved from duty, both in here and those that watch the cameras. It's a small window, but if we can subdue the guards in here, with so many out there trying to get home, we can get lost in the crowd."

"And how do you suggest we get out of this cell to subdue those guards?" Wesley asked.

"With this," the boy said, stealing the granola wrapper away from Fred. "The wrapper is made of aluminum. Aluminum conducts electricity. Those are electronic locks. Just like the bullet did earlier, I can take this wrapper and… voila, the door is open."

Fred stood looking at the door amazed. Wesley was impressed by the boy's ingenuity. All they had to do now was wait for the right moment.

***

At midnight, things played out exactly as the boy had said. Four guards came in to relieve those that had been standing watch. As the guards were swapping out positions, those that were in the cell fanned out across the holding area, hiding in plain sight. They placed themselves in strategic places, that way when they were given the signal, they could all strike at once. They waited for the first four guards to leave, and then with perfect harmony took down the last four.

Wesley walked over to the boy to commend him for his plan. Behind him, some of the prisoners were changing into the guards' uniforms. The others were gathering chains and hoods from the far wall and linking themselves together.

"This part of your plan, I liked," the boy told Wesley. "It's a way for us to get more people out without drawing a lot of attention."

Wesley nodded and found his place in the line of prisoners. They still had to hurry before the cameras were back online. As they pushed open the door, a small sigh of relief came over Wesley. The once fearful prisoners had found hope in the strength and bravery of the boy.

"I've had an eye on you since you got here," the boy said quietly as they walked through the door. "You seemed different than the others who come through. I had a feeling you would be the one to try to escape. If we're going to go through with this, I feel like I should at least know your name. I'm Damien."

"Wesley."

"Well Wesley, let's rock and roll."

12

THE CITY LIGHTS BURNED BRIGHTLY that night. It was the first time Michael had seen them in so many years. Metropolian. Everything was different. The horrors of war had long been forgotten. So too had been the unity among the citizens. Self-indulgence ran rampant through the city like wildfire. Drunkenness, gluttony, lust, and every self-pleasing venue were available at every street corner. There was no humility, no consideration for others, no morals. Lost was a time when people had looked out for the common good of all people. Violence was everywhere. Brawls would erupt on the streets simply because someone's smile offended them.

Michael felt sick to his stomach. Rebecca would have been appalled at him for even being in such a place. Michael felt her bible pressed against him. Such a thing did not belong there. Vasher and Tobias strolled through it as if it was nothing. Michael felt anxious. His eyes shifted steadily from one side of the street to the other. He had wished that they could have stayed in the car and drove through the area.

The smoky haze was almost as dense as fog. The streets seemed to be forever wet. Michael waited for there to be another explosion of violence with him caught in the crossfire at any moment. He stayed close to Vasher and Tobias. Tobias still had his gun, which Michael regretted. It would have given him more peace of mind if he was better protected. He could understand now why they had banned guns after the war. In such turmoil, there would be no one left standing when the gun smoke settled. Michael wasn't sure where they were headed exactly. Tobias had promised him a way to reach Amanda. He was still holding on to that promise, hoping that she would have information on Allie.

They were leading him to a Metropolian detention center. Michael was unsure of how he felt about it. On the one hand, the guards could offer some protection from the unruly citizens of the area. On the other, he could find himself back in the Federal Police compound he had just come from. The closer he walked to the center, the more his hopes for safety fell. In the shadows, he saw the detention center guards making deals with the very ones Michael wanted protection from. They were no less corrupt than the citizens. Michael had never seen such lawlessness.

"We're going in," Vasher said, pointing to the door of the detention center.

"Are you crazy?" Michael exclaimed. "I'm not going in there. They'll arrest me for sure. I thought you were on my side?"

"Look around you, Michael. Does anyone here seem to be concerned about what's going on around them? This is a detention center for petty crimes. The Federal Police are hardly even involved in this place. While you may be a wanted man, they have their own agenda for wanting you.

Very few people know about it. Besides, these people won't even look at you in that uniform. I promise."

Michael followed him up the steps of the detention center apprehensively. Had Tobias not have helped him escape from the compound, he would have ditched them as soon as they had left the car. At this point, he saw no reason not to trust them. If they had wanted to have him arrested, they would have let it happen then.

Vasher boldly strode up the steps, slinging the door open. The room inside went completely silent. The people were frozen in time. All eyes were on them. It seemed even the local guards were afraid of the Federal Police.

Tobias played into their fears. He walked over to the receptionist's desk. With a fierceness Michael had not seen from him, he began barking orders at the woman. She had been on the phone, oblivious to their presence. She immediately tensed and gaped at Tobias. Vasher followed suit and slammed a set of orders on her desk, causing her to drop the phone. It bounced off her desk, skidding across the tile floor.

"Two prisoners were transferred here by the Federal Police earlier this evening. They are to be released into our custody," Vasher told the woman.

She jolted from her chair and ran to the warden's office, carrying the papers. The two stood stoically, waiting for her return. The room was still. Silent enough to hear a pin drop. The others in the room went out of their way to avoid eye contact with them.

The receptionist returned shortly, followed by the warden with two prisoners in tow. They were wearing the typical white jumpsuits but without the hoods. Michael was relieved when he saw that one of them was Amanda. Tobias had kept his promise, and he was one step closer to finding Allie. Michael looked at the other captive with her.

He looked familiar to him as well. He was one of the ones they had picked up in the raid on the village. Michael wondered what their purpose for him was.

There was no time for questions. Vasher was quick to sign the release forms. He began leading them out of the station. Not a word was spoken on the walk back to the car. Amanda looked terrified, but the other one was hiding a glimmer of a smile. He worried Michael. He knew there was more going on than he had been told, but for a survivor of such a horrific attack to be hiding a smile, it made him edgy. Michael knew Tobias had his own reasons for wanting to help him, but he couldn't figure out his intentions. It wasn't kindness, Michael was sure of that. Somehow, this other prisoner was involved.

"That was fun," Tobias said when they had reached the car, his carefree persona returning.

"I think you tend to let the power of our positions go to your head," Vasher scolded him.

"Hey, I'm not the one slamming stuff down, and making a woman throw things halfway across the room."

"If you two are done bickering, I just want to say I hope no one followed us to this piece of junk car. If they did, this whole little ruse has been for nothing," the prisoner said.

"Hush, Evan. You know we do this all the time. Michael, meet Vasher's brother, Evan," Tobias said.

Michael was stunned that the prisoner was a brother to someone in the Federal Police. They seemed to be on opposing sides. Michael began using what he knew to try to tie the strings together. Tobias said that this was something they do all the time. The two of them must have been part of an underground operation to help free those wrongfully accused by the Federal Police. That would explain why they were helping him. The village must not have been a terrorist camp, but instead was somehow associated with them.

Michael didn't know how long the two had been doing it, but they seemed very proficient in their craft. Given their behavior around the other federal officers and Vasher's rank, it was unlikely anyone suspected anything. Part of his job was to direct transfers concerning his flights, which gave him access to move prisoners around as they needed. Michael considered himself lucky to have crossed paths with them.

"How did you know they were coming?" Evan asked.

"How do you think? She told me," Vasher said. "I always keep my earpiece in while I'm flying. What happened?"

"I don't know. Everything was going fine. The villagers welcomed us. They anxiously awaited us bringing them freedom. We were planning our evac home when the comms went down. Next thing we know, we see you guys. If we had known, we would have stood down."

"No, I'm glad you didn't. There was no way for me to really help without blowing my cover."

"When Tobias ran in, I realized what was going on. How many could you save?"

"You and four others. Two were from the village."

"That's a terrible shame. I've never seen the Federal Police come on us that fast. Of course, I see your mission didn't go quite as planned," Evan said, nodding toward Michael.

Evan had confirmed it. They were after Michael. If they weren't Federal Police, he didn't know what they could possibly want from him. He pondered what was so exceptionally important about him. It seemed no matter who he came across, someone wanted him for something.

While he appreciated the help in getting out of the compound and into Metropolian, Michael spent the drive planning his next step. He still had his daughter to find, and he didn't feel he had made much headway in it. It had been over four days since she had been taken, and he knew time was running out. Michael dreaded to think of what she was having to endure in his absence. At least he had found Amanda.

He looked over at her and tried to ask her about Allie. She hadn't spoken a word since they picked her up from the center. She refused to acknowledge Michael or even look him in the eye. He knew getting her to help him would be difficult, but he didn't expect her to be quite so cold to him. He was sure she blamed him for everything, and she had a right to. It was him they had come after.

The car came to a stop. Through the window, Michael saw an old relic of a building. It appeared to be well over a hundred years old and contrasted sharply with the brightly lit glass boxes that made up the buildings surrounding it. Massive concrete columns rose up to about the building's center. *Metro Station* was emblazoned in lights just above the columns.

A cold shiver ran up Michael's spine. This was the place where everything started. This was where Cade had died and Michael's life spiraled out of control. He had wanted to run after getting out of the car but seeing the train station pulled at him. He had to know what all this was about.

"There's a change of clothes in the trunk," Vasher told them, already getting out of the car. "Michael, be sure to put that uniform in the suitcase. We may need it again."

Amanda must have had the same idea as Michael during the drive. While everyone was preoccupied, she took the opportunity to run. She darted through the cars of the parking lot, but her age proved a disadvantage. Tobias caught up to her and locked her in his arms.

"If you want to live, you'll come with us," he said.

Amanda struggled against him but gave up her fight. Vasher handed her a set of clothes to put on. She protested having to disrobe in a parking lot in front of four men, but they gave her no other choice. They couldn't take the chance of her running off again. She would pose a threat to them getting caught. They walked casually into the train station, with Michael keeping Amanda on a short leash. He held her arm and kept her pressed against him.

Michael kept his head down, following closely behind the others. In the bustle of the train station, it was easy to get lost in the crowd should someone notice him. There was a constant movement of people as trains came and went. The green uniforms of the station guard were interweaved among them. Vasher purchased them all tickets, and they walked to the platform.

Michael looked at his ticket. It was for the same place Cade had wanted him to go. It was déjà vu. The same train station, the same platform, the same destination. Wherever it was they were going, it was evident that he was intended to get there at some point.

Paranoia weighed heavy on Michael. He kept looking back over his shoulder. He couldn't help but check around every corner as he stood waiting. This was the first place he had ever encountered the Federal Police directly. He waited for the moment they would spring forth and attack. He watched for signs of little black darts to stick into one of his companions. His fears were simply that. The train arrived on schedule. Michael was glad history did not repeat itself as he boarded the train.

Michael took a seat next to Amanda. He wanted answers. He had played the game of "follow the leader" for far too long. She resumed her quiet indignation toward him, staring blankly out the window at the long dark tunnel beyond it. Michael pressed harder. His questions becoming stern and harsh. Still, she said nothing. Her anger seemed to stem far beyond just her anger toward him. She once would at least give him the satisfaction of an argument. Whatever the Federal Police had done to her had crushed her spirit.

"It wasn't supposed to be like this," she said, finally breaking her silence. "I knew they were coming. They had given me the letter and told me where to start looking for you. They gave me permission to go into the Forbidden Zone just to make sure you were still there. They were supposed to come arrest you."

Michael was in shock. Amanda had been more than angry with him. She had sent the Federal Police to his house. Michael's blood boiled. His nostrils flared as he gritted his teeth, and his hands began to tremble. He had trusted this woman. He had let her into his home when she claimed to be a refugee seeking shelter. She was the reason his wife had been killed. She was the reason his daughter had been taken. Michael gripped her by the throat and pressed her against the window. Vasher and Tobias tried to pull him off of her. He released. It wasn't in his nature to attack a defenseless person, especially an older woman.

"I'm sorry, I didn't know it was going to be like this," she said, trying to catch her breath.

"They used her Michael. It's what they do. They prey on people's emotions, using them to infiltrate targets of interest. It saves them effort and manpower," Vasher told him. "She should be dead right now. You owe us for saving her life. I just hope you're worth the effort put into setting up all of this."

"Listen, I don't know what you have planned, but no scores will be settled until after I find my daughter," Michael said. "Now tell us what you know, Amanda."

"It all happened so fast. They stormed the place. We were completely surrounded. They went for the older lady first. They caught her off guard tending to those stupid trees. She ran, but I don't think she got very far. The black lady ran to help her. She picked up a shovel and was swinging it wildly, but…" Amanda winced at the thought. "They left her there. Your daughter was hiding in the rubble of the house. Her mother fought to protect her. That's all I know."

Michael waited for her to continue. He wanted more. He didn't care about the details that happened before he and the others arrived. He wanted to know what happened after.

"A little girl told me they brought Allie into the holding area with another woman. I know that was you."

"I'm sorry, Michael. I really am. I don't know what happened to her. I blacked out when they caught me and woke up in the room he found me in," Amanda said, nodding at Tobias.

Michael slumped back into his seat. His hope was lost. He had spent so much time following a dead-end lead. He had failed his daughter. Michael cursed his rashness. He had never taken the time to plan his course of action. He acted on pure impulse. For all he knew, Allie could have still been at the compound he so hastily abandoned to stay close to Amanda. He hung his head down in shame, covering his face with his palms.

Tears streamed down his face at the thought of never seeing his family again. In his determination to find Allie, he neglected to ever take time to grieve for Rebecca. She was his rock. She had kept him grounded. He felt as if the whole world had been ripped from underneath him. They were to have celebrated twenty years of marriage next month. He and Allie had been planning a surprise party for her. Now both of them had been taken from his life.

He closed his eyes. He wanted to sleep. He wanted relief from the pain that pulled at his heart. He felt as if it were broken into a thousand pieces on the floor. She had become so much of a part of his life for so long, he couldn't imagine his life without her. Was it to be nothing but running and hiding from the Federal Police? Was he condemned to live the rest of his life a fugitive and alone?

"Don't worry Michael," Tobias said, placing a hand on his shoulder. "Your daughter, your brother, your next-door neighbor's kid, anyone you're close to they'll keep alive to draw you out. If you help us, we can help you save them."

"What is it you want me to do?" Michael sputtered, still sobbing uncontrollably.

"You don't worry about that right now. You just focus on getting your head back on straight. We still have a long road to go."

"If they would keep the ones close to Michael alive, why would they kill me?" Amanda asked.

"You were a loose end. A liability," Vasher said. "The Federal Police can only go on record as killing or capturing terrorists to maintain their image. Officially, Michael doesn't exist. He was executed six years ago. To be able to legally capture him, they needed evidence, which is what you gave them."

"They also didn't know exactly where he was. Their intel stopped at just having a place in the Forbidden Zone. Instead of trying to search it out themselves, they put a tracker on you and let you lead them to him," Tobias said.

"To cover up their hand in all of this, they would have staged your death, and no more would have been said," Vasher added. "They would be free to legally carry out their agenda with Michael."

Amanda huffed at the thought of being played by the Federal Police. Neither she nor Michael was aware of the underhandedness of the Federal Police. The knowledge of their inner workings shared by Vasher and Tobias astounded him. Surely a simple guard and a pilot wouldn't be privy to such sensitive information.

The longer Michael was around them, the more his suspicions about them grew. There was a much bigger picture in place, and he could only see a small portion. Still, Tobias had helped him get this far. There was no use in turning back now. He had run out of options.

The train skidded to a stop at the end of the tracks. Michael hadn't noticed that they had long passed the destination on their ticket. They were the last passengers still aboard. Vasher grabbed the suitcase as he and Tobias led them off the train.

They were at an abandoned underground platform. Two tracks went through it, but by the amount of debris on the other track, Michael could tell it had not been used in years. The ceiling above it had at some point collapsed, leaving a gaping hole above. Vasher and Tobias hopped down onto the forgone track, walking along the rails to avoid leaving footprints in the dust.

The tunnel was dark. The overhead lights seemingly burnt out when the track was decommissioned. They walked for what seemed like a mile in darkness. The path lightened as they neared a small lamp hanging above a metal service exit door.

"Through here is what I want you to see, Michael."

Vasher pulled a key from his pocket and unlocked the door. Michael peered in as the door swung open. Inside was a system of rooms full of people. Everyone was busy. Some were seated, typing away at computers. Some had maps displayed on large screens on the wall. Others were in heated discussions over planning operations.

Michael was amazed at the sight. He had not seen so much commotion in a room since he had left the compound, but these people didn't look like Federal Police. They lacked the unity and precision. Their work together was more sporadic. They were all dressed in plain clothes instead of the black tactical uniforms he had been used to seeing. This must have been the underground operations Tobias and Vasher worked with.

"Welcome to Defiant."

13

GUNFIRE EXPLODED. The plan had to be abandoned. Wesley crouched behind a large black armored vehicle. It was built like a tank with heavy metal plating surrounding its exterior. Three rows of tightly spaced, hardened rubber tires provided adequate cover from underneath. Their slight distance apart allowed him to look through at the situation. They were pinned down. Wesley, Damien, and Fred had been separated from the others who were trapped near the exit gate of the compound.

Wesley watched as more guards surrounded them. Bullets flew in from all directions. Ground troops fired from below, while the watchtowers fired from above. There was no way to help them. He saw one of them emerge from behind the van they were trying to steal, with hands in the air. He was gunned down before Wesley's eyes. There was no mercy. They offered no quarter for the ones they captured.

Wesley wasn't sure what had tipped them off. Maybe they had left too many loose ends. Maybe it was the guards they had left imprisoned in a cell. Maybe breaking out of the cell tripped an alarm. Or maybe they had just taken too much time to execute the plan. The others had to cross the drive in plain view of the watchtowers. Wesley and Damien were supposed to be right behind them. With Wesley still regaining his strength and Damien helping Fred to keep up, they were too slow.

Wesley cursed himself for being too weak to help. He was a trained fighter, and yet he felt the most useless. If it wasn't for the boy, he would likely be either dead or still trapped in a glass cage. Wesley looked over at him. Damien kept his composure better than most men he had met. His steely gaze was locked on to the other prisoners. His fists were clenched tight, and yet he knelt there just watching.

"We have to get out of here. There's nothing we can do for them. If we don't move, they'll be on us soon," Wesley told Damien.

"I know, but they're my friends. I have to do something."

"If you want to help them, honor their sacrifice, and get out of here. What do you know about this thing?" Wesley asked, pointing up to the massive vehicle they were hidden behind.

"A torro? It's built for ramming things, but we're not going to make a high-speed getaway with it."

Wesley acknowledged Damien's concerns, but under the circumstances, a well-armored battering ram may prove to be useful. The door used electronic locks with a panel of buttons just above the handle. Wesley looked for signs of wear on the buttons to determine the code used to unlock the door. On his third try, he heard the latch release.

"Unauthorized access," the onboard computer screeched repeatedly as Wesley climbed inside. He must have triggered an alarm when he entered the wrong codes. Sirens began to blare from the vehicle. He had to work fast.

While Damien stood watch, Wesley crawled beneath the dashboard and cracked open the control panel. He had hot-wired a few cars in his younger days but never one as sophisticated as this. Wires and circuit boards lined the control panel.

He ripped out a few wires. None of them carried an obvious amount of current. He tried again. Still no use. For all he knew, he was pulling out wires vital to the vehicle's operation. In his frustration, he punched the plastic casing around the control panel. That caught Damien's attention.

"Tie the blue and red together. Then connect the white ones," he said.

"How do you know all this?" Wesley asked.

"Not my first time stealing one of these."

Sure enough, doing so caused the two wires to briefly spark. The sirens stopped. The computer had become silent as well. He looked at the screen in the center of the dash. The system was restarting.

"Time to go," he told Damien as he pressed the ignition button on the screen. Damien climbed into the vehicle just as the guards swarmed around them. Bullets were flying, bouncing off the vehicle's armor. One caught Fred's arm. The pain caused him to faint. Damien reached down and strained to finish pulling Fred into the torro.

Wesley pressed the accelerator to the floor. Damien was right. The vehicle was not equipped for speed, as it slowly began moving forward. Guards climbed on top of the torro. They were trying to enter the code to open the doors. To their dismay, Wesley had managed to disable the locks by accident.

He kept driving straight, heading for the fence. He was shaken as the torro vibrated and rocked to its side. Wesley looked through the darkness and saw more Federal Police arriving outside of the fence. These weren't just the guards of the compound. They came equipped for war. More torroes had come, along with heavily armed cars. Helicopters were approaching in the distance.

"They've got reinforcements," he said as they were bringing out the heavier artillery.

They were firing rockets at them, aiming for the tires. The ram on the front end of the torro provided extra protection, absorbing most of the blast. Wesley didn't know how long the armor could hold out against it, especially if one made a direct hit on the tires. Damien began going through the options on the screen. He found the weapon systems and activated the control for the gun mounted on the roof. He began trying to provide cover fire until Wesley could get them out of there.

"This thing has to be able to go faster," Wesley said, still pressing the accelerator down.

The torro moved at a crawl as more rockets continued to fly at them, shaking the behemoth of a vehicle. He began to search through the control panel as well. He found the problem. The vehicle was in a high torque ramming mode. He switched it to standard driving mode and immediately noticed a speed increase. He barreled through the fence, plowing through the lines of Federal Police vehicles and onto the highway.

The Federal Police gave chase. The torroes, cars, and vans pursued them on the ground. Helicopters followed them from above, raining bullets and missiles around them. Wesley weaved his way through their explosions. The cars were a threat to them. They were gaining speed on the still much slower torro. Wesley decided to test the abilities of its ramming features. He turned hard left and steered it straight into a dense forest. The impact jarred them, but he kept going. The cars and vans couldn't traverse through such terrain, and the helicopters had poor visibility through the treetops. Only the torroes were left to contend with.

Wesley tried to maintain a fast pace through the forest, but the continuous impact and the climb and fall over the stumps made it difficult. They were constantly tossed about inside the torro, pulling hard against the harnesses of their seats. He barreled his way through, trying to outmaneuver the officers behind him. He darted back and forth in a zig-zag pattern between the trees like an antelope evading a cheetah. It seemed to be working. The officers were beginning to fall behind.

Wesley checked his rear view on the dashboard screen. As he watched them, he began to have an eerie feeling. It was as if they were slowing down on purpose. Before his eyes could regain focus on what was ahead of him, he felt a sudden sensation of weightlessness. Damien was screaming at him. In his haste, he had driven them over a ravine.

The torro flipped end over end, rolling down the steep edge. It came to an abrupt stop upside-down next to a river bank. The heavy front end pulled it into a downward angle over a muddy ledge. Water lapped up against the cracked window, seeping in slowly.

"Is everyone alright?" Wesley asked. His ears were ringing, and his vision was blurry. The taste of blood filled his mouth as he spoke.

"I'm fine, but my legs are pinned," Damien said.

Beside him, Wesley saw that an ammunition box from the back had gotten loose and crashed into the seats in front of it, breaking them free. Damien was buried beneath

145

it, still strapped into his seat. The weight of it pressed him against the small windshield of the torro. The extra seat and the ammunition box were crushing the lower half of his body. Water began to pool around his face as he strained to lift his head out of its icy reach.

Wesley tried to fight against the pull of his body weight to release his harness. As he worked with it, he heard groaning behind him. The jolting of the crash had awoken Fred.

"Where am I? What's going on? Where's Maud? I've been shot." Fred was screaming hysterically. He was fighting against the harness Damien had over-tightened. He rocked in his seat trying to break free, kicking frantically against the back of Wesley's seat.

Wesley managed to undo his own harness and dropped down to the top of the torro. It shifted underneath him, knocking him over. It was teetering on the ledge, held only in place by its nose lodged against an underwater root of a long-dead tree.

"Fred, you have to try to stay calm. This thing is unstable, and I have to help Damien," Wesley said.

"Forget the kid, I've got to get back to Maud," Fred screamed, continuing to fight against the harness.

His jerking caused the already leaning torro to slide on the muddy riverbank, putting more strain on the root. Water poured in faster. Damien began sputtering and coughing, unable to hold his head up higher than the water.

Wesley gently twisted his body to try to lift the munitions box. It was too heavy, and in such a confined space, he couldn't get any leverage. The box was wedged between the seat and the door. He tried to open the door to push it out, but the metal casing had bent on impact, jamming it. Time was running out. Water had risen up over his ankles. Any deeper and Damien wouldn't be able to breathe.

He had to think fast. Damien was already gasping for air. He dropped to a knee to see if there was a way to pull him out from under the pile. It looked possible if he could find a way to release his harness. The latch was by his legs, buried beneath the pile. He searched for anything sharp to try to cut the straps but couldn't find anything. The munitions box was full of bullets for the top-mounted machine gun. The other boxes were out of reach. Even the broken window, being made of bullet-proof plastic instead of glass, wasn't sharp enough to cut through.

His search proved fruitless and a waste of valuable time. It was no use. He couldn't do it alone. He went back to Fred, who had finally calmed down with the calamity happening around him.

"Damien saved our lives at the compound. He needs us to save his. I can't do it alone," Wesley said.

Fred nodded as Wesley pulled himself up on the back of the seat in front of him.

"Pull yourself up into your seat while I undo the harness. Press your feet hard into the seat I'm sitting on," Wesley said.

He was relying on Fred's grace to gently drop down without shaking the torro more. A feat that was made difficult by having a large man hanging upside-down in a chair. He tried to help as much as possible as he guided Fred to walk down the back of the seat in front of him. One slip, one hard fall, and Wesley was sure the torro would slide on into the river. They had to be careful.

"What do you expect me to do? A somersault to get down?" Fred asked when his feet had reached midway of the seat.

In Wesley's mind, that was exactly what he had pictured. He didn't account for Fred's lack of athleticism. Wesley looked down at Damien, who was completely submerged. His mind raced to come up with a better plan.

"Put your hands against the roof, and let your feet drop. I'll catch your feet while you put your weight on your hands."

Fred put his arms down. Wesley braced himself to catch his feet. Everything was working until Fred winced at the gunshot wound in his arm and toppled over. He crashed into the side of the torro. The sudden impact broke the root that held it in place, causing it to slide into the river.

Water gushed in, the pressure breaking apart the fractured windows. The torro tipped over on its side. Wesley fell against Fred. Both of them fought to stay above water as it began to fill the interior. Damien was still submerged.

Wesley dove under the surface after him. Damien was still in the corner, his head floating in the water. With the munitions box no longer trapping him, Wesley pulled him up seat and all. He wasn't breathing. Without thinking, Wesley slammed the seat against the side of the torro with Damien still strapped in and began performing CPR. The torro turned back on its nose from the weight of the ram. He pulled him to the side again and resumed. The turn had bought them more time. It had trapped the air in the solid back end, stopping the water from rising.

"The doors are jammed. We're trapped," Fred said, bobbing back up out of the water.

Wesley was so focused on saving Damien, he didn't think about how they were going to escape the icy coffin of the torro. The front windows were much too small to crawl out of, and with the doors jammed, there seemed to be no exit. Wesley continued to try to resuscitate Damien.

If it wasn't for the box of ammunition, we could all find an escape together, he thought. That thought gave him an idea.

"Look for a hatch on top. If they kept the ammo for the gun in here, there should be a way to reload it."

Fred began searching. The water had almost completely filled the torro before it stopped. It was just beneath Wesley's neck. Its frigid grip was taking a toll on his body. He couldn't imagine how Fred was feeling, being completely submerged in it. He couldn't worry about him, though. Damien still needed his attention. Abruptly, Damien coughed, water pouring out his mouth. He looked at Wesley with a look of both fear and thankfulness. Wesley quickly snatched the harness free, releasing him from the chair.

"Hatch is open," Fred said as his head popped up. "Looks like it might be a long swim up."

The three dove through the hatch into the cold blackness of the river. The current pressed hard against their backs as they swam upward. Wesley emerged first, followed by Fred. They grabbed on to a floating log as it passed by. Damien was slower in coming up. He struggled just to tread the water. Wesley stretched out his hand to pull him in, but he was too far out of reach. His head bobbed up and down out of the water as his arms splashed around him. The cold water and fatigue had gotten to him. He slipped beneath the surface.

Wesley felt a sudden bobble in the log. Fred had been watching him too and dove down to rescue him. In the dim light, Wesley couldn't see any sign of them. No shadows beneath the surface. No bubbles of air rising up. Nothing. As Wesley readied himself to dive in after them both, Fred burst up from the water with Damien in tow.

"I am not going to let you drown today," Fred said as he fought to swim toward the log.

He was in no condition to try to rescue anyone after spending so much time submerged in the near-freezing water. He struggled to keep swimming. Wesley caught his hand and pulled him and Damien in.

The three held on as they floated down the river. They were all too tired to risk swimming to the bank. The morning air on their cold wet jumpsuits left them shivering. Still, they held on for their lives. Wesley knew they had to find a way to get to dry land and out of the frigid waters.

"Paddle toward the bank. It's the only way we'll survive," he said as he started kicking his legs. The cold was already beginning to make them feel numb, and the adrenaline from the escape had worn off. He and Fred kicking in tandem pushed the log toward the bank. Damien was attempting, but his kicks were labored.

With each kick, Wesley knew it brought them that much closer to safety. He willed himself to one more kick. One more kick. He told himself that over and over again. His entire body felt like it had been stabbed by a thousand needles. The cold replacing his limbs with appendages of pain. He looked to either side of him and saw the same look of agony on the others' faces that he was feeling. Just one more kick.

Wesley's eyes were beginning to feel heavy. He fought to stay awake, but the lack of sleep mixed with the night's activities and the cold water left him exhausted. He steadied himself on the log so that he wouldn't fall off. He tried to get a tighter grip but had lost all dexterity in his hands. It didn't matter. They had to keep going.

Up ahead, he could see grass rising from the water. A marsh jutted out from the bank. If they could reach the marsh, they could crawl to dry land.

"Th-there," Wesley said through chattering teeth.

When he didn't get a response, he turned to look at his companions. Damien was hanging on to the log but was no longer alert. Fred was still attempting to kick but slow and sporadically. It was up to Wesley to save them. He mustered all the strength within him to keep going.

Just as his legs made the last stroke they possibly could, he felt it. Dead grass and mud. They had reached the marsh. Only a few more feet and they'd be on dry land. They could make it. He pulled the other two along with him, his legs and hands paralyzed from the cold. Having given every ounce of strength within him, he collapsed at the water's edge. The icy water lapped up against his limp body. He was so close.

14

MICHAEL WAS IN AWE of everything he had seen. Tobias had led him through their safehouse, giving him the "tour" as he called it. Everywhere they went, people were busy orchestrating something. Vasher stood in the center of the main room, waiting for them to return.

"Defiant's job is simple. We want to save the world," Vasher said.

"Save the world?" Michael asked, still trying to take it all in.

"We want to save it from the oppression of the Federal Police. They say they're protecting national security, but really, they're just protecting their own assets. That's why we have eyes and ears among them. We're trying to bring them down from the inside."

Michael looked at him dumbfounded. He had never met anyone who would openly admit to being against the Federal Police. Though he hated the Federal Police himself, to confront them was treason. He had stumbled onto something much more than just freeing the wrongly accused. The Federal Police were an extension of the nation's government. To oppose them was to oppose the Federation. The terrorists had shared the same philosophy.

"You're a terrorist group, aren't you?" Michael asked, balling up his fist. As much as he hated the Federal Police, the terrorists were no better. They had savagely taken Rebecca and left her to die in the Forbidden Zone. They were ruthless and killed anyone they came across unprovoked. There was no way he would ever join forces with such barbarians.

"Man, you actually bought the lie that there are terrorists running around out there? It's been eight years since the war," Tobias laughed at Michael's tenseness. "All propaganda to sell their existence. You've been living in no man's land too long."

Michael's eyes widened as Tobias' words echoed those Cade had told him years ago. It was evident this was the place Cade had wanted him to come to.

"I don't know what this place is or why you've helped me, but there's only one thing I care about. I'm going to get my daughter back."

"Listen to yourself. You condemn us for standing against the Federal Police, but we're not the ones who took your family," Vasher said. "I need you to trust us. We're trying to do the right thing."

Trust was not something Michael wanted to give out freely. There was so much more going on around him, and none of it made sense to him. Vasher had made a valid point. Regardless of their status, the Federal Police were no less wicked than the terrorists in fulfilling their agenda. They had not lived up to the promise that was made of them by the government.

"I don't know that I can," Michael admitted.

Even if this was the place Cade wanted to bring him to, he was apprehensive. Although he had once trusted

Cade, he had been accused of trying to plant explosives at a government building. That was the story that had been told to him by the Federal Police. Now, he didn't know what to believe. Although he had been leery, he was learning not to trust anyone. The world of black and white Michael had lived in was quickly becoming a thousand shades of gray.

He and Cade had joined the war together when the terrorists took Rebecca. It was their vow to stop the terrorists at all cost. He couldn't believe that Cade, even amidst the paranoia and delusions he suffered from, would join them.

"Jake, I hate to interrupt, but there's a lot going on at Camp Talon," a girl sitting at a computer said to Vasher.

She may have been twenty years old at most. With her hair pulled back in a short ponytail and her plaid over-shirt rolled up to her elbows, she seemed even younger. She sat with her feet crossed in her chair, focused on the screen. The light of it flickered in the lenses of her black frame glasses. Something about her put Michael's mind at ease about his suspicions of them. She seemed to be genuine.

"What is it?" Vasher asked.

"There's a prison break, led by a Zone Four prisoner going by his inmate number. Probably the same one that shot at Camp Delta."

"Michael, meet Watch," Tobias said. "We call her that because she watches over us as well as what the Feds are doing."

"Pull up the security footage for us," Vasher said, walking to a large monitor on the wall.

Watch immediately began typing. The sound of keys, like the patter of rain, emanated from her fingers as they flew across the keyboard. In seconds, the monitor was aglow with a still image of a man. On the side panel, small screens were filled with different camera angles as the event played out.

"Know him?" Vasher asked Michael when the images appeared on the screen.

"That's Wesley! We have to help him," Michael said.

"Man, you just want to help everybody don't you?" Tobias mocked. "Isn't there a little girl you're wanting to help too?"

The question struck Michael. It was true. His compassionate heart had always led him to want to help people when they needed it. He never thought he would have to choose between his best friend and his daughter. He knew which one he had to help. He knew Wesley would understand and hoped that if the situation was reversed, he would make the same choice. Wesley could take care of himself, Michael thought, justifying his decision. Vasher must have been able to read the look on his face. He told Watch to clear the screens and begin a new search.

"Don't worry about your friend," Watch said. "Looks like he got away from the compound. They've put out orders for a search team. I've already got some guys out looking for him too. Hopefully, we'll get lucky. Now about this girl, I need some info."

"Thank you," Michael said. "Her name is Allie. She's six years old, about four-foot-tall, with blondish hair and green eyes. I'm pretty sure she was at the compound Tobias saved me from."

"She sounds like me when I was her age," Watch giggled as she began keying in the information. Michael could see the similarities between them. She could have passed for an older version of Allie. Perhaps that was what put his mind at ease about her.

Screen after screen passed over her monitor. Michael was impressed that she could read that fast. He watched her dig through files of sensitive Federal Police information. A sense of joy was rising up in him. For the first time, he felt he had a solid lead to where Allie was. With all the information available to Watch, surely, she would be able to tell them exactly where to find her. She would also know what awaited them in the process of getting to her.

Watch stopped typing. Michael sprang to her, waiting to hear what he had longed for. His joy quickly fell. The look on Watch's face wasn't one of joy or accomplishment, but of horror.

"I've found her, but..." Watch began. She hung her head, her hands falling from the keyboard to her lap.

"But what?" Michael was hesitant to hear the answer. His nervousness caused his hands to shake. He was afraid to know what had made Watch have that kind of reaction. Whatever it was, it couldn't be good. Michael feared the worst.

"They've taken her to Myers. He's claiming her as...as his own daughter. There are adoption papers on file."

Michael was outraged. Not only had the Federal Police kidnapped his daughter, but their leader, the secretary of security was trying to pass her off as his own. He couldn't imagine how she felt. She had to be terrified. He pounded his clenched fists hard on the corner of Watch's desk, almost toppling over her computer. While he was glad Allie was alive, he knew after this long, she had to feel abandoned there. He ran to the door. He wasn't going to let her stay a captive in their wicked hands.

"Where are you going?" Vasher called out to him as soon as he opened the door.

"To find Myers. To get my daughter."

"We know where he is. He's the only politician to actually live in Metropolian, but you'll never get there."

Vasher turned Watch's computer monitor toward Michael. On the screen was an aerial image of Metropolian. A fortress was at its center, spanning three city blocks. Watch zoomed in tighter on it. Black suits crawled across its exterior like ants. Guns were mounted atop its high walls. Fencing barricaded it from the rest of Metropolian, making it an island among the commercial buildings.

"Myers uses the Feds as his own personal security team," Tobias said. "If anyone suspicious even gets close to the fence...well, you get the idea."

"I'm still going," Michael said as he stepped through the door, into the darkness of the tunnel.

"If you try it, you're only going to get yourself killed, or worse, captured. I told you, if you help us, we'll help you get her back," Vasher said.

"I'm not leaving her there any longer. I'm going to get her."

As his foot touched the track, he heard a faint click behind him. Something about the sound ran a chill down his spine.

"No, you're not," Vasher said in the same serious tone he used at the detention center. Michael turned back to look. Watch had turned away with her face buried in her hands. Tobias stood frozen, watching. Vasher had his sidearm aimed center of Michael's back. "You are too valuable of an asset, and we worked too hard to bring you here to let you fall back into the hands of the Feds. Now come back here and sit down. We have work to do."

15

WESLEY OPENED HIS EYES. His joints ached, but he was alive. The warmth of the fire eased the tension in his muscles. The soft glow reminded him of the winter nights he had spent in the shack with his friends. He thought he was dreaming. The cold icy clutches of the river had been replaced by a warm and cozy home. This place was different from the place he had once called home, though. In its modern grandeur, it lost its heart. The light gray walls were cast in an eerie orange tint that danced with the flames. The fire seemed to be suspended in midair against the wall.

Bleary-eyed, he sprang up from the hardened couch he was lying on, trying to figure out where he was. Damien and Fred were missing. He was alone. Or was he? He wiped his eyes with the back of his hand. A woman was sitting opposite of him, watching him sleep.

"Who are you?" Wesley demanded.

"My, my. No need to be so fussy. Enri, he's awake," the woman called to the next room. "My name is Jezebel. They told us to be on the lookout for a couple of escapees through these parts. Never thought one of them would be so handsome."

She placed her hand on Wesley's knee, gently rubbing against it with her thumb. Wesley brushed her hand away, but the incident made him aware that someone had changed his clothes. He was no longer wearing the white prison jumpsuit, but navy-blue khakis and a wild floral shirt. If this was truly the style of Metropolian, Joanna would have been furious. Wesley felt like he was wearing a clown suit.

He stood to his feet and thanked Jezebel for her hospitality. Although she had most likely saved his life, he was still suspicious of her. For all he knew, she was just biding her time until the Federal Police came to retrieve him. There was also the man, Enri, she had mentioned. Wesley wanted to make his escape while he had the chance. He still had to find Damien and Fred. He walked to the door, only to find it biometrically locked.

"Going so soon?" Jezebel asked.

"I have to find my friends."

Before Wesley could say another word, Fred walked through the door of the connecting room drying his hair with a towel. He was still wearing his white jumpsuit. He was followed by a rather short fellow with a small pencil line mustache adorning his upper lip. Fred only stood a head taller than Wesley, but he seemed to tower over this man. It became apparent that they didn't have any clothes to fit his height and size. While Fred carried himself with such happiness over the situation, the other man had a more serious look.

"Wesley," Fred exclaimed, wrapping his arms around him, towel and all. He could feel the moisture from it on the back of his neck. "I'm so glad you're up. You've been out for a while."

"Who are these people?" Wesley asked, barely above a whisper.

"They say they're part of some secret group, and they were sent to find us. Something about it seems fishy to me," Fred said, pressing his lips almost into Wesley's ear. "The guy behind me has been watching me like a hawk."

"How did we get here, and where's Damien?"

Before Fred could answer, someone nearby cleared their throat. Enri was standing next to them, only a few inches away. He gave them a look as if to say the hug had gone on long enough. Fred took notice and released his arms from around Wesley, before taking a seat on the couch.

Fred's suspicions of the couple only amplified those of Wesley's. He took the opportunity to walk to the nearby window. He pretended to be gazing out over the wooded land in the morning light. In reality, he was examining the window, looking for a way out. It was a single pane with no obvious ways of opening it. If he were to try to escape through it, he would have to break it. As he continued to study it, he felt a hand on his shoulder. The bright red nails sharply contrasted the pastel print of his shirt.

"You like them, honey?" Jezebel asked, waving her fingers at him. "They say only the politicians ever get to be showy, but they don't know about my little secret stash. Makes me feel more like a woman." She placed her hands back on Wesley, sliding them down to his chest.

"Don't touch me," Wesley snapped as he batted her hands away. She looked at him sternly and furrowed her brow. Wesley couldn't help but grin as she glared at him with her arms crossed. It was obvious this woman wasn't accustomed to not getting her way. His grin only infuriated her more. She stormed off into the other room. Enri stood watching without a change of expression.

"There was another one with us in the river. Where is he?" Wesley asked him.

"I'm sorry, but your friend has suffered some serious injuries. He is currently resting comfortably in a room out back," Enri said.

"Then we have to go get him."

"If you move him, you will likely only injure him further. Regardless, I can't let you leave yet. The others are coming. We had orders to find you and keep you until they could take you."

Fred jumped to his feet. He caught Enri under the chin in the crook of his elbow.

"Thanks for saving our lives, but I think it's time we got going now," he said, squeezing Enri's neck a little tighter. "I don't know who they are, but nobody is taking me anywhere."

Jezebel reemerged from the other room, wielding a shotgun. She aimed it straight for Fred. She had obviously been eavesdropping on their conversation, stewing in her anger over Wesley's rejection.

"Put my husband down," she exclaimed, pumping the shotgun menacingly. The stray bullet fell to the floor with a thump, taking her attention off Fred. She looked down briefly at it. Wesley could tell that she was inexperienced with a shotgun by her reaction.

"Listen, lady. You've done got on my last nerve," he said, pulling the gun away from her.

Terrified, she fell to the floor, trying to crawl away. Fred let out a sigh of relief at the sight of Wesley holding the gun. Before they had a chance to regroup, Wesley told Fred to press Enri's hand onto the lock, so they could escape. Despite their size difference, Enri struggled against him, biting into his arm. Fred slung him to the floor, placing a knee directly on his sternum. Enri fought to breathe from the pressure, but still, he was relentless in his efforts. Irritated, Wesley used the shotgun to blast out the window, shattering it into a thousand pieces.

"That's okay. I've found my own way out."

Wesley hopped over the wall and through the frame. Fred was quick to join him, although not as graceful as Wesley in going through it. A few pieces of glass caught his leg, causing it to bleed.

Outside, they realized they were in a small cabin built near the river bank. It was on a slope with the rear of the house being toward high ground. Wesley began running toward it, hoping that Damien really was in a room back there.

Behind the cabin was a small shed built between the trees. As they ran toward it, Wesley caught a glimpse of something white. It was dirty, but it was still bright enough compared to the wooded area to catch his attention.

Damien was in there.

He was chained to a table inside the shed. His arms were stretched high above his hanging head. Straps held his waist and legs in place. Wesley charged for the shed. His only thought was that he hoped Damien was still alive.

When he reached him, he immediately checked for a pulse. It was faint, but it was there. He shot at the tops of the chains. The wooden table disintegrated from the impact of the bullets, leaving two gaping holes. He then unbuckled the straps. Fred hoisted him onto his shoulder, slouching slightly under the weight.

Carrying Damien made it difficult for them to climb the steep slope. Wesley knew they didn't have much time. Whoever it was that the couple were waiting on, would most likely be arriving soon. He opted for them to run alongside the river in hopes of finding a more level spot to reach the mainland. Wesley led the way, darting through the trees and shrubs looking for any danger that could be lurking ahead. Fred trotted along behind him. Wesley offered to help carry Damien as Fred's panting breaths grew louder, but he refused.

A twig snapped on the ground just ahead of them. Footsteps.

Wesley knelt down behind some shrubs and ordered Fred to do the same. Fred was trying to quiet his breathing, but Wesley still had to put a hand over his mouth to muffle it further. The footsteps were getting closer. He tried to look between the branches of the bush, but the limbs were too tightly tangled to get a clear visual. Whoever it was would be on them in a matter of minutes. They drew up tight against the plant, being careful not to disturb it and give themselves away. Their only hope was that the strangers wouldn't be alerted to their presence and just pass them by. No such luck.

A soft groan permeated the silence of the woods, seeming to echo from every tree. Damien was waking up. The footsteps grew quicker. They had heard it too. Wesley steadied the shotgun in his hands. With only one shot left, he had to make it count. A man emerged from above the bush. Instead of wasting his only bullet, Wesley swung the end of the weapon at him. The stock caught him on the chin, causing him to stumble backward.

"Whoa. Whoa," screamed a woman running up behind him. "We're on your side. We're part of an underground group that was tasked with finding you."

"I've heard that one before," Wesley said, resetting his gun and taking aim.

"Just come with us. We'll explain everything on the way."

"Yeah, that's not going to happen. You have one more chance to get out of here."

"Michael told us to…"

"Michael's dead. Times up."

The woman fell to her knees. She began to sob, hiding her face in her hands. The sight pulled at Wesley's heart, but he couldn't relent. For all he knew, it was a ploy on his emotions to get him to let his guard down. He continued to watch her. It was as if she was softly pleading for her life. The sight made Wesley feel like a monster. He lowered the gun slightly. Without warning, his fears were realized. The woman jumped to her feet, snatching the gun out of Wesley's hands. It was now trained on him.

"Listen here, bub. If you want to stay here and become an example for the Federal Police, it is no sweat to us. We were told to come get you so that Michael could focus on his own job. Now you have a choice. Stay here and die or come with us. I promise you, if we wanted you dead, you would be," the woman said, handing the gun back to Wesley.

He looked at it in his hands, stunned. With all that had happened in the last few days, he found it hard to trust anyone. He weighed his options, which were highly limited. As he looked toward Fred, even he seemed to give him a nod of approval. Damien was in desperate need of medical attention, and these people also seemed to have knowledge of Michael's whereabouts.

"Lead the way," Wesley replied reluctantly. Given the circumstances, it seemed like the best option. He only hoped that these people weren't somehow associated with Jezebel and Enri. He kept his eyes peeled for a trap.

They led them farther down the riverbank to a vehicle hidden near the edge of the trees. The man took the burden of carrying the still groggy Damien from Fred's tired shoulders. So far, the coast looked clear. Wesley noticed he kept hearing a voice. He looked around, but no one was saying a word. He listened closer and realized the woman seemed to be talking to herself.

Great. We're about to get in a van with a crazy woman. Perfect, he thought.

As he looked at her a little more keenly, he noticed it. A small earpiece was affixed just underneath her hair. Whoever these people were, they weren't working alone. Wesley picked up his pace to shorten the gap between them. He tried to inconspicuously eavesdrop on her, hoping to reveal just who exactly they were.

"I can't confirm one-hundred percent it's them, but he does look like the guy in the picture. He's wearing a ridiculous shirt, so I have no idea what his inmate number is," the woman was saying into the device. "He's suspicious enough of us as it is. I can't just interrogate the man. He's got a gun."

"Interrogate me?" Wesley asked. "Says the woman talking on a cellphone, which I'm pretty sure is still monitored by Fed computers."

The woman stopped in her tracks. She slowly turned around with her mouth gaping. Fear seemed to grip her. It was obvious she didn't want her conversation overheard.

"It's...it's encrypted. Our tech girl is really good with this stuff."

She pulled the device from her ear and handed it to Wesley. He looked at it briefly before putting it to his ear. The silence on the line was broken before he could even say hello.

"Wesley, you don't know me, but my name is Watch. I'm called that because I watch the Feds and I watch my teams. Right now, you have about a dozen officers forming a search party about a hundred yards behind you.

We're trying to save you as a favor for Michael, but if you don't get your stubborn butt in that van, you're welcome to go back to being a human pin cushion. Now go."

Before the voice on the phone could say anything more, Wesley caught a glimpse of a line of black uniforms coming through the trees behind them. He ducked low, pulling the others down with him. They only had a few seconds to make it to the van, assuming they could remain unnoticed with the stained white jumpsuits Fred and Damien still wore. They crawled on all fours, trying to stay beneath the cover of the undergrowth.

Wesley breathed a sigh of relief as his hand touched the cold metal exterior of the van. As soon as he did, bullets began to pepper its sides. The Federal Police had found them, but unless they had additional support nearby, they wouldn't be able to catch up. Wesley scampered into the van, slamming the door behind him. He checked to make sure the others were ready to go as the van lunged forward at tremendous speeds. He had never seen a van have that much acceleration from a dead stop. He felt the pressure against him as he leaned back into his seat.

All was quiet outside as he gazed through the window. They had caught the Federal Police off guard. There were no helicopters buzzing in the distance. No cars or torroes giving chase. Behind them, he saw the line of black uniforms shrinking in the distance.

"Alright, now that that's over, who are you, really?" Wesley asked. "It's obvious you're not Federal Police, so what? Terrorists? Traitors?"

"We're members of an underground organization known as Defiant," the woman said. "Our mission is to restore the world to the way it used to be, before the oppression of the Federal Police."

"I'm not sure if I should thank you for your service or be concerned. The Federal Police are monsters for what they've done to me and my family, but do you not know what the country was like before? Before the Federal Police, there was chaos. I was a cop. I saw it firsthand. People would violently protest against us while we were just trying to keep them safe. No matter what we did, we were blamed for something. When the Federal Police came, they brought order with them. There was peace."

"If the Federal Police are so grand, why did you leave to hide out in the Forbidden Zone?"

"Because I had to! They burned down my house and forced me into isolation."

"And yet you want to do nothing about them."

Wesley hesitated. Though he was indignant about the Federal Police, he knew that they had served a purpose. He had seen their job as a necessary evil for the good of all the people. The formation of the Federal Police had secured the victory against the terrorists. Their presence was meant to provide a sense of security among the civilians.

They may have ruled with fear, but they brought order and unity. That was their purpose. Peace was worth the sacrifice paid for their tyranny. Their formation also disbanded the local authorities, leaving him without a job. When Joanna resigned from her position in the fashion industry, Wesley took it as a chance to escape.

"As much as I would love to take down the Federal Police, starting with Colonel Hempton, I don't want things to go back to the way they were," Wesley said.

"You say you know how things were, but do you know how things are now?" the woman asked, motioning for him to look out the window.

Wesley's eyes followed the end of her finger. The sight made him sick. They were nearing the edge of Metropolian. A thick haze filled the air. Grime hung from the dilapidated walls. Bile lined the streets. Violence was everywhere.

"What happened here?" Wesley asked, looking on in horror. It was a far cry from what he remembered.

"The rich and powerful happened," the woman said. "Myers built Metropolian as a city that could sustain itself. Its entire economy was kept within its borders. It was the prototype. Then the classes happened. The higher class no longer wanted to associate with the lower class. The poor would steal from the rich, claiming the rich had stolen from them first. Each side claimed intolerance."

"What did they do?"

"They didn't want another war to start among the citizens," the man said. "They divided it up into districts based on social class and occupation. There are six districts. The upper class has five. The rest..."

"Welcome to the slums of Sybarite," the woman said, gesturing with her arms. "It's the biggest district, taking up almost a third of Metropolian. Those that live in this district are your factory workers, laborers, those with blue collar jobs. It has some of the most important jobs, but it's also the most forgotten. Wages here are almost non-existent. With everything being so taxed, most of what they make is paid to Imperia."

"Why don't they petition the government, or try to raise their wages?"

"Everything is based on percentages," the man said. "The factory sends what they make to the retail district for final assembly and preparation for sale. That district inflates the price from thirty to fifty percent of what Sybarite sold it to them at. So, if they raised the price of unfinished goods, because of the percentage, the retail price would go up even higher. It would offset the gain. The only ones that would come out ahead would be the retail district, and the government after the stuff is taxed twice for going in and out of a district."

"Things just don't work that way," the woman said. "Instead, a lot of them turn to less moral methods for making money. Gambling, drugs, crime. Every unimaginable thing you can think of, just to try to survive. Even the local prison guards are in on it. Nobody cares here. The Federal Police don't even care what goes on in this district, so long as there's no one trying to cross over into a different district without approval. Once they classify you, you just have to deal with it. It's how they keep it contained."

Wesley looked on. He couldn't imagine being forced to live in such an immoral society. From the look on the woman's face, she obviously had firsthand experience with it. She wouldn't even turn to look out the window. Wesley assumed that was the reason she was so set against the Federal Police. They had held her captive in such filth.

"Just a few miles up the road, we'll have to go through a checkpoint to cross districts," the man said. He had parked the van in an alley and was making his way through to the back of the van. He came back holding several sets of Federal Police uniforms. "I'm going to need all of you to put these on and try not to make eye contact as we pass through. Natalie and I have IDs so as long as none of you look suspicious we shouldn't have a problem passing through."

Wesley kept his head down as they approached the checkpoint gate. Two officers checked the IDs of the man and woman. Natalie waved them off as they looked at the van and their other passengers. The man eased the van forward. Once they were clear, Wesley lifted his head. The sight was drastically different than what he had seen. It was clean and modern. The buildings seemed to be crystalline sculptures reaching to the sky.

"Clerica. The business district," the man said. "The district where everyone always wears a suit and tie, and don't dare let anyone catch your tie be slightly loose. They'll think you're a little too relaxed and you'll be forced to file things for hours upon hours. At least in Sybarite, nobody really cares."

"Oh hush, Maps. Clerica is a cakewalk compared to what I had to go through," Natalie snapped at the man.

"Wait, if the Federal Police are so strict about people not moving between districts, how do people get anything? How do people eat?" Wesley asked, trying to get an understanding of this new world he had found himself in.

"Computers, man. It's the way of the world," Maps said.

"It's really only Sybarite that they restrict people from leaving. The rich can do whatever they want," Natalie retorted.

"You know, not everyone in the other districts is rich. Though, it would have been nice," Maps said. "Clerica handles the shipping of things. If a factory worker needed a new tire, he would order it online from the retail district. Clerica would then move it to where it needed to be and then charge them for it. Clerica is at the center of all the districts so it's easy to move things about. It's also built around the train station."

Maps pointed up to the Metro Station building as he began to park the car in its overnight lot. Once they had parked, Natalie disappeared, only to return with a wheelchair for Damien. Wesley didn't want to know where she had gotten it from, or from whom she had most likely stolen it.

Careful to avoid suspicions, they casually walked through the train station, pushing Damien along with them. He had yet to fully regain consciousness and laid slumped in the seat. The two led them to a train.

"Where are we going?" Wesley asked.

"We're taking you to see your friend," Natalie said.

Wesley hoped that she was being honest. He really wasn't concerned where they were physically headed to at the moment. Even with all he had seen, he only had two thoughts in his mind—finding help for Damien and reuniting with Michael.

16

ICHAEL LOOKED DOWN the short barrel of the handgun pointed at him and shook his head. It seemed no matter where he went or who he came across, he couldn't find anyone not willing to kill to fulfill their own agendas.

"You have three seconds to come back inside and close the door," Vasher said.

Michael refused. He would rather take his chances alone than with someone who could turn on him in an instant. Bringing down the Federal Police was not his intentions. All he wanted was to find his daughter and be left alone. He had enjoyed his life tucked away in the depths of the Forbidden Zone. Outside his secluded home, it seemed everyone either wanted him or wanted him dead, and he didn't know why.

"Michael, I don't want to do this, but I cannot let you fall into the hands of the Federal Police. If you do, everything we've worked for will be in vain. Everything Cade died for will be lost."

Cade. The name resonated in Michael's ears. So, it was true that he had been there. Michael sorely wished he would have just talked to him all those years ago. He wished he had known what he was involved in. Any information would have helped him now.

"Do you even remember Cade?" Vasher asked softly, with a hint of sincerity in his voice.

"Of course I remember him," Michael said. "He was killed by the Federal Police because he was working with you."

Vasher's eyes widened. His focus was fixed on Michael. So much so, it made Michael anxious. Even Watch was peeking out from behind her hands, staring at him. Michael recalled his words. None of it seemed to bear much significance. Surely, they already knew the Federal Police would kill anyone working with Defiant. They would classify them as terrorists just as Michael had done earlier.

"You remember?" Vasher asked. A glimmer of a smile flashed across his face. "Then they succeeded in activating you."

"What?"

Michael wrinkled his forehead in thought. They weren't concerned with what he had said, but merely that he remembered. Although it had taken some coercion from Amanda to recall the event, they couldn't have expected him to not have any knowledge of his friend at all. He also didn't know what Vasher meant by saying that they were "activating" him. He was no robot that could be switched on by command. He did remember the pain he felt in his mind when the memory came back to him. Perhaps that's what Vasher meant.

"We found out who you were, and that the Federal Police had intentions of activating you," Tobias said. "When you came into the holding cell at Camp Delta dressed as a guard and not a prisoner, we weren't sure if they had actually managed to."

"What do you mean by 'activating' me?"

"Ever have a word that felt like it was on the tip of your tongue, but no matter how hard you tried you couldn't remember?" Watch began, trying to explain it. "Basically, activating you means they're telling you the word."

"It's not quite as simple as that, but the idea is solid," Tobias said. "The Federal Police have a way of suppressing certain memories. The memory never really goes away, it just takes a lot of concentration. So, to bring it back, they typically give a person a combination of right and wrong information. It forces the brain to work through the details, breaking through the memory block."

Michael thought about how he had remembered the incident. No matter how hard he had tried, he couldn't remember what happened to Cade prior to reading the letter Amanda had. As soon as he had read it, it was like Watch had said. All the blanks were filled in. The letter, riddled with its inaccuracies, had allowed him to remember the day vividly.

"I don't understand," Michael said. "Why would they make me forget something only to have me remember it later? What do they even want with me?"

"You don't know, do you? You don't even know who you are," Vasher said, lowering the gun to his side. "It didn't work."

Disappointment spread across Vasher's face. He sighed heavily and turned to walk away. He no longer seemed to care that Michael still stood in the doorway or that he might try to run. The thought crossed Michael's mind, but he felt he was getting close to discovering why everyone was after him in the first place. He had to wait a little longer. He had spent so much time running blind. If he could finally glean some information about what was going on, he would be much better equipped for what was still ahead of him. It seemed that whatever advantage Vasher thought he could give him had vanished, and that concerned him.

Michael stepped back inside, loudly slamming the door to get Vasher's attention. His curiosity churned within him. What had they made him forget to have Vasher say that he didn't even know who he was? What was so important that everyone was after him to remember?

"Be glad you don't remember the horrible thing you've done," Vasher said gruffly.

The words cut deep. The truth was, Michael did remember. The thought had haunted his dreams for years. The screams of the innocent that echoed in his mind. The effect it had on Cade. He had never forgotten. It was the reason he hid in the Forbidden Zone. The others in his unit would talk about it like it made him some sort of a hero. They never would let it go. When he finally found Rebecca, he could barely look her in the eye. He wasn't the same man that he was before she was taken. There was no way he could let her find out about what he had done. He took her deep into the Forbidden Zone, far away from the memory.

"It was war," Michael said. "I didn't have a choice."

"Didn't have a choice? You almost singlehandedly gave the Feds the country on a silver platter."

Michael grew angry. As much as he regretted what he had done, he was sure there was no way it could have had such an effect on its own. The Federal Police weren't even as strong then. There was no way his actions could have led to them gaining such power.

"One attack could not have led them to take over."

"What are you talking about? This is about the virus you created."

Michael was stunned. He just stared at Vasher with his mouth agape. There were no words left to argue with him. They weren't even referring to the same event. Michael was sure Vasher had him confused with someone else. He didn't know how to create a virus. He didn't even know where to begin. He was a chemistry professor, not a biologist.

"Is that why you and the Federal Police want me? Because of some virus?"

"This is pointless," Vasher said, waving his hand in dismissal. "He can't help us. He doesn't even know he created it."

Vasher walked out of the room. Disappointment seemed to ooze out of his every pore. It was obvious he was counting on Michael to be his solution. Michael was angry. His life had been torn apart by something he was sure he had never had any part of. He was just another scapegoat for the Federal Police and a false hope for Vasher. His reaction also meant that he was no longer interested in helping Michael. Tobias followed him closely, trying to encourage him, but he was unaffected.

"Unless you know how to bring back his memory, Toby, there's nothing he can do to help us. He's not Cade."

"Listen, Jake, I know you miss him but don't just give up. I mean, we did at least find him again. And besides, if the Feds are after him, there's got to be a way," Tobias reassured him.

Michael could tell that at some point in time Vasher and Cade had become close, although he wasn't sure how. Despite everything that had happened, he knew this was where he needed to be. This was where Cade had wanted to bring him. This was where everything started. The only way out of this mess he had found himself in was to follow through. Before he could tell Vasher of his change of heart, a familiar voice stopped him mid-stride.

"Michael? You're alive."

Michael turned and saw Wesley entering through the doorway. He and four others emerged from the darkness of the tunnel. Michael ran to him and embraced him tightly. He was glad to see a friend. He was glad to finally come across someone he could trust again, even if that person had left his face scarred.

"Alright. No need getting all mushy," Wesley joked, pulling Michael's arms from around him. "But I am glad to see you. A lot of people have been looking for you."

"I know. It apparently has something to do with a virus they think I created, but it doesn't matter. They think I can help them. But they have helped me. I found Allie. She's at the secretary of security's fortress. I'm hoping they'll help me go after her."

Wesley looked at him like someone waiting for the punchline of a bad joke.

"I know it sounds crazy, but..." Michael began.

"You think?" Wesley snorted. "I've been running to save my life and you were worried about giving someone the flu. Now you think you can take on the commander of the Federal Police. That's a lot more than crazy. You used the same foolish thinking at the compound and look where that got us. I was shot and captured." Wesley placed a hand on his shoulder. "You don't even know what they're capable of."

"I've seen them bomb villages without mercy."

"No, my friend," Wesley said, his tone becoming much darker. "Bombs are quick and painless. I've watched them kill. Death is not the thing you should fear. I've felt their torment. They can make you feel as if you were dead, but unable to die. I can promise you, you don't want to try to do this."

Michael studied his friend. He could see the seriousness in his eyes. He could sense his fear. He started to ask him what they had put him through but decided against it. It was evident that he was still struggling with it himself. He chose the second most logical question that came to his mind.

"Who were they?" he asked, looking for the others that he had seen with Wesley. They had disappeared into a room, pushing a boy in a wheelchair through.

"Friends I've made along the way. I've got to go help them," Wesley said, already beginning to walk toward them. "Come with me. We need all the help we can get."

Michael wanted nothing more than to save Allie but getting to her was next to impossible. He knew what he had to do. Although he had no trust in Vasher, he did for Wesley. He knew he couldn't do it alone. They needed to stay together.

I'm sorry Allie, but it looks like it's going to take me a little longer, he thought. *Just hold on for me. I'm coming. Becca, I promise I won't let you down. I will get her back somehow.*

Michael turned and walked begrudgingly behind Wesley. The two exchanged their adventures along the way. They were both amazed that they each were able to escape the Federal Police and end up in the same place. Wesley had called it luck, but Michael informed him of Defiant's plan to bring him there.

***

When Michael returned to the main room, he saw Vasher reclined against Watch's desk with his arms crossed, glaring at him. The others in the room stopped to look at them also. Indignation adorned their faces. The room was still. There was no bustle of planning. No patter of keys being typed. Wesley ventured past him, amazed at the sight of it all. Michael hung back in the doorway. He felt responsible for letting them all down.

"Is there no way to make him remember?" the woman Wesley called Natalie asked.

"It's not in his file," Watch said. "They never recorded how to bring back the rest of his memories. My guess is so that we couldn't use him. Now it's just to wait and see."

Vasher pounded Watch's desk and paced across the room. Michael wished there was something he could do. Wesley had convinced him that he needed their help, and it seemed the only way to get it was to give them something in return. All any of them seemed concerned with, however, was the virus. The tension was high. Everyone huddled around the room, softly mumbling to each other. Michael would catch snide glances being cast at him. It was as if the whole room blamed him for everything.

"What is so important about this virus anyway?" Michael asked, finally having enough. Watch strummed a few keys on her keyboard, lighting up the monitor on the wall. Information slowly passed across it, along with pictures from Federal Police servers.

"The virus is how the government ended the war," Watch said, explaining what she had put on the computer. "It's how they suppress memories. They implanted it in the food and water supplies that went into the cities. They wiped away the reasons for fighting and covered up their ascension to power. The blanks it left was filled in with propaganda by the media."

"If it makes you forget, how do you know all of this?"

"Just like with any virus, some people are immune to it. We call those that are Resilients. Some are born immune, while some develop it later. Right after the virus began its outbreak, many of the first Resilients banded together to form Defiant."

Michael watched as the names of the founding members flashed across the monitor. The names scrolled by too fast to read, but beside each name, most were labeled as deceased. It seemed as if the life expectancy of most Defiant members was rather short. Those that hadn't been killed were hidden away in safe houses. Only one of the founding members was listed as still active. The screen changed too quickly for him to see who.

"What happened to them?" Michael asked.

"The virus is the Federal Police's ultimate weapon. With it, they can make allies out of enemies. Anyone who is found out to be a Resilient is often killed or experimented on."

***

Watch's words peaked Wesley's interest. He walked over to the monitor beside Michael. He had endured his share of their experiments. The reason they kept asking him about colors had become clear. They were testing him to see if he remembered them. He wondered if the others he had seen in the holding cells were Resilients. Those like Fred who had been trapped in compounds for years, or Damien. There was no way for them to know for sure. He couldn't ask them if they remembered forgetting. Unlike Fred though, he remembered the experiment. He remembered the chemical they had poured into him.

"The virus, if it was implanted in food and water, I'm assuming it's kept in a liquid form? Something that could be injected with a syringe?" Wesley asked, gaining everyone's attention. "Does it feel like fire as it enters your bloodstream, followed by a pain so intense it feels like every fiber within you is being ripped apart?"

The room fell silent. Vasher stopped pacing. All eyes were on Wesley as if he had said something astounding. Vasher walked to him and studied him carefully. Even Michael looked at him perplexed. Wesley waited for an answer. He wanted to know what it was they had injected him with.

"What do you know?" Vasher puzzled.

"I'm not sure what I know. They kept locking me in this room, asking me about colors. They would show me a set and then ask me to repeat them back. Each time I did, they would get mad and inject me with more of some chemical."

"They're already doing trials?" All the color left Vasher's face. His mouth fell agape. "Watch, run a search to see if you can find anything about the trials."

Immediately, she began typing, cycling through screen after screen on her computer.

"Nothing. There's no mention of it on any of the Feds' servers."

"What is it?" Wesley demanded.

"That's a new strand we've heard rumors about. It was designed to attack only specific memories," Vasher said. "Picture us standing in this room. With that virus, they can erase you from our memory as if you were never here. It was only supposed to be a rumor. We haven't seen anything official. There was no way we could know they were already starting trials."

"I don't know about any of that, but you said it was a new strand. Is that what the experiments are for? Creating a better virus?"

"Some of them yes. The virus is also losing its effectiveness. More and more are becoming Resilients. They're trying to change that. That's why they need Michael," Vasher said. "They've been working off of Cade's revisions…"

"Cade helped build the virus?" Michael interrupted.

Wesley could tell he was in deep thought, going through the connotations in his mind. He knew Michael and Cade had been close. He wondered why Michael didn't remember the virus. Or did he and the memory was stolen from him?

17

"THANK YOU, DR. ANDERTON."

Michael nodded as an older man was walking out of the laboratory. He and Cade were now the last two still working at such a late hour. The sun was barely noticeable against the bright fluorescent lights as its remnant sank behind the nearby buildings.

"Thank you, Dr. Anderton," Cade mocked as he threw a crumpled ball of paper at Michael. "You're not even old enough to have that title."

"I got my Ph.D. when I was twenty-two, thank you."

"Slacker. I got mine at twenty-one," Cade laughed, sticking his tongue out at Michael.

"You also didn't get married or have twins in the middle of getting it," Michael said, returning Cade's gesture. "You try writing a dissertation with two newborns having a screaming contest."

"Well excuse me, Mr. Smarty-Pants. If you're so smart, why is my virus kicking your cure's butt?"

Michael pursed his lips. It was true Cade almost had his virus ready for human testing, while his cure was still struggling to be palpable. In his frustration, he stood up from his workbench and walked to the screen hanging on the wall to do more calculations. He applied so much pressure on the stylus, it squeaked as it rubbed against the glass of the screen. He was determined not to let Cade outdo him. He had a good reason for his cure.

Cade sat behind his microscope still laughing. He was always giving Michael a hard time. The two had become very close in the last year when a drug company decided to fund Michael's research. His idea had shown promise at creating a viable cure, but it needed a carrier system. Cade was working his way up to being at the top of his field in viral medicine and jumped on the chance of headlining such a major breakthrough. The two challenged each other regularly. Although they each had their own reasons, they desperately wanted the cure to succeed.

"Pick a neuron," Cade said, smiling.

"Huh?" Michael said without breaking stride in his calculations.

"Pick a neuron. I want to see if I can get the virus to zap it."

"Cade, I don't have time for your silly games." He didn't really care what Cade was up to. He was focused. His frustration grew with each calculation. Each time he thought he had something figured out, the screen would tell him something was invalid. He was on the verge of sitting on the floor and working in the dust. It at least wouldn't talk back.

"Well, I got bored waiting for you to finish up over there. I'm trying to see if I can get the virus to only target certain neurons that I choose. It would let us bring back only specific memories."

Michael quit listening. He wished he could be like Cade and not have to be quite so serious about it. Cade was only taking part in the project for the recognition it would bring if they succeeded. He didn't really seem to care when it was finished. Michael didn't have that luxury. He was on a deadline. It was a matter of life and death.

He had watched his father slowly slip away for the last several years. The symptoms had started to become noticeable when Michael was still a senior in college. He would notice that his father would lose his shoes almost daily, and then get angry with Michael when he would get them for him. He also caught him sitting in his car as if he were lost in his own driveway. He had since progressed to the point where he no longer recognized his own grandsons.

The thought pushed Michael on. He had to finish his cure before it was too late. It had become his life's work. When the symptoms first started to appear, he promised his father that he would create a cure. While everyone else thought he just had big dreams for himself after graduation, Michael devoted his life to it. He geared his entire post-graduate studies to learning about the disease. He spent every spare moment trying to discover a way to reverse its effects. If it wasn't for Rebecca's persistence, he was almost positive he wouldn't have his family.

The thought of her eased his tension, until he thought of her at home alone with the boys. She always hated when he would work late. She would fuss at him about raising their sons alone. He wanted to be a good father, but he knew he had to finish his work. He constantly reassured her that once it was finished, things would be back to normal. He truly believed that. He just needed more time.

He set the pen down after another failed attempt. He needed to try to smooth things over with Rebecca. Every minute he waited was another minute for her frustrations to grow. He told Cade he was going to walk downstairs to make a phone call. Cade responded with another joke about him giving up. Michael shook his head and walked out.

"Hey, sweetie," Michael said softly into the phone.

"Michael Anderton," Rebecca's voice yelled back, loud enough to distort the small speaker wedged in Michael's ear. He knew she would be unhappy, but he had never made her nearly as mad as she seemed to be. For her to raise her voice meant it was something serious. "Have you heard about the new law they just passed? They're closing all the churches. They claim they promote hate and violence. Can you believe that?"

Michael wasn't surprised. There had been so much conflict in the last decade, everyone was looking for someone to blame. Claims of religious intolerance had been at the forefront of it for years. The whole country seemed to be on the brink of a civil war. The civil unrest was only amplified by the media's skewing of stories for better ratings.

"Maybe it's for the best," Michael said. "Maybe now that they can't just blame religion, they can get to the heart of the matter and settle everyone down."

"For the best?" she screamed into the phone. "You can't legislate God out of existence. All they're doing is throwing morals out the window just to appease a few whackos."

"In better news, I heard that our mayor...what's his name...Myers is trying to take the Metropolian Project national. You know the whole self-sufficient city. It's supposed to help the economy, because other than taxes, all the money stays in the cities. After seeing what he's done with it for Chicago, I think it could work. I mean, who would have thought in this economy he could make Chicago twice the size of New York City."

"Don't change the subject. Especially not to talk about Myers. I know he's done a lot for this city, but I don't trust him. Something in his eyes."

"He's a politician. They all look the same. Once the government gives Myers enough votes to start more mega-cities, everything will be different," Michael reassured her. "Heck, maybe he'll even run for president. He'd definitely have my vote."

He had seen his ad campaigns. He constantly promised the people that he would bring order back to the country. Even without the votes, there was rumor he was already working with New York and Philadelphia about starting other self-sufficient cities. They were trying to gain ideas and insight into what worked best for the people. The entire city loved him. Rebecca had her doubts about him, though. Something about him didn't sit well with her.

"Everything's going to work out fine. I promise. Just have a little faith," Michael said. He heard Rebecca giggle on the other end of the line.

"Look at you. Mr. Science-can-explain-it-all telling me to have faith. I must be finally getting through to you."

It was never that Michael didn't believe in God. He acknowledged that there could be some higher power out there somewhere. He just liked the idea that he was in control of his own destiny. He was also far too busy to concern himself with such things. He told Rebecca that maybe once he finished the cure, they might start a bible group since the churches were being shut down. He had promised he would eventually find time to read it more. Rebecca was thrilled at the idea. With his wife appeased, he apologized for working late and walked back upstairs to the lab.

"How bad are you in the dog house tonight?" Cade smirked.

"Not as bad as you're going to be if we don't hurry up," Michael said.

"Still waiting for you. Equations didn't solve themselves." Cade pointed to the screen.

Michael loathed looking at it. He had hoped that taking the break to talk to Rebecca would help. It didn't. He was tired of calculating. All it seemed he got to do anymore was work with formulas. Cade was having fun doing real-world tests. He could see the fruits of his labor taking place. He could watch it move and grow under a microscope. Michael was jealous.

Two years he had spent on the project, and he was still doing calculations. He looked at the screen, then looked over at the beakers on the counter. He had solved most of the problem already. He convinced himself that maybe some real-world testing would prove to be the breakthrough he needed to finish. He grabbed his beakers and some pipettes. Behind him, Cade was putting on safety goggles and turning on the ventilation.

"I know what I'm doing," Michael said.

"So that's why that board up there has been screaming 'invalid' for the last hour and a half."

Michael refused to pay him any attention. He began mixing his compound, slowly combining the chemicals from his formulas. Everything was going smoothly. He turned back and gave Cade an "I told you so" look. As he neared the undetermined part of his formula, things began to go haywire. Smoke billowed from his flask. It burned his nostrils like fire as it went up his nose, causing him to cough rigorously. Cade took cover beneath his desk. Just as it seemed the compound was about to explode, the smoke dissipated. The liquid in the flask settled to a calm.

"See…works…" Michael sputtered, still coughing.

"That's debatable," Cade said, peeking out from behind his desk.

Michael put his hand up to the flask. No heat was radiating from it. In spite of the near explosion, it was as cold as ice. Michael was relieved. A scalding hot compound would do them no good, even if the cure did work.

"Combine it with your virus and let's get the show on the road. I'd like to get home before breakfast," Michael said.

Before long, Cade produced the infused virus and readied it in a syringe. He had prepared a cadaver brain for initial testing, but Michael stopped him. He handed him a large mouse instead. He wanted to test it on a live brain to see how well it worked in producing acetylcholine, the chemical in the brain that allows a person access to their memories. Cade injected the serum, but not without protest. He had gotten attached to the mouse. Within seconds of the injection, the mouse began to convulse violently. It thrashed about inside its cage before it fell completely still.

"Good job, Michael. You killed Bob. You owe me a mouse."

"Run a test for me and tell me what happened. I may be able to fix it, and we can test it again."

"You can get your own mouse first," Cade said as he drew blood from the dead rodent. Michael walked back to his calculations. Witnessing the compound's reaction and effect had reinvigorated him. He wanted to understand what kind of compound the reaction had created that his computer had claimed was an impossibility.

"Mike, you need to check this out," Cade said before Michael could even begin. "Your compound is backward. It doesn't cause the brain to create acetylcholine, it absorbs it from around the neuron. Bob died because he forgot everything. He even forgot how to breathe."

Michael pounded his fists on the desk, hard enough to cause his knuckles to bleed. Two years of work and his cure caused the problem it was intended to fix. Michael slumped to the floor. He felt like a failure. He kept thinking he was close. He kept pushing. The whole time, he had it all wrong. He didn't know how to reverse it. Cade tried to make light of the situation, but it made little difference to Michael.

"Stop beating yourself up. You didn't fail. You just made something else by accident. I've been working with my virus to only target specific neurons. What if we put that together? Got a bad memory? No problem. We've got you covered."

"That's fine, but that doesn't help my dad," Michael said, his face dropping. Cade placed a hand on his shoulder, trying to comfort him. Cade had known the reason for his determination, but he was doing what he could to make him feel better. Michael knew that. He took solace in the fact that he had a friend who cared enough to try.

18

MICHAEL'S HEAD WAS SPINNING, flooded with the same pain he had felt before. His mind was waking up. He remembered the virus. Wesley had dropped to a knee beside him. He cradled his head, trying to help him up. Vasher stood over him smiling. It was as if he knew a piece of his memory had been unlocked. Not that it mattered, he didn't know any more about how to reverse its effects than he had before. He had failed again.

"I can't help you," Michael said, lifting himself up from the floor. He squeezed his eyes tight to try to relieve the pressure in his head. "My formula failed. I designed it to regain memories, not suppress them. Cade was the only reason it was even usable."

Unmoved, Vasher slowly rubbed his chin as if he was in deep thought. Michael had disappointed him so many times, he knew he was going to give up on him. He was not the salvation Vasher was hoping for.

"That must be why they went for him first," Vasher said, still thinking. "If only we could have gotten you both here then, we may could have beat this thing."

"It's a virus. Can't you just come up with a vaccine or something for it?" Wesley interjected.

"We've tried that. It doesn't bring back a person's memories. It only prevents them from losing more, and that's only for a few people. When the Federal Police discovered the number of Resilients among them, they captured Cade. They forced him to create a virus that would mutate and adapt. It makes vaccines useless."

"What's so important for them to remember anyway? I mean, it's natural for people to forget things."

"Either of you ever heard of the Red Riders?"

Michael looked at Wesley. It was clear from his blank expression that neither of them knew the name. Michael wondered why they were of any importance.

"The Red Riders started out as just a motorcycle gang, but they grew into a freedom fighter movement. We were at war with the Northwyn Province of China and were losing badly. It caused animosity among the people. They had already been bickering with each other on the internet for a decade about social issues. Everyone had their own side. There was mass murders, violence, and hysteria in our own streets. The government finally acted. They couldn't afford to look weak when Northwyn wanted so badly to destroy us."

"What did they do?" Michael asked.

"They stripped people of their gun rights, their religious rights, basically anything that caused an outrage. Of course, all they really did was stir a boiling pot. It was true that such things did cause radicals to act, but when the government began stripping people's rights, the silent majority spoke up. The Red Riders revolted against a corrupt government and the Federal Police. The government fought back by claiming that the Red Riders were Northwyn terrorists."

"Were they?"

"Not a lot is really known. Some say the Red Riders struck first. Others the Federal Police. When the Red Riders bombed Washington and killed the president, it split the nation into all-out civil war. The Federal Police's response was to level every state associated with the Red Riders, thus creating the Forbidden Zone. Then with the virus, they were able to erase them ever existing as well as the atrocious thing the Federal Police had done."

Wesley was silent, trying to take it all in. Michael was pale. He felt as though he was going to be sick. The weight of guilt overwhelmed him. He and Cade had acted nobly then, only to have their creation lead to a massive coverup of the destruction of the nation. His life's work was to save his father, whom he had failed.

Michael had been forced to watch the slow deterioration as his father's mind slipped away. Day by day, he would drift farther from the world. Michael had to endure the agony as everything and everyone his father ever knew passed away. All the while, he knew that the cure he had worked so hard for had failed when he needed it most. Depression crept into the corners of his mind. The one goal he had strove so hard for had not only failed but took away the lives and freedoms of countless people. The thought was too much.

"I'm going to stop Myers, no matter the cost," Michael said through gritted teeth. "He killed Becca, took Allie, and used my life's work for his own evil. He has to be stopped."

Michael's anger raged within him, which spawned hatred. Michael had never been one to hate anyone, but he felt justified in hating Myers for all he had done. The image of Myers sitting in the dark room Tobias had called the Void flashed before his eyes. The plump, little man, who combed his gray hair to the side to hide the ever-growing bald spot. His eyes like that of a snake waiting to attack its prey. Michael couldn't believe so much evil could rest within one person.

"We've tried," Vasher said. "We don't have nearly enough manpower for brute force. We've tried taking out key places. Cade even tried to bomb their research lab, but it's no use. Nothing we have has been strong enough to make a dent in Myers' forces. That's why we put so much hope in reversing the virus."

"Right now, I don't care about any of that. Myers is my priority. If you want to stop the Federal Police, cut off the head."

"We've already told you that was impossible. Myers keeps himself hidden away in his fortress, and there is no way in."

Michael pounded his fists on a desk. He refused to give up. Myers had taken away from him everything that he had ever cared about. He looked over at Wesley, who stood in silence. He could see the fire burning within him. With all they had been through, he knew Wesley would help him. The others may have been too afraid to stand up to Myers and the Federal Police, but his friend had lost just as much to Myers. The two of them would charge the front gate if they had to. Michael was sure Wesley wouldn't approve of that, but he was willing to try anything.

The thought had given him a possibly viable idea, though. He pulled Wesley to the side out of earshot of the others. He didn't want Vasher to dismiss it before he had a chance to think it through.

"That's crazy, Mike," Wesley said, reeling from Michael's plan. "You want to turn yourself in?"

Wesley's reaction caught the attention of the others, especially Vasher who was quick to keen in. His only goal seemed to be keeping Michael out of the grasp of the Federal Police, leaving him to be less than thrilled with Michael's plan.

"Let me explain," Michael said. "The Federal Police want me alive, so we use that to our advantage. If we go up to Myers' fortress, they'll be much less likely to shoot on sight once they notice that it's me. To keep them from just arresting me, I need a Defiant member to take me hostage."

"So, then they kill a member of Defiant and still take you prisoner," Vasher said flatly.

"Strap him up in a bomb vest with a dead man switch. They kill one of us and their prize goes out with us," Natalie said, offering a solution. "If it works, it's a chance for us to get eyes inside his fortress, or possibly take him out."

"No. No bombs," Michael blurted out. The thought was despicable. Although he was willing to risk his life for a chance to take down Myers, he was not going to have a bomb strapped to him. He hated bombs in general.

"The bomb will be more for show than anything unless one of us is captured. We can't let Michael fall into their hands."

Michael felt like a pawn in their game. It seemed his opinion no longer mattered. Everyone else in the room was nodding along to Natalie's idea. Everyone, except Wesley, who seemed to share in Michael's discomfort.

"And then what?" Vasher asked. "How do you plan to take down Myers? Or is this about your daughter? The fortress covers almost three city blocks. How do you expect to find her? Security cameras are on a closed system. We have neither eyes nor ears inside. And if you do find her, what's your grand plan for escape?"

"If Myers is keeping Allie, there has to be a reason. He'll bring her to me. If he's so adamant about me helping him further his virus, he'll try to leverage her. Once I have her, we run. You could have troops surround the outside of his fortress."

"I don't think you understand their security. There are cameras surrounding the exterior, so we can't provide that kind of backup. They'll see us coming, even if we could manage to get enough troops into Metropolian to help. Also, the only way in and out of the fortress is through the main gate, which they won't let you just run out of. It won't work."

"Then I'll figure it out once I'm in there. But I'm doing this."

"No. It's too risky."

Michael growled in frustration. He hated knowing that Allie was there. He had found her, so he was going to find a way to get to her. He wouldn't leave her there any longer in the hands of Myers.

"Talk to me about this system," Damien said, rolling his wheelchair among them.

"Damien. You're awake," Wesley said, rushing to him.

"Yeah, just remind me to shoot the French guy next time I see him."

"The fortress isn't linked to any outside networks, so there's no way for me to hack it," Watch said, breaking up their moment.

"So, all you need is a link?" Damien asked. His eyes moved with his thoughts. "Got a spare router? All someone has to do is plug it into their system once they're inside, and you can backdoor your way in."

Watch smiled and nodded in agreement.

"And how do we manage to get someone in place to plant the router?" Vasher asked.

"We'll still have to work on an extraction, but I have a plan that should work perfectly for getting someone inside," Wesley said. "It's one we actually used to use on the police force for getting into difficult places. Ever heard of a Trojan horse?"

"I'm all ears," Vasher said.

***

As Michael sat in the back of the car with a bomb strapped tightly to his chest, nerves began to overtake him. His hands were trembling, so he kept them folded on his lap. With every building that passed by, his fear grew, but so did his determination. Each building that passed was one step closer to Allie. His fear wasn't what they would do to him, but that he wouldn't be able to save her. He had come so far to get to her, he wasn't going to let the Federal Police stop him from finally reaching her.

Maps pulled the car into an alleyway. Just up ahead was Myers' fortress. Michael's heart sank at the sight of it. Although he had seen an image of it, he never expected it to be so large. The red brick was commanding against the concrete backdrop of the buildings behind it.

It spread out wide. Its edges were hidden behind the buildings on either side of the street. Black suits lined every crevice of the fortress. Rod iron fencing shaped like spears jutted up from a low brick wall encircling it. Looking at it, Michael felt lucky he was able to enter the prisoner compound. If they had guarded it as well as they were guarding Myers' fortress, he and Wesley would never have made it out alive.

Michael could feel his heart beating beneath the vest. It seemed with every pulse, the vest grew tighter, making it harder for him to breathe. Natalie and Maps urged him on. Seeing the trigger in Natalie's hand only made matters worse. To try to stay calm, he kept reminding himself of his mission and why he was there. Each step took him closer to what he had waited for.

"Halt! This is a restricted area. All violators will be shot on sight," one of the Federal Policemen called through the loudspeaker from atop the watchtower next to the gate.

"I have someone you want," Natalie yelled back, shoving Michael forward. They fired a warning shot. The bullet ricocheted off the ground in front of Michael, causing him to stumble back. The guards didn't seem to be too concerned with who he was, despite the great efforts put forth by the Federal Police to capture him. "Are you really willing to shoot Michael Anderton?"

There was no word back from the fortress. Tension ran high as they awaited a response. Minutes seemed to tick by. Natalie repeated his name to them, and still, there was nothing. Michael wanted to move forward but was afraid it may lead them to shoot at them again. He was ready to go. His entire plan hinged on this moment, waiting for them to lead him into the fortress.

The front gate groaned as it slid open. It sounded as if it had been some time since it was last opened. An ominous figure emerged from behind its iron bars, too far away for Michael to see any details. Silence enshrouded the fortress as the figure strode by. It was obvious he carried an air of importance with him. Against the bright concrete street, Michael began to make out the lush purple robe. Myers.

Three officers were with him. One simply to hold up the bottom of his robe to prevent it from dragging the ground. They ambled down the street, oblivious to the weapons Natalie and Maps had aimed at them. In Michael's mind, he could see a twitch of a finger and ending the problem, but he couldn't do it. Even in anger, he couldn't take another man's life in cold blood, and he still needed him. Myers was going to lead him to Allie.

"Mr. Anderton, how nice to see you again. Oh, please put those down so we can talk like civilized men," Myers called, motioning to Natalie and Maps to lower their weapons. A smile was proudly worn on his face as he approached. "We've been looking for you. I'm so glad we found you. I just wish it wasn't under such dreadful circumstances."

Myers pulled at the seams of the vest strapped to Michael. In a panic, Natalie lifted the switch held firmly in her palm. The two guards trained their weapons on her. Maps lifted his in response. Myers lowered his head and rubbed the bridge of his nose between his thumb and forefinger.

"You people and your guns and your bombs. The war is over. Come join us and you can stop living like dogs."

"I'd rather live like a dog than your slave," Natalie said, spitting on him. In an instant, the guards moved, and Maps was taken down. Michael looked down at him. Maps laid face down on the ground unconscious. A syringe was still stuck in his shoulder.

"Insurrection will not be tolerated. Join us or face the consequences," Myers said.

"I'll show you consequences if you strike us again," Natalie screamed, waving around the detonator. The sight made Michael feel ill. His stomach felt as if it had risen into his throat as his eyes danced around following her hand.

I wish we had used a decoy bomb vest, Michael thought, although he knew it was for security they used a real one. If either he or Natalie was captured, they wouldn't be able to use him to enhance the virus or possibly torture his daughter when he couldn't.

Myers chuckled. There was no fear in him. He had mocked them for using guns and bombs while he hid safely behind the artillery of the Federal Police. He thought he was untouchable, staring death in the eye. Michael had to control his mind to keep it from wandering back to the place of wanting Myers dead. He wanted terribly to wipe the grin off his face.

"What is it you want, dear, to come all this way in such a brash fashion?" Myers asked.

"A trade," Natalie said. "You track us down and hunt us like animals, but we pose no threat to you. To prove it to you, we're offering up your most wanted person in exchange for our freedom. We want to live by our own rules, outside of Federal Police jurisdiction."

Michael watched Myers' expression. There was a gleam in his eye. He looked like he was taking the bait. The plan seemed to be coming together. That was until there was a push on Michael's back. He stumbled forward, nearly planting his face on Myers' chest. One of the officers slapped him across the face at Myers' instruction as he unruffled his silk shirt. Michael was taken back. He couldn't believe Natalie had pushed him like that.

"Take him, and I'll take your order of amnesty. Everybody wins," Natalie said.

"Hardly," Myers scoffed.

Michael felt betrayed, as if Defiant had been playing him all along. He felt like a mere pawn in a game set forth between Defiant and the Federal Police.

Michael looked back at Natalie. With such an intense focus in her eyes, it was as if she were looking into the very soul of Myers. She stood steadfast with her jaw clenched tight. Michael had stumbled into a feud between these two groups that had spanned for years. Natalie hated Myers for all he had apparently done to them. Or was it personal? The look in her eye showed the same emotion toward Myers that Michael himself felt for him.

Michael knew the reason for his anger. This was the man that was ultimately responsible for Rebecca's death. The man now responsible for keeping Allie prisoner. He had to keep his feelings in check for her, but he wasn't sure about Natalie. At Myers' reply, it was as if she would trip the bomb for the spite of it. Just to prove to him that he wasn't in control.

Before Michael could think another thought, Natalie dropped the hand holding the detonator to her side as her other hand brought up her pistol. In a flash, its bullet pierced the forehead of the officer standing closest to Myers.

"I'm not asking twice," she said.

Michael was taken back. He couldn't believe Natalie shot a Federal Police officer without so much as a second's hesitation. There was no apprehension, even with so many guns aimed at them. If Myers had not been in such close proximity to the bomb, Michael was sure they'd both be dead.

"Come now, let's take this inside and discuss the terms like civilized men, with dignity," Myers said unfazed by Natalie's actions. "Clean this mess up. It's bad for public image."

With a snap of his finger, Myers turned his back to Michael and Natalie and began walking back to his fortress. One guard picked up the dead body while the other picked up Maps. They fell in line behind Natalie, urging her and Michael into the fortress.

This was it. Michael's plan to get them inside was working, he just needed to figure out his next move and fast.

19

HOVERING OVER Watch's shoulder, Wesley stared at the computer screens. The scene outside the fortress looked tense. Maps and an officer were both on the ground. Wesley wished he could hear what they were saying. Watch sat in front of him with an earpiece wedged in her ear. She was having to strain to make out the words.

"How are they doing?" Wesley asked.

"So far so good. They're talking," Watch said.

Vasher breathed heavily behind them. He was pacing back and forth. His hand nervously rubbed his chin.

"This was stupid," Vasher said, never breaking stride. "I understand wanting to protect family. I get that. But there is so much more at stake here. And we let our most valuable asset walk right into the hands of the enemy. Your plan better work."

Wesley could only hope. He waited in apprehension, repeatedly tapping his thumbs above his interlaced fingers. He hated sending Michael there alone. He should have gone with him. He didn't trust these Defiant characters. Who were they really? An entire organization seemed to have materialized out of nowhere. They were devoted to bringing down Myers, the Federal Police, and perhaps the entire bureaucracy. Both organizations seemed pitted against one another over a single target—Michael.

The whole idea that Michael could somehow be behind a virus that targets memory seemed a little absurd. What really puzzled Wesley, though, was why now? Why after eight years of just trying to survive in the Forbidden Zone did they come for him? It wasn't as if they were looking for him. They knew exactly how to hit him. The thought of the burning shack, of Joanna lying before its ashes made him shudder. He tried not to dwell on the thought any further.

"They've taken them inside," Watch said. "They're taking Maps to the infirmary like we had hoped."

"What was that they injected him with?" Wesley asked.

"That's their weapon of choice, so to speak. Think of it like an instant amnesia. The more of it they inject, the farther back the memory wipe seems to go. Thankfully, Maps is a Resilient, so other than a slight headache, its effects are pretty minimal."

"That's why they're in such a hurry to revamp their serums," Vasher said. "Resilients can't really be controlled by memory drugs."

Wesley watched the screens as Watch cycled through the exterior camera feeds.

"Anything yet?"

"Not yet. Give him time."

***

Maps laid still on the gurney. He steadied his breathing and kept his eyes shut tight as he listened to everything around him. Two men were talking. He wasn't sure who they were, but it seemed like everything was going to plan.

"This one's been wiped," one of the men said. "He came in with the other terrorist. Make sure his nap is a little more permanent."

"I thought Myers wanted them left alive," said the other.

"And I thought you liked your job."

"Listen. I'm Richard's personal physician. If you want something like that done, take him to the north wing. Let LeFleur do it."

"He's here. Get it done."

Their conversation made Maps nervous, but he knew he had to wait for the perfect time to strike. Unlike his colleagues, fighting was not his specialty. Natalie would have dispersed of them both in an instant. Although she could play the sweet girl when it was beneficial, Maps knew the truth. She was as hard as nails and never let anyone stand in her way. That was most likely why Vasher had sent her to be Michael's escort. That, however, meant Vasher also had a lot of faith riding on Maps' ability to stealthily escape that room.

Maps peeked through slits in his eyelids to try to survey the room. One doctor was all he could see, but that doctor was getting closer. Too close for Maps' comfort. He panicked and jolted up off the gurney. His forehead smashed into the nose of the doctor, causing him to crash into the side table and onto the floor. The doctor screamed, blood already oozing from his nostrils. To silence him, Maps grabbed the nearest thing he could find, a specimen jar, and smashed it against the side of the doctor's face. It landed with a thud as glass collided with bone. The doctor's screams intensified. No. Those screams were coming from the hallway. Guards.

Jumping up from the floor, Maps raced for the door but was immediately pulled back. The doctor had wrapped a clear tube around his neck and was holding it taut. Maps struggled. The more he fought, the tighter the doctor's grip would get and the more the tube strangled him. Maps threw his weight back, kicking the gurney and knocking it to the floor. It was his hope to land on the doctor. No such luck. His full weight landed on the corner of the nearby cabinets just beneath his shoulder blade.

Maps wheezed, both from the sudden blow and the lack of air flowing into his lungs. He could feel his pulse pounding in his neck as if it were going to explode. Heat filled his face as the blood pooled in his cheeks. It was no use to anyone for him to be a Resilient if he couldn't escape that room. Perhaps it was the lack of oxygen to his brain or the anger welling within him, he did the only thing he could think of to do. He reached over his shoulder and flicked the doctor on the nose.

Tears flooded the doctor's eyes as both hands instinctively grabbed his face. Maps took his opportunity and buried his shoulder into the door as it was opening. The guard squealed in pain as three of his fingers were abruptly pinched in the door frame. Keeping the door pressed with his body, Maps slid a heavy metal table in front of it. It wouldn't keep them out long, but he had gained a few minutes to think. The doctor no longer paid him any attention, as he was solely focused on his face. Maps looked at the other doors in the room and then the window. He had to stay inside the fortress, and the guards would find their way to another door soon. Without a moment's hesitation, Maps climbed on top of the metal table and shimmied himself up into the air vent.

The warm air-conditioned wind hit him in the face. Its effect immediately made his mouth dry but turned his eyes into faucets. Tears streamed from both eyes, making it difficult for him to see. Such was already hard enough in the dark metal vent. Without letting it phase him, he pressed on, passing up room after room. He was sure the guards would be onto him being in the air vent and would most likely check the nearest rooms.

With each room he passed, he would peer into it through the grates of the vent and take a mental image of the room. In his mind, he would memorize details about the room and its relative position within the palace. That way once the current job was done, he would be able to draw a map of the facility.

Shouts from the guards echoed throughout the maze of metal ducts. They knew he was in the air vent, but with such a vast compound and so many connected channels, the air conditioning became its own network. The same ductwork serviced both the top and bottom floors of the palace. It would take them hours to search the whole area. Maps kept crawling until there was only silence.

Through the vent, he saw a small, quaint room that was painted bright pink. White and blue flowers adorned the walls, haphazardly hung throughout. The covers of the bed were tousled, obscuring the images of the unicorns decorating it. If Myers was keeping Michael's daughter anywhere in the palace, that had to be the place.

Maps carefully pried open the vent and took a better look at the room. No one was in sight. He squeezed through the vent as quietly as possible. In the corner of the room, he noticed a laptop also covered in unicorns. This time in the form of paper stickers that seemed to have faded. The layer of dust on the keys suggested that the computer hadn't been used in quite some time. He took advantage and connected the router to the computer as he had been told.

Hope you're getting this, Watch, he thought.

He slipped his hand into his shirt pocket, pulling out a small earpiece. Patiently he waited for Watch's voice to ring through the tiny speaker, letting him know that she was in their system. He couldn't risk calling her to let her know that the router had been installed. The Federal Police were always listening in on communication devices. Without a secured connection, he would be telling them exactly where he was and what their plans were. Instead, he waited.

"We're good to go, Maps," Watch said, ending the low roar of the static.

"That's great. What do you see?" he asked.

"Surprisingly, not much. There's an amazing lack of cameras within the palace."

"I suppose Myers likes his privacy. Do you have any blueprints of the building or anything?"

"Those I have. Give me your location and I'll get you where you need to be. I do have Natalie and Michael on a camera feed. They're sitting with Myers in the banquet hall."

"Keep an eye on them and I'll start searching for the girl. Judging by the looks of this room, I shouldn't be too far away. Once I find her, I'll rendezvous with Natalie. How far do I need to go to get to the banquet hall? I'm on the second floor in a small bedroom. Six rooms north and four rooms east of the infirmary. There's a window in here so I know I'm in an outer room."

"Let's see…You're in Myers' living quarters, meaning you're about halfway across the palace from them. The banquet hall is at the entrance to the palace in the south wing. You're in the east wing, which is very isolated according to the plans. The only way out seems to be a connecting room at the center of the palace."

***

"How much have you been able to pull from the servers?" Vasher asked Watch.

"So far not much. At this point, getting in seemed to have been the easy part," she said. "There are so many layers of encryption, I feel like I'm trying to reconstruct the whole system one byte at a time. I've had to focus most of my attention on getting the blueprints to help guide Maps."

"Mind if I take a look?" Damien asked, rolling his wheelchair next to Watch's desk.

"Sure. Pull up a…" she paused, catching herself mid-sentence. "I'm sorry. I didn't mean anything by that. I can be so dumb sometimes."

"Don't worry about it," he said, smiling. "Hopefully this is only temporary, because I'm literally going to kick that little French guy's butt."

Watch giggled and handed him a keyboard. As he began typing, she felt a twinge of reluctance. She was Defiant's best hacker and had never needed help before. It didn't seem right. Myers' security was posing a bigger challenge than she was used to, though. Having the competition spurred her on.

She watched as his fingers flowed across the keys. It was as if they could think on their own. Never slowing down, never pausing. Just flowing like water from a stream cascading over a flat stone. She was amazed at his talents.

"How did you learn to do that?" she asked.

"My dad," he said, never looking away from the screen. "He was a software engineer with a couple of military contracts from the government. Before they killed him, he taught me everything he knew. From then on, I've spent a lot of time hacking the government looking for proof it was them and why. I had almost gotten close to an answer just before they caught me."

Watch's heart filled with empathy at Damien's sincerity. She could understand his determination. She continued to sit there, watching him.

"What's your story?" Damien asked, catching her off guard.

"Huh?"

"How'd you learn to do all of this?"

"I- I taught myself," she said abruptly. The words came out harsher than she intended, but hers was a story that was better left untold. She leaned back in her chair and folded her arms.

"I'm sorry, I didn't mean to offend you."

"It's okay. Since you're doing so well with that, I'm going to move over to another computer and start helping Maps."

20

M YERS SAT at the head of the long banquet table, casually resting on his elbow. On either side of him stood two Federal Policemen, acting as his personal bodyguards. Their hands were folded in front of them. Cold, lifeless eyes watched Michael and Natalie as if they were waiting for one of them to so much as breathe wrong to spring them into action. Myers paid them no attention. His careless, nonchalant attitude only infuriated Michael.

"Oh, Michael, I must say it is very good to see you again," Myers began. "I hate that it has to be under these conditions. I would have never guessed that you would show up at my home, however. Even if you were escorted by this...bulldog." He curled his lip into a disgusted snarl at the uncouth sight of Natalie.

"This is not a social visit," Michael snapped, slamming his fist onto the table. "You have something of mine, and I'm here to get it back."

"Settle down. Settle down," Myers said, dismissing Michael's outburst. "I have business to discuss."

It was as if Myers was looking through Michael. Looking past him. His eyes were on Natalie standing behind Michael's shoulder.

"What price are you expecting of me for bringing him here?" he asked.

"I've told you what I want," Natalie said. "I want you to put into the system an official pardon. I want all members of Defiant absolved from any wrongdoing in the eyes of the government and the Federal Police. And I want you to free my sister from Sybarite."

"That's a large price you've placed on one man's head."

"That one man is Michael Anderton, and I know how important he is to you. He's currently at the top of the Federal Police's most wanted list. A list that also comes with a rather large reward attached to the arrest of such people on it. I brought your number one to your doorstep. I'm not asking for money. All I want is freedom for Defiant and my sister."

Michael looked over his shoulder at Natalie. He was surprised by her resolve but admired her ability to stick to the story she began outside. At least Michael assumed it was a story. They had never discussed the details of what they were going to do once inside, other than completing their missions. Michael figured it was more of her improvising.

"Since you did bring him to my doorstep, as you so eloquently put it, what's stopping me from killing you and taking him?" Myers asked.

Natalie raised the detonator. Both guards immediately drew their weapons. Michael gritted his teeth and squeezed his eyes tight as he waited for things to escalate.

"If I die, he dies. You die," Natalie snarled. "Here's how this is going to work. You put in the order. I see it go through with my own eyes. Then I walk out of here. Once I feel like I'm safely out of your sight, you'll see the lights change on the bomb. That's your cue to know it's been disarmed."

"You drive a hard bargain. If you had only chosen a different side, I'm sure I could have found a nice place for you within my empire. Felix, take some rookies to Sybarite, find this sister, and escort her to the train station."

At Myers' order, one of the guards holstered his weapon and began walking toward the rear exit. He was grumbling under his breath. It was clear that he was not thrilled about being ordered to go to Sybarite.

Something wasn't right. Natalie was going way off script from the way they had discussed things going. Maybe Michael was being paranoid. Perhaps Natalie was skillfully clearing the room. That had to be it. He gave her the benefit of the doubt. He couldn't read her. Her face was stone. No expression. No gleam in her eyes. No deviousness. Nothing but intense focus on Myers. Whatever was on her mind she kept well hidden. The only thing that Michael could see was her drive. It was clear this mission meant more to her than she had led him and the rest of her team to believe. He wondered where her teammate, Maps, was and if he was truly coming for them.

***

"I'm at the end of a hallway, Watch," Maps said into his earpiece.

"Excellent. Have you ditched your Defiant look yet?" Watch asked.

"Left that gear in the closet of the little girl's room. I'm now fully camouflaged in the ridiculous uniform of the Federal Police." Maps stood in front of the mirror at the end of the short hallway, going over his appearance. "Do you ever feel like they try too hard to look like someone important, with their black tactical outfits and their body armor? I feel like I'm going to draw spontaneous gunfire any minute. But that's okay. I look like a burnt marshmallow."

Maps adjusted the uniform, preparing for his next part in the plan. Thankfully, Defiant had uniforms handy that they could use when needed. He had kept it hidden beneath the more rugged gear he had worn in.

Usually, it was only Vasher and Tobias that infiltrated the Federal Police since they were actual members. Without any intel on the interior of the fortress, this job required someone with a special skill set. Watch may have been able to access the blueprints thanks to the wormhole he installed, but that wasn't risk-free. If those prints were inaccurate or if they happened to lose connection, the job would require someone with a great sense of direction. Someone who could memorize paths and details about rooms along those paths.

Maps had always accredited his skills to his time spent in Clerica, managing shipments all across Metropolian. The truth was, it was a natural gift he was born with. His photographic memory allowed him to easily glance at a room and place it on a map he could create in his mind. He did tap his pocket to make sure he was at least carrying his fake ID card. That should get him by if not inspected too closely.

"Focus, Maps. Any sign of Michael's daughter?" Watch asked.

"So far, nothing. I was hopeful when I saw the little girl's room, but no luck. It was empty, and it didn't seem like anyone had been in there for a really long time."

"Keep your eyes open. It's going to be hard to get Michael out of there emptyhanded. Right now, it looks like they are still in the banquet hall. Myers is filling out some paperwork. As soon as he uploads it, I'll have Damien check out what that's about. For now, take the door to the right. That will take you deeper into Myers' living quarters. That would probably be the best place to start."

"Oh, sure. Let me go organize the man's sock drawer."

Maps eased the door open and peeked inside. Life-sized images danced across the wall of the television. Other than that, the room appeared empty. No one sleeping on the couch. No one hugging the burning fireplace. He walked casually to the door on the opposite side of the room. The lights were out, but he could clearly see it led to the kitchen. The darkness boosted his confidence that the next room was vacant.

With dauntless courage, he strode through the doorway only to be met almost immediately by a figure standing in front of him. The person was short, slim built, with long, curly hair. It was a woman. The sudden glimmer of light shifted his focus off the woman and onto the knife she had pressed within an inch of his face.

"Who are you, and what are you doing in my house?" the woman demanded.

"I...I'm...Officer Watson..." Maps stumbled, reaching for his ID. "You...Your husband asked me to..."

"My husband knows better than to allow an officer into my home. You have an entire fortress to run around in, playing cops and robbers or whatever it is you do. This is my home, and you are not allowed here, nor are you welcome."

Maps took a step back. He could feel the coolness of the steel radiating from the blade still pressed toward his face. Whoever this woman was, she had tenacity. She braved threatening a Federal Police officer just to protect the sanctity of the rooms she called her home. However, she had the advantage and was clearly far above any officer of the FPD.

As she followed him back into the den, the light illuminated her face. There was a fierceness in her eyes. The same fierceness as a bear protecting its cub from an intruder in its den. It was then he understood why.

"Mommy, who is that man?" a little girl cried, emerging from the shadows of the kitchen. Her hair was disheveled, and she was dressed in pink pajamas. Her matching pig slippers oinked with each step she made. It was evident she had been asleep.

"Drink your chocolate milk, dear, and go back to bed. Mommy's talking right now." The woman was careful to keep her body between Maps and the little girl, hiding the knife from her view.

The little girl pouted but then disappeared through another doorway in the kitchen. Maps hoped that the girl leaving would ease the woman's tension but to no avail. She didn't budge. She didn't even so much as blink. That made Maps even more nervous. With the woman so intent on hindering him from exploring any more of that part of the living quarters, he thought it best to abandon the mission and excuse himself from the room. Cowering, he eased his way back out through the doorway. He was relieved when that seemed to appease the woman and she let him go.

"Watch? You there?" Maps asked into the earpiece once he was back standing in the hall. The tension of the moment had caused his heart to race, leaving him short of breath. "What's Myers' marital status? I was just met at the door by a rather unpleasant female."

"Um…" The pattering of keys could be heard in the background. "Records show Myers as being currently divorced. He's gone through so many wives, it's hard to keep straight."

"You may want to update that, because this woman claimed to be his wife. Also, kids? Just to verify, he doesn't have any, right?"

"No. That's why I figure he's put in the adoption paperwork for Michael's daughter. Wait. Here's something."

Maps waited patiently, taking the moment to catch his breath. He could hear Watch through the earpiece typing vigorously. Whatever she had stumbled on must have confirmed Maps' fears.

"C'mon, Watch. The suspense is killing me. Is it…?"

"Myers does have a daughter. Everything on her is redacted, even in his own system. It's like they're trying to erase her."

"The woman was fiercely protecting a child. Is she Michael's or Myers'?"

"She has to be Michael's," Watch said. "I'm almost positive."

"Then we have a major problem."

21

"JUST THE TWO OF US at last," Myers said to Michael. A grin adorned his face, spreading across it full length. He seemed to be very gleeful about the situation. Michael sat stiffly in the hard, mahogany chair next to the large banquet table. His hands were laced, held beneath his nose by the armrests of the chair. His eyes fixed on Myers.

It had been some time since Natalie had left out with the other guard. Michael couldn't believe she had left him there. None of that trip had gone like he had pictured. The plan was to infiltrate the palace, save his daughter, and escape with the help of Maps. Not once did he see himself alone in a room with his mortal enemy.

Michael sat there and stared at Myers, with his beady eyes and large round cheeks. He reminded him of a balding chipmunk. All he could think about was the hundreds of different ways he could attack Myers in that banquet hall. He was unprotected. For the first time, Michael had an opportunity to go on the offensive and no one could stop him. As much as he wanted to, it was he who restricted himself. He had to buy enough time for Maps to rescue Allie and figure out an escape. He had to hope at least that was still going according to plan. He also didn't want to risk having a fallout with Myers that would end up detonating the bomb.

He looked down at the bomb vest still strapped to his chest. There was no weapon that he hated more than a bomb. He hated how imprecise they were. Bombs were unbridled weapons of destruction. Bearers of collateral damage. As a sniper, he liked weapons with pinpoint accuracy. When he was in the war, he could eliminate a single target in a group. How he wished his crosshairs were pointed at the glistening marble atop Myers' forehead. Michael had resigned himself to when that bomb was disarmed, nothing would stand in the way of him avenging his family.

A change in the lights caught Michael's attention, breaking into his thoughts. Natalie had disarmed the bomb as promised. Michael's focus returned to Myers. With the bomb disarmed, he was free to remove it. Free to carry out the fantasies that had been playing through his mind.

Something was wrong. Myers' eyes widened as he hurriedly tried to back up from the table, knocking the chair to the ground. He tripped over it and fell to the floor. It didn't slow him as he scampered to get away. Michael looked back down at the bomb vest. He saw the lights flashing. A whirring sound began to emanate from it. The timer strapped to his chest began counting down.

Michael's life flashed before his eyes. It was as if all time had begun to slow. His hatred of Myers no longer mattered. Myers was just a little man fearful for his life. He regretted not getting to Allie in time. He regretted never getting to tell Rebecca that he loved her one last time. When he looked down, he knew he had been betrayed. Natalie didn't have a grand plan to help him. She didn't have a plan to disarm the bomb. She left to detonate it.

In that moment, Natalie's whole plan had become crystal clear. She had played him. She was able to bring Michael and Myers into the same room with a bomb. She had gotten Defiant pardoned and free from the tyranny of the Federal Police. She had gotten her sister brought out of Sybarite. And she had gotten the two men she blamed for her misfortune to willfully be the instruments of their own demise. Michael couldn't believe he had been too stupid to have seen it earlier. Now it was too late. He closed his eyes to wait for what was certain to come.

Time passed on. The whirring stopped as soon as it began. He was still alive. The bomb had failed. Carefully, he began trying to remove it. He didn't want to press his luck that a sudden jar wouldn't still cause it to go off. Once he was free from the clutches of death, he set out for Myers. In his fear, Myers had managed to crawl out of the banquet hall. Michael was amazed by how fear could make even the stoic head of the Federal Police become a weaseling coward in an instant.

Michael peeked out the door. The hallway was clear. It seemed that everyone in the area fled for their lives with Myers. For now, his revenge would have to wait. This was his chance to reunite with his daughter. The guilt of not getting to her he had felt outweighed the anger and hatred he felt toward Myers. Michael reached into his pocket and pulled out an earpiece. He hesitated. With Natalie having tried to kill him, he could no longer trust Watch or Maps or anyone working with Defiant. He was on his own.

Michael shoved the earpiece back in his pocket. He studied the hallway for a moment. Everywhere looked the same. Maroon wallpaper and rich wooden trim lined every wall that he could see. Doors spread out along it. The fortress was a labyrinth. There was no possible way for Michael to know where to even begin looking. Rooms were connected by doors connected to more rooms. Behind each door stood the potential to find the Federal Police. Cameras monitored his every move. It couldn't dissuade his determination. He wasn't about to let anything stop him. He had come too far. He had already faced insurmountable odds since the day at the shack. Now, he knew that somewhere in the building was his daughter. His focus killed his fear.

I'll tear this place apart brick by brick until I find her, Michael told himself as he barged in through a doorway. Finding it to be an empty office room, he pressed on, trying other doors. Door after door, room after room, he continued his search. He ducked behind furniture or hid behind drapes whenever the Federal Police got too close. The cameras were a problem. They seemed to be everywhere. He did what he had to do to avoid them.

All in all, though, things seemed too quiet. Michael expected there to be more resistance inside the fortress. He resigned himself to believe that with the perimeter so secured, they were a little more relaxed on the inside. That was fine with him since it gave him more freedom to search the grounds.

The more he searched, the less he found. Michael grew agitated. His search was proving unproductive. He began searching through papers left in the offices for clues but to no avail. All he could find was fluff and propaganda. It praised the work the Federal Police and Myers had done not only for the city of Metropolian but the entire nation.

Even the library Michael had come across had adulatory books on the accomplishments of the Federal Police. At the end of the library, Michael found what looked to be the most promising. A large mahogany door recessed into the wall ever so slightly. Figured designs had been routed out from the rich grain of the wood. Emblazoned in golden letters across it, it read *Office of the Secretary of Security.* Michael had found Myers' office. If there was a clue to be found, that's where it would be.

Of all the doors he had come across, few had been locked except for that one. Michael wasted no time. He kicked the door as hard as he could next to the handle. Splinters filled the air as the frame around the door split.

No lavishness was spared in the design of the office behind the door. The room was the largest that Michael had seen in his search since he left the banquet hall. Thick heavy tapestry draped the large stained-glass window. It perfectly matched the lush emerald carpet spread along the floor. At the end sat a heavy wooden desk. Michael surmised it to be Myers' personal desk, and it, therefore, should have the most valuable information.

Michael closed the door behind him and began searching through the desk. Nothing. More bogus papers. No, wait. There was something on the back. Something familiar. Michael flipped over the paper, and in a child's handwriting, he saw the note.

Deer Daddy, this big scary man told me to rite to you. I miss you daddy. When are we going home? I don't like it here. Everybody's so mean. They won't let me go outside. I miss climbing grammy's trees. I found a rabbit a few days ago. He was nice. He let me pet him. I named him Mr. Fuzzyboots cause he had white feet. I've been sneeking some of my food to him. I'm sorry daddy. Don't be mad. I wanted to show him to you. I couldn't let Mr. Trent see him tho. He wanted to hurt him. Maybe you'll get to see him soon. I'm ready to go home. I love you daddy.

Tears streamed down Michael's face as he read the letter. Each word pulled at his heart. He couldn't believe he had left Allie alone for so long. She had been at the mercy of Myers and his goon squad masquerading as cops. He was going to find her. He was going to get her home. Although he could no longer trust Defiant, Watch had been honest. His daughter was here. The letter was proof.

At the corner of the desk, he saw a photo of Myers shaking hands with the potentate in front of the new capitol building in Imperia. It was the day Myers had been selected as secretary of security. The wide smile plastered across his face was nauseating. Michael flung the picture across the office, shattering the frame on the floor.

He was frustrated and heartbroken. He had searched every room that he could access and found nothing other than the note. It occurred to him that Myers had his fortress intentionally built in sections. Based on the amounts of propaganda, Michael figured he was in the common area where Myers met with other politicians and diplomats. There was one more door he couldn't get through. It was biometrically locked, and no amount of brute force could cause that door to budge. That's where he needed to be.

"Eh'hm"

The sound sent a cold shiver down Michael's spine. The familiar calm, aged voice, like the swinging of a wooden gate. Myers.

"Enjoying my desk, are we?" Myers asked in his typical nonchalant way.

"Where is she?" Michael exploded, holding up the note.

"Come now. Now that the ruckus has passed, let us resume our conversation," Myers said without a change in his voice. Myers was a man who could order a massacre, all the while swirling wine around in a glass. To him, everything was business. A means to further his own ends. That only infuriated Michael further. He wanted answers. He didn't have time to play games. He didn't have time to indulge in Myers' desire for control.

Michael sprang for Myers. Papers flew up from the desk as he ran over the top of it. Long before he could ever reach him, a guard emerged through the doorway and tackled him to the ground.

"Foolishness," Myers said. "We have work to do."

22

"WHAT'S GOING ON IN THERE?" Wesley demanded. "I thought we could trust you people. She tried to kill Michael!" He was furious as he watched the events unfold on Watch's monitor. Damien froze at Wesley's outburst. Watch began trying to search out more information as to what happened. Vasher stood with his arms folded, watching as everything had happened.

Without thinking, Wesley balled up his fist and struck Vasher beneath his eye. The blow caused him to stumble. He reached up to tend to the sting and then looked at his red-stained fingertips. Wesley had drawn blood.

"Natalie. She's gone...rogue," Vasher said. "I never expected this. I knew she had had a hard life growing up in Sybarite, but I never knew she still had family there."

"I never should have trusted you," Wesley sneered. "I should have been the one to go in there with him."

"You want to talk about trust? Who are you?" Vasher pointed a finger at Wesley's face. "I don't know you. Michael was an asset. You were just baggage. For all I know, you could be an FPD sleeper agent. And you want to talk about trust. For years Defiant has run in secret, standing against the Federal Police. Now we have three outsiders standing here in our midst. One is a brainiac, who's already taken over Watch's computer, and very well could be planting a virus in our system. Another one thinks he needs to be involved in every little aspect of our work because he's a 'friend of Michael's.' You expect me to buy that on trust, and yet I don't get the same courtesy?"

Wesley's face fell. He didn't want to admit that Vasher was right, but he had never tried to look at it from his point of view. He wasn't there to witness his escape from the Federal Police. He didn't hear the pain in Fred's cries over Maud. He didn't see the sadness on Damien's face as his friends were captured. He hadn't shared a house with Michael for the last six years. To Defiant or the Federal Police or whoever, all Michael was, was an asset for what was somewhere in his brain. To Wesley, he was a friend.

"And you were the one who almost got several of my men killed in your ill-conceived assault on Camp Delta," Vasher continued.

"What are you talking about? I was alone in the woods, attempting to draw their attention, so Michael could sneak in. They were on me in seconds."

"You were not alone in those woods. I ordered my men to stand watch over the compound should something go haywire in his extraction. Then some idiot started shooting. He put the whole place on high alert and forced my men to engage. When they had to retreat, it left me and Tobias without any backup. You're lucky we were able to get him out quietly."

"Guys I hate to interrupt, but we have more serious problems," Watch said with nervousness in her eyes. "Myers is taking Michael to the eastern wing where there's almost no camera access. Maps is there but he is having

225

his own issues. He may have found the girl, but it seems that's not all he found."

Wesley and Vasher put their differences aside and rushed over to see what Watch was looking at on her computer. Myers and Michael had disappeared from any available camera view, which concerned them. All the while, Maps and Watch were trying to piece together information on the mystery woman.

"I told you this was not a good idea," Vasher scoffed. "Have you been able to identify her yet?"

"Nothing yet," Damien replied. "There's no info on the servers and without any way to see in there, we don't know what she looks like. I can't even find an open webcam to try to hack."

"What about audio? Did we get anything from Maps' phone?"

"I don't know how much help it'll be. Without something to compare it to, it still doesn't help us."

Vasher urged Damien to humor him. He agreed and played the voice over the loudspeakers. Everyone within earshot listened in to see if they could recognize the voice. Only one did. Wesley. His eyes widened at the sound of familiarity. It was a voice he knew all too well.

"I have to get in there," Wesley shouted, already running to the door. "Tell your man to run as far and as fast as he can. Michael has no idea what he's about to walk into. The Federal Police expected this. They are in control right now."

"We've been over this," Vasher hissed. "There's absolutely no way we can get you inside. This is the first chance we've ever had to even get inside ourselves."

Wesley stopped midstride. Turning on his heels, he marched toward Vasher. The swagger in his step, the tightly clenched fist, Vasher could only gawk at him.

Wesley was not amused by his lack of cooperation. He had had enough.

"You are the freaking Federal Police," Wesley shouted, grabbing Vasher by the shirt collar and throwing him onto the desk. The room stopped. Everyone was silent with trepidation. No one knew whether to defend Vasher or stay out of the way of Wesley's wrath.

"Wesley, I…"

"I don't want to hear it. Michael told me all about your little scheme with Mr. Huckleberry over there. Moving prisoners in and out as you need it. Don't tell me you can't get me inside. Don't lie to me. Myers' fortress has been infiltrated by Defiant. I can almost guarantee they've called in every available unit by now to assist. All you'd have to do is show up. So don't stand there playing your man-in-charge trump card, lying to me, saying we can't get inside when the truth is you don't want to. What are you so afraid of?"

By the time Wesley had finished ranting, he had Vasher pinned to the desk beneath him. Wesley's snarling face was only a mere few inches away from his. Vasher wasn't having it. He was not going to be embarrassed in front of his constituents. He pushed back, shoving Wesley off him.

"I was Federal Police long before I was ever Defiant. I know how they work. I've seen the way things go down with them. Believe me, when I tell you something won't work, it won't work. Now, I've worked too hard getting us to where we are. I worked my way from the ground up to be able to do what I do. I'm not going to throw that away, just so you can go play hero."

Frustrated, Wesley left their hideout, slamming the door behind him. He refused to sit idly by while the Federal Police had their way with his best friend. The virus wasn't their ultimate weapon. It was their mind games. Michael wasn't prepared for the one they were about to play with him.

The single light cast an ominous glow inside the long dark tunnel. He didn't need Defiant. He had come this far on his own. He was going to help Michael regardless. He had to make amends for attacking him in his anger. Before Wesley even realized what he was doing, he was sprinting his way almost to the end of the tunnel.

"Slow down, will ya? My legs don't quite move that fast," Fred shouted from the darkness.

The thought of Fred coming along appealed to him so that he didn't have to go alone, but he couldn't slow down. He couldn't afford to miss the train back to Metropolian. Michael's life depended on it.

Wesley's patience or lack thereof made little difference. The train was nowhere in sight. Fred's heavy breathing was the only sound he could hear. Each gasp sounded as if he were absorbing all the air around him like a vacuum through a straw. With the strain in each breath, it was evident that he was not accustomed to such rigorous activity. The wait gave him some time to recover. It seemed as if the train was taking an eternity to reach them. In all honesty, Wesley didn't even know the train schedule. He just knew that was the only way in and out of the place. He was relying on luck to get him back.

"This is taking too long," Wesley exclaimed, throwing a rock at the tracks. "I'm walking it."

"First off, you're crazy," Fred exasperated between breaths. "I can't even catch my breath, and we're at the last stop. Do you know how far that is away from where you want to go? A really, really long way."

Wesley was unfazed. He hopped down onto the tracks and began walking down the tunnel. Fred sighed both in frustration and exhaustion. Salvation rang out through the tunnel. A smile of relief spread across Fred's face. The train was approaching. Wesley climbed back up on top of the platform. Fred snickered.

"So, what are we going to do when we get there? Go up and ring the bell?" Fred asked once they were seated on the train. Wesley looked at him with a faint grin on his face. He withdrew his hand from his pocket, revealing Vasher's Federal Police badge.

"I had a feeling he had it on him. I just had to get close enough to steal it."

"That would be a pretty good idea, but that photo on it is a few shades too vanilla if you know what I mean. Besides, didn't we do this already. I feel like we've done this already. This whole impersonating the Federal Police thing. I seem to remember it leading to swimming and, I don't know, getting shot," Fred said, rubbing his arm.

"You're not the only one they've shot, and let me tell you, what they can do is so much worse. Unless you've spent any time in the Void, you have no idea what they're capable of. Physical pain is one thing. You can block it out. Turn it off. Be numb. When they get in your head, there's nowhere to run. That's where they get you."

"And we want to do this because?"

"Because they're going to do so much worse to Michael. Imagine if Maud was standing there in front of you. Taunting you. You could see her just as clear as me and you. But she's not your Maud. Your Maud's been lost. She's on their side. They're forcing you to either resist them or save her, but to save her means you lose yourself. What do you do then?"

Fred gazed at Wesley as if he could see the pain and fear that he hid behind his eyes. Not another word was said. Wesley's eyes danced as he watched the rubble and devastation whip past the windows. Fallen buildings laced the skyline. The eerie abandonment, the shadows of former life flew by one after the other.

That was all that Wesley needed to see to still his resolve. He couldn't let Myers win. He couldn't let the Federal Police win. He couldn't let Hempton win. This was the world they had created. The death and destruction scattered about as reminders of their capabilities. He was going to stop them, no matter what it took.

23

"WATCH, TALK TO ME," Maps said into his earpiece. The last words he had heard from her was her telling him to abandon his mission and run. He didn't know what had happened, but whatever it was he knew it had to be big.

The static made him feel uneasy. It wasn't like Watch to forsake them on a mission. He had come to rely on her. She was his eyes and ears around every corner, watching his back. It had become quiet in the fortress. In most circumstances, that would have been comforting, but that only fed into his fear of the unknown. At least when the officers were shouting and running, he could have a general idea of where they were. He knew where to put them on his mental map. In the silence, he felt both alone and surrounded.

As he entered a large room, he found himself on a balcony. The balcony encircled the room, with large pillars every so often to support the high ceiling. Judging by the number of doors dotting the walls and the elaborate skylight above, he surmised he was in the center of the fortress. He assumed it was the connecting room Watch had told him about. That meant he was no longer in the living quarters of the palace.

The floor beneath him had guards posted at several of the doorways. Maps eased his way behind a pillar, watching them just out of sight. He assumed that wherever the guards were, was somewhere he needed to be. He had explored a large portion of the eastern wing, even as he crawled for his life in the air vent away from the officers chasing him. He had plotted out his extraction route as well as found the location of Michael's daughter. All he needed to do now was find Michael and get the girl away from the mysterious woman. He knew that Michael was in the banquet hall of the south wing. Finding the center of the building helped him to get a better reference point to further his search.

He watched the guards closely, trying to judge which door to take and the best route to sneak by them. As he watched, two guards burst through one of the side doors. They were dragging along a woman. Blood streaked the light-colored carpet behind them as they walked. Maps looked closer. It wasn't the woman he had seen earlier, but through the blood and sweat, he still recognized her.

Natalie.

Maps' heart raced. He watched as they dragged her through the room. He ran behind another pillar, trying to stay out of sight, watching to see where they took her. While the guards were distracted by them, he ran down the stairs. He hoped his disguise would get him through. As he approached the door, one of the guards stepped toward him, placing a hand on his chest.

"You can't go through here," the guard said.

"I- I have to," Maps said, trying to look past him.

"You can't go through here," the guard repeated, placing his other hand on his weapon. "Who are you? I haven't seen you in this sector before."

"Right, right. I'm sorry. Wrong floor." Maps pointed up at the balcony he had come from.

He hurried back up the stairs and entered through the same door they took Natalie through but on the floor above. It was his hope he could find another air vent to crawl into so that he could follow them. The room was nothing more than a long hallway that seemingly only led to a door at its end. Maps ran for it, hoping that by some small miracle, it would lead him downstairs undetected.

No such luck or luck of any kind for that matter. Maps searched the room, all five square feet of it. As he entered the doorway, his nose all but touched the wall in front of him. He spread out his arms, only to realize the walls weren't far beyond the door-facing.

This makes no sense, he thought to himself. *Why would anyone build such a long hallway, that only led to a room smaller than a closet?*

He ran his hands through his short brown hair, thinking. He knew he couldn't waste time pondering the use of such a room. Natalie was in danger, Michael was missing, and he had lost contact with Watch. The mission had failed. He had to get to Natalie. He couldn't let something happen to her and it all be in vain.

He sprinted back down the hallway to the central room. Once again hiding behind the pillars, he surveyed the room looking for another route. The guards were still in the same places they were, so there was no way for him to follow them directly. He had to find a way there from the second floor.

He barged through the door next to the one he had just left. The sight took him by surprise. The world on the other side of that door was completely different from the rest of the palace he had seen. Gone was the maroon wallpaper emblazoned with the golden floral print. Gone was the rich mahogany trim. Gone were the lavish drapes that adorned both windows and picture frames. Everything was white, brick, sterile. The room vividly reminded Maps of the nurses' station he had visited on multiple occasions as a child. He waited for Ms. Matilda to turn the corner at any moment asking him if he was ready for his shot.

As he walked through, he realized that it was more than the mere decor that reminded him of the nurses' station. Through tiny glass windows, he could see patients strapped to their beds. Many of them stared wide-eyed at the ceiling as if the act of blinking was more effort than they could put forth. On the far wall, he saw a sign that said, *Center for Wellness.*

The cure for wellness seems more likely. It's like they're treating wellness like a disease here, Maps thought. *What's with this place? This guy lives here, runs the Federal Police here, and what? Has his own hospital?*

The more things he discovered inside the palace, the more questions he had. Metropolian had hospitals in every one of its sectors. Why did Myers need one in his home? And what made these patients so special to be here? The screech of the intercom silenced his questions.

"Dr. LeFleur, we have a Code Gray. You're needed to the operating theater. However, patient is critical."

Code Gray? Maps thought. He tried to remember some of the codes he had heard during his visits to Ms. Matilda. *Code Blue, someone was dying. Code Red, there was a fire. Code Gray? Code Gray… someone was being… combative. Someone was being combative, and they were critical.* There was only one person he knew that could be critical and still put up a fight.

He scanned the wall for a directory and then ran for the operating theater. He was sure it had to be Natalie. From the amount of blood she was covered in, he wasn't surprised she was critical. He wished he knew what they had done to her. In that condition, he wasn't sure what he was going to do once he found her, but he knew he had to get there. He had to be there for her.

***

Myers' guards led Michael through his fortress. He couldn't stop staring at the back of Myers' head. He kept his fist clenched as he walked, although he knew he couldn't do anything about it. He had to keep waiting. They were at least moving. His hope was that Myers was taking him to his daughter. Myers turned back to face him and shook his head.

"Michael, you really must stop seeing us as the enemy," Myers said, placing his hand gently on Michael's shoulder. The touch repulsed him, but there was no use resisting. "These terrorists that live on the outskirts may think they have the best of intentions. They maybe even convinced you of such, but I can assure you that terrorists are all they are. They don't understand our order. Our ways. They only want to see anarchy reign supreme. You've seen that they've tried to kill us both. Is this who you really want to align yourself with?"

"I don't care about them. I don't care about you. I don't care about the feud between you. I'm here for one thing and one thing only. I'm here for my daughter," Michael said. "And while they may be terrorists like you say, they weren't the ones to kill my wife, kidnap my daughter, and burn my house to the ground. And for what? Because of some virus I barely remember even working on, who even knows how long ago? Because you want a better mind control serum? No. I will not be a part of it."

Myers crossed his brow puzzled. He nodded at the guard by the door who promptly left. Michael watched Myers intently. Of all the emotional responses for Myers to have, confusion was not the one he expected. Still, it didn't matter. He had spoken his peace, and he awaited the fallout from it. He was absolutely sure about two things—he would get Allie back and he wouldn't help them with their virus. Nothing could change his mind of that.

"There was a time I thought we were on the same side. We were working for the good of all mankind," Myers said. "It seems there's been some misinformation given. We didn't kill your family. We're keepers of the peace. Our mission is to ensure the peace and tranquility of not just the United State Federation, but the citizens within it. If it were not so, do you think we would have not eradicated this rebel organization? The war is over Michael. Come home. You've been stranded in the wilderness too long. The terrorists are by and large defeated. Peace reigns not only in Metropolian but in all the USF. We won."

The light touch of Myers' hand on Michael's shoulder became a tight grip, shaking him as if to wake him up from a dream. Michael was unmoved. For eight years, he lived in fear of the Federal Police. For eight years, he dedicated his life to helping those that wanted an escape from their iron grasp. He remembered Myers' face emerging from the shadows of that dark room they had held him in. He couldn't believe him.

A voice invaded his anger, collapsing it into itself. A voice so familiar, so gentle, as if a breeze were blowing through subtle chimes calling him home. Allie.

"Daddy? Is that you?" she cried from behind him.

Michael turned around to see her. It had felt like it had been a lifetime since he had last heard her voice. So much pain, so much anger, so much wanting, all faded away. It was all worth it to lead him to this moment. As soon as he turned, everything came to a screeching halt. His thoughts, his body, his heart, all were frozen in time. He had seen a ghost. A spirit of the past stood before him to haunt him. His still heart broke into a thousand pieces. A sight so angelic it sent a cold shiver down his spine.

"You see, Michael, we haven't killed anyone," Myers said.

"Rebecca? Is it really you?" Michael was in disbelief. It had to be a trick.

"I was beginning to wonder when you were coming home. Allie and I have been worried sick about you," Rebecca said.

"Coming...home?" he asked, shifting his weight backward.

"I apologize, Rebecca," Myers said. "We've had Michael under a lot of stress lately. We'll have him back to his old self soon. Why don't you two head back to your chambers? I'll bring him by in a little while."

Rebecca smiled at him, while Allie ran up to Michael and wrapped her arms around his waist. His eyes welled with tears. Streams began to roll down his face, dripping off his chin and onto Allie's forehead.

"What's wrong, Daddy?" Allie asked.

"Nothing, sweetie," Michael said, trembling. "I've just missed you so much. And I'm so glad to see you again."

"Are you coming back with us?"

"Not just yet," he sighed. There was nothing in the world he wanted more than to take their hands and get as far away from the fortress as he could. Seeing her face, though, he realized how foolish he had been. No matter what he did, he couldn't risk putting them in danger.

He had never felt pain like he had the day he thought Rebecca had died. He couldn't bear to relive that moment again, with either of them. He would have to play along with Myers. Michael stood statuesque as he watched Rebecca and Allie walk away under their own free will. They weren't being forced or led away by guards. They simply said their goodbyes and walked away as if all this was somehow normal. Their actions pulled at his curiosity. There was something he was missing. He was sure of it.

"Now Michael, that should be evidence enough that I'm a man of my word," Myers said. "Come, we have some things we need to discuss."

24

T HE TRAIN HURRIED down the tracks. The scenery outside its windows had changed. The devastation had disappeared. Here, everything was in order. Wesley knew they were getting close to Metropolian.

"So, what was it that got you so rattled back there?" Fred asked, ending the tense silence between them.

"The voice," Wesley said. "It was Rebecca's. Michael's wife."

Fred furled his brow. His eyes darted back and forth, and so did his finger. It wiggled, miming the motion of his eyes as if solving an invisible puzzle in the air.

"You mean to tell me that he's been running around everywhere looking for his daughter, and this whole time she's been with his supposedly dead wife?" Fred asked.

"That pretty much sums it up," Wesley said. "And that means there's a whole lot more going on than we realized. Michael would have died to save his daughter. If they have Rebecca too, there's no way to know what he'll do for them. Last time he thought he lost her, he literally went to war."

Fred smiled, then chuckled, and then all out laughed.

"What in all of this could be so funny?" Wesley asked.

Fred continued to laugh hysterically. It was as if Wesley's concerns for Michael had been some kind of twisted joke to him.

"Do you not see it?" Fred asked, wiping the tears from his eyes when he finally stopped laughing.

"Do I not see what?"

"Michael's been so focused on his kid. You've been so focused on protecting him. Defiant's been so focused on doing whatever it is that scary rebellious organizations do. No one's ever took the time to step back and say 'huh.' Lee Harvey Oswald, John Wilkes Booth, that strange guy that was on TV with the mask, do you know what all these guys had in common? They're all patsies. They're all guys setup or paid off by the government. You realize we are two guys on a train to go break into the home of the secretary of security. That's right up there with the secretary of defense, secretary of state, you know, the really big wigs of the United State Federation. Not only that, but this guy also just so happens to be the guy in charge of, I don't know, the entire national police force."

"What's your point?"

"Well, let's put that into perspective. You have Metropolian, which might as well be modern-day Rome. You have Agridemesne. You have Burghalan. You have Canton. And that's just your major players, not including all the countless independent towns and cities scattered about. The point is you have a country of two hundred plus million people. We right now... We are me and you. We are going against that. How we've made it this far... If it wasn't illegal to say it, I'd call it divine intervention. Or else we're the patsies. Have you ever thought maybe we're just all getting played by the big wigs with power?"

Wesley thought for a moment. Maybe he had been too focused. It all happened so fast, and everything had been such a whirlwind. He had to stay focused, or it would have been too much. The loss of Joanna would have gotten to him. In his mind, he could see her smile, hear her laugh, and see her eyes light up. Then they faded. Those beautiful brown eyes faded into the lifeless ones looking at the sky. He saw Hempton's snickering grin. Smoke rising from the barrel of the gun clenched in his hand. This wasn't governments, or patsies, or hidden agendas. This was about revenge. Unlike Michael, Wesley knew his wife was dead. He held her cold body in his arms. Watched as his tears mixed with the blood and soot on her face. He was going to avenge her, no matter how insurmountable the odds.

"Even if we are getting played, what would you have me do? Sit by and watch them destroy my best friend's life, just like they have destroyed mine?"

"Listen, Wesley. I'm sorry. I'm just telling you like it is. These guys are scary, and they're powerful. Worst of all, they know it. I just want you to be ready to realize that this probably won't work. I mean, let's face it. These guys have been ruling the country with an iron fist for eight years. What chance do we really have?"

Wesley mulled over Fred's words. He knew the odds of failure were high. Those odds seemed to go from giants to mountains the closer they got to the station. As the train made its descent into the underground tunnel, Wesley glimpsed several black helicopters encircling the train station. Torroes were gathered at the front door. The Federal Police were waiting.

"We have to get off this train," Wesley said, sizing up the window.

"The train's still moving. Why are we getting off?"

"I think you may have called it on this one. Feds are at the station."

"How is that even possible? You just kind of took charge and got on the train. How did they know we were coming?"

Fred climbed up on the seat at the end of the train car and inspected the clearly disabled security camera. He twirled the frayed cables between his fingers, and then pressed his eye into the socket above the dangling lens.

"I'm pretty sure Defiant has disabled all the surveillance on the train," Wesley said, amused by Fred's study of the camera. "If not, their hideout would have been found out a long time ago. No. Something else is going on. I can almost guarantee they're gathering to go help defend Myers. I told Vasher they would send in every available unit after Defiant made a show there. Whatever it is they're about to do, I don't care to be here to find out what it is."

Wesley pried open the train door and leaned out to look at the ledge below. It was only a few feet wide. Just wide enough for one person to walk alongside the tracks.

"Get ready. This may hurt a little. We've got to jump," Wesley said.

"How do we do that without splattering ourselves against the wall?"

"Like this."

Without hesitation, Wesley jumped through the door as the train was slowing down. He rolled across the concrete. Fred leaned out the doorway to watch. He closed his eyes and gripped his bottom lip between his teeth. He jumped through the door but didn't tuck his arms and legs in to prepare to roll. Instead, he plopped down onto the concrete tiles, and the sheer momentum caused him to flail about. Wesley walked toward him as he was attempting to stand up. He had managed, but his head was still at his feet with his midsection in the air.

"I think my rib's broken," Fred said, attempting to straighten out. "Yep, it's broken."

He slouched back to his knees, hugging himself tightly. Wesley felt guilty for Fred's injury, but at the same time, was also thankful that they had managed to stay a step ahead of the Federal Police. He would have been in much worse condition if they would have caught them on the train. He reached down and gently lifted Fred by his shoulder.

"We have to get somewhere safe," Wesley said.

"I can't breathe," Fred wheezed, clutching his side with one hand, while his other hand kept him propped up on his knee. Then, his face turned deathly white. Wesley didn't think Fred had hurt himself that badly. It was possible, though, that he was hemorrhaging internally. It seemed that no matter how hard he tried to protect those around him, everyone kept getting hurt.

Fred slapped him on the arm without moving from his bent position. He was pointing at the train. Then Wesley saw it. What made him so pale wasn't from his injury, but from what he saw on the train. Standing in the last car, next to the rear window, was the black tactical uniform.

***

Vasher had resumed his pacing behind Watch. So much so, it was making her even more nervous. She was doing everything she could to figure out why she had lost communications.

"I still haven't been able to reestablish comms with Maps yet," Watch told Vasher. "I'm not sure what happened. There was some kind of interference and then static."

She was frustrated with herself. This was probably the most important mission they had embarked on, and she felt like she was failing. She felt as if the weight of the entire mission was resting on her shoulders, and the pressure was getting to her. The levels of encryption she had encountered on the files had surpassed her skills. She could only pull up spotty surveillance, and now she had lost communications. Though she would never admit it, she was the best at what she did, but at the moment, all her skills were coming up short. She felt like an amateur first learning how to code.

She looked over her monitor at Damien. He would struggle but was able to break through the encryption. Whether it was admiration or jealousy, she didn't know, but she continued to watch him work. She watched him pull the little yellow pencil off the top of his ear to do a quick calculation and put it haphazardly back, oblivious to anything else going on around him. He was in the zone. She imagined that's how she often looked leaned forward into her computer with her feet crossed beneath her.

Maybe it was a touch of admiration. She had been surrounded so long by guys with guns, and plans, and tactics, and here was Damien, content and happy. Despite being this tall, handsome guy, he wasn't a thrill seeker. He was a geek.

Damien looked up from his work. His eyes met her gaze, and he smiled. Watch flicked her eyes back to her screen, but the red in her cheeks were a dead giveaway, she just knew it. She could feel the heat radiating in her face. What had gotten into her? How could she allow herself to even begin to entertain such thoughts? It was him.

He was the reason she couldn't concentrate. He was the reason she was failing at her job.

The more she thought about it, the more frustrated she became. Soon she was pounding her keys so hard, each line sounded like a barrage of firecrackers.

"Everything okay over here?" Damien asked, rolling up beside her.

"I'm fine. I don't need any help," she scoffed, making no attempt to hide her frustration. She was upset at how good he was. She was upset at herself for ogling over him for it. She was upset that the mission was failing and there was nothing she could do to help. Like the rolling of thunder, she typed out the most incoherent line of text as fast as she could, before throwing her keyboard to the floor.

"I'm sorry. I didn't mean to upset you...again."

"What? No. It's just-" Watch rested her head on her hands, before drooping it down and pushing her glasses back to meet her ponytail. "How are you so good?"

"Excuse me?"

"For the last four years I've been with Defiant, I've hacked every server, cell phone...egg timer used by the Federal Police, but I cannot get through Myers' encryption. You, you're just typing away like you're writing out last night's essay assignment."

"Well, to be honest, I have an advantage. Remember when I said my dad taught me all about computers and coding? It's his code I'm hacking. In one of those government contracts, he was tasked with writing the security software for the fortress."

Watch was relieved that it wasn't her skills that were failing her. That helped her to regain some of the confidence in herself. Hearing that his dad taught him how to code or that he taught him anything, however, made her jealous for a completely different reason. She didn't let it affect her though. She repositioned her glasses on her face and crossed her legs in her chair.

"Let's do this," she smiled. "I could use some help."

"Alright, what do you need?"

"First off, I need to reestablish comms with Maps, then I need more surveillance access. I know Myers has to have more cameras inside than the few I've found. It would be a lot easier to find Maps, Michael, and his daughter if I had eyes inside. After that, we need to download any internal records on the Federal Police. What their plans are, where their strongholds are, anything that may give us an advantage."

Damien nodded and set up his computer next to hers.

"Let's do this together," he said.

The two worked in tandem, so much so, that their typing seemed to synchronize. Whenever one would hit a roadblock, the other would offer a solution. Such ability was new to Watch. She had grown so used to doing everything herself, it seemed strange to be able to ask for assistance. Damien kept her pride in check, keeping her going when her frustrations would boil over. Before long, the fortress' entire system was laid bare to them.

Financial records, personnel files, and the inner workings of the Federal Police were finally accessible. Myers kept detailed reports on everything. It was no wonder why they kept it hidden from the outside world. Watch felt like they may finally have an advantage over the Federal Police.

As she dug deeper, some things seemed out of place. Myers kept a dossier on every officer listed as a palace guard. She assumed that he wanted to be sure he was surrounding himself with the best people. She kept digging through files until she found one that caused her to stop typing altogether. Damien questioned her reasons for the abrupt hesitation.

"Go grab a hard drive from out of that cabinet over there," Watch said, pointing to a row of filing cabinets on the far wall.

As Damien rolled his way over to the cabinets, Watch quickly slipped a memory stick into her computer. Never taking her eyes off Damien, she downloaded the file to the memory stick, before deleting it from the server entirely. No one in Defiant needed to read that file, and she was going to make sure no one did.

25

MICHAEL WALKED STEP FOR STEP with Myers. His head was swimming. He was still in shock over seeing Rebecca. He couldn't think straight. He had been on a roller coaster ride of emotions, from pain to loss to anger to hate. He didn't know how to add joy to it. But even so, Rebecca was alive, and Allie was safe. His worst fears had been only that. He was glad that they hadn't put her through the same things as the little girl he had met. He couldn't say the same for Rebecca. Something with her was off. She was so calm and collected and even called the fortress home. That was what bothered him the most. They had never lived there. Michael was sure of that. He could only assume they had injected her with the virus and messed with her mind. He had to find a way to get away from Myers and back to his family.

"What did you do to Rebecca?" Michael asked, stopping Myers in his tracks. Michael stood glaring at the back of his head, waiting for a reply. He needed to know what they did, so he would know how to fix it. "You injected her with your memory virus, didn't you?"

Michael grabbed Myers by the shoulder, turning him around until they were face to face. Myers looked up at Michael with a solemn face.

"I see that the rebel group has been filling your head with nonsense," Myers said. "Very convincing, aren't they?"

"I know the virus exists. I know me and Cade had a hand in making it, and that's why you want me here so badly. You want me to help you make it better, so you can kill me, my family, and all of Defiant just like you did to the Red Riders." Michael pulled Myers closer with every word until he was towering over him. His hands gripped the purple robe so tight as to leave permanent creases in the fabric. Myers was unflinching. He remained stoic, but Michael saw a little twinge at the mention of the Red Riders. "I know it was you who ordered the strike, killing millions of our own citizens."

"Oh, my. No." Myers shook his head, brushing Michael's hand from his collar. "See what I mean about nonsense? The rebels are trying to force you to see me as the enemy."

"They didn't have to. You kidnapped my family."

"A necessary action, in exchange for your cooperation. Besides, this is much more accommodating than that scrap heap we saved them from." Myers lifted his hands as a grand gesture of his palace. "I am not a murderer, Michael. My job as secretary of security is to keep the people safe from whatever may come against them. Sometimes that requires me to make difficult decisions, but I always do it with the best intentions. I do it for the good of the people. As far as the Red Riders, you have no idea what they had done, and yet I ordered the Federal Police to detain them, to arrest them, to hold them until they came to their senses. Come with me and let me show you my generosity."

Myers led him through the wing, back to the large central room. Michael looked up at the stars shining through the skylight. They walked up the stairs to the balcony that encircled the room, to a door that led to a long and narrow hallway. The hallway led to only a single door. The room on the other side of the door was small. Smaller than even a closet. Myers squeezed his way in and urged Michael to do the same. Michael stood in the tiny space, rubbing elbows with the man he hated more than any man that had ever lived. He couldn't believe he had ever let himself get here.

"Shut the door please," Myers commanded. "Be careful who you trust, Michael. For wolves lie in sheep's clothing, and lions are but little lambs."

Michael turned back and swung the door shut. As soon as it clicked, the room filled with a loud hum. The walls began to expand on both sides. Michael felt his body moving as if he was in an elevator but traveling forward. The wall in front of him split like a curtain, revealing a medical center below.

"I'm sure you recognize her."

***

Maps barged in the door to the operation theater. Nurses scurried about within. No one seemed to notice him. No one, except Natalie. Her gaze fixed sharply on his. She was standing on top of the operating table, wielding a scalpel. She was kicking and slicing at anyone who got near her. Blood poured profusely from her side as if it had been laid open by a large blade. With such a wound, Maps knew why they considered her critical. He wasn't sure how she was even able to stand and defend herself. He ran to her to help her in any way he could.

One step. Two steps. Three. Maps was stopped hard. A metal pan clipped him above his left eye, the corner catching him in the temple. He stumbled looking for the thrower. To his surprise, all the nurses were hunkered down. There was no one there but Natalie.

"Natalie, it's me. I'm here to save you," Maps said.

"Get away from me," she screamed, hurling more things at him. Maps took cover behind a supply cabinet. Fear and adrenaline had to have gotten to Natalie. She was too riled. It was as if an animal instinct had taken over. There was no way for Maps to get to her without agitating her further. With her wound, he knew she wouldn't be able to hold out much longer. He would wait her out. The nurses were too terrified. He could grab her and have them out before they realized what happened.

Above the screaming, another sound filled the room. A loud hum, followed by the creaking of metal. Maps peeked over the supply cabinet and saw an observation room emerging from the wall. Two men were occupying it.

Great, Maps thought. *Could today get any better? Natalie's gone crazy, and I'm stuck behind a cabinet with Secretary Myers watching everything. Well, at least I found Michael.*

Maps raised up to look over the cabinet once more. He could see that Natalie was fading fast. The hand with the scalpel hung loosely at her side while she examined the blood that covered the fingers of her other hand. A look of dazed bewilderment had replaced the fierce anger she had worn only moments ago. She slouched down to a knee, nearly falling off the operating table.

"Oh, *ma chère*, what have you done to yourself?" asked a man in a white coat as he walked through the door. A thick French accent was heavy upon his tongue, and a thin mustache adorned his upper lip. "Come now. Come now. Let's get this off our patient so we can see what we are working with."

The man motioned to the nurses to remove Natalie's gear. Slowly they began to emerge from their hiding places, afraid of another outburst. They stripped her down to only her tattered tank top. The light gray of it stained a dark burgundy on her side. Maps winced at the sight.

"Do we know the cause of such a profound laceration?" the man asked his nurses, pointing to the gash in Natalie's side.

"Yes sir, Dr. LeFleur. She attempted to scale the fencing when the Federal Police tried to detain her. She slipped onto the spired top, piercing the lower abdomen, and slicing upward as she fell." The nurse demonstrated the incident with her hands following the wound.

The doctor called for x-rays and other tests to be run to check for internal damage as other nurses began attaching hoses and monitors to Natalie. Maps watched from behind the cabinet, hoping that they would be able to save her. Seeing her in such shape tore at him.

She had been his partner for as long as he had been with Defiant. She was the reason they had ever found him. One night he had been working late, orchestrating deliveries to Sybarite, when a certain order caught his attention. It had originated from a bogus address in Clerica. The fake address peaked his curiosity. He had to know what it was. At such a late hour of night, the building was vacant, so Maps took it upon himself to investigate.

He went downstairs to the loading dock and began shuffling through the packages until he found it. Slowly, he cut open the tape to reveal the contents. Inside was a small locket with pictures of a man, woman, and two girls.

Beneath the locket was a note that read, *your guardian angel.*

The next morning, Maps went to his superiors and asked to be part of the day's delivery team, making up an excuse about correcting an error he made. He had to know more about the package. He had never been on a delivery run before and was completely unaware of the way of life in Sybarite.

Terrified was an understatement as to how he felt when their van crossed through the gate. Trembling, he took the package up to the apartment it was addressed to. He recognized the woman that answered the door as one of the girls in the locket, however significantly older. Her hair was matted, and her eyes were sunken in. One was completely blackened. Bruises covered both of her arms.

Maps felt sorry for the woman, and remembering the note made him sad. This woman looked as if she needed a guardian angel. When she pulled out the locket and the note, her face lit up. It was as if for the first time, she was able to smile. Maps didn't know then, but Natalie was just outside the window, watching as well. She had been the one to send the locket to her sister as a promise that she was coming to save her. She had told Maps how badly she wanted to give it to her herself, but because of Natalie's connection to Defiant, she didn't want to risk putting her in danger.

Maps' life had grown mundane, sitting behind his desk day in and day out. Seeing Natalie's sister light up in such darkness she was living in brought hope to him.

As they approached the gate back to Clerica, the Federal Police stopped them and injected them with liquid fire. The other delivery men drooped down in their seats asleep, but Maps panicked. He opened the door and ran from the van. His head was throbbing, and he could feel the heat radiating from his veins. He didn't know what the Federal Police had done to him, but he was afraid. Soon they were giving chase to him. Maps surrendered, curling up into a ball on the ground. That was when Natalie swooped in and saved him. She was the reason he discovered that he was a Resilient, and she led him to Defiant. They had been inseparable since.

As Maps saw her lying helpless on the operating table, he wanted to swoop in and save her just like she had done for him. He couldn't let anything happen to her. In all the time of being partners, he had been too scared to tell her how he felt about her. She was so strong and fearless. He never saw himself as her type, but he should have told her. He cursed himself for not saying those words to her. There was nothing he could do for her now. She was in the hands of Dr. LeFleur.

***

Michael looked down and saw Natalie standing on top of the operating table, fighting off the nurses. She was, without a doubt, defiant to the end. He watched as her wounds began to overtake her, pulling the strength from her hands. He wasn't sure how to feel. Wesley had told him that she had saved his life, but then she had also turned on Michael and tried to end his.

"You see. This is the way of the rebels," Myers began. "They're like savages. They can't see that they're fighting against the very ones trying to save their lives."

Myers had surprised Michael by showing that to him. In his mind, he had painted the Federal Police as instruments of death. He saw them as being ready to pull the trigger on anyone or anything that stood in their way without question. But here was Natalie surrounded by doctors and nurses trying to save her life, after she had attempted to kill both himself and Myers. This wasn't the actions of the monster he had pictured Myers to be. He was showing compassion to his enemy. He watched Myers from the corner of his eye. For a few brief fleeting moments, he could see him let his guard down. The stoic, straight-laced Myers showed genuine concern as he watched the doctors try to save Natalie's life. Maybe he did have it wrong.

Michael couldn't believe he was entertaining such thoughts after all that he had been through. His hate for the man had raged so fiercely. Seeing Myers show compassion reminded him that he was human. Michael needed to know his reasons. He took a deep breath as his hate began to dissipate. Maybe it was time he finally got some answers. He was safe. His family was safe. That was what mattered to him. Defiant was just a means to get them back. He was tired of running. Tired of hiding. If he was that important to everyone that he came across, he wanted to know why.

"Okay, Myers," Michael began, hanging his head. "You win. What do you want from me?"

Myers turned and looked at him with a smile so wide it was borderline cartoonish. His round cheeks, swelled underneath his eyes, only added to the ridiculousness of it. He tapped Michael hard on the shoulder as a congratulatory gesture, before pressing a button to retract the observation room.

"I'm so glad you have finally come around. Come. We don't have much time. Let me show you your new laboratory."

Michael had been led around so much of the fortress, he had grown accustomed to following Myers on his grand tour. He had also grown accustomed to the same decor until he walked into the Center for Wellness. They passed by corridor after corridor of patients, some appearing far better off than others. The blank stares and nearly lifeless eyes of some made Michael feel eerie. One room stood out against the rest of them. This particular patient's window was covered, so he couldn't see in. The doorway, however, was lined with daisies and little pink unicorns.

Myers never missed a beat. He marched on until he reached a large door that was biometrically sealed. He strummed a few buttons on the control panel and placed his hand on the screen.

"Give me your hand, Michael," Myers said, placing Michael's hand on the scanner. "Here it is. You're new home-away-from-home. Everything you need is in this room, but if you need more, don't hesitate to let me know. You have unlimited resources. Your assignment is that important."

Michael surveyed the room. Every wall was a calculation board. Two long workstations lined the center. One station had computers, while the other had microscopes and lab supplies. It reminded him a lot of the lab he and Cade had worked in, only this one was much bigger with much better equipment. Although they had gotten funding from a drug corporation, they had still been working out of the university's lab.

"Why is it so important that you've gone through all of this so that I can make your virus better? I mean, don't you have enough control over the people? How is this going to help you gain more?" Michael asked.

"Michael, you have it all wrong," Myers said. "I don't want to make it better. I want you to help me stop it."

26

"STAY BEHIND ME," Wesley said, stepping between Fred and the train. He stretched his arm out as if to shield the still slumped over Fred. His eyes were focused on the officer in the last car of the train.

"Where else am I going to go? We're in a tunnel, on this little tiny ledge, and you see this?" Fred asked, pointing to his side. "This hurts."

Glass sprayed down onto the tracks as the officer shattered the rear window of the train car. He climbed through the opening and down onto the hitch near the tracks. He turned toward the car, before jumping down onto the tracks, running with it to slow his momentum. Wesley tensed, waiting to have to confront the officer. The officer faced him and began walking along the tracks toward him. Wesley clenched his fist. If it was a fight the officer wanted, he was going to give it to him. The officer walked steadily closer. Wesley readied himself to take the offensive.

"Wesley, wait. Look," Fred said, pulling at him. He began motioning at the wall. "Look. Door. Service exit."

With the amount of Federal Police gathered at the train station, Wesley agreed. Retreat was probably the best option. He helped Fred through the door. As he closed it behind him, he saw that the officer had begun sprinting toward them. Wesley slammed the door shut and kicked the handle, breaking it off onto the floor. Behind them, he could hear the shouts and pounding as the officer was trying to beat down the door. They had bought a few minutes, but with Fred wincing with every step, they weren't very fast.

Wesley looked up at the pipes running along the walls. He knew that the underground lines formed a catacomb. It would be easy to lose the Federal Police if they ventured farther inward. If they weren't careful though, they could also lose themselves. Nevertheless, they had to keep moving. He propped Fred up on his shoulder, being careful not to put pressure on his side. Fred's height made it difficult. With him being taller than Wesley, he couldn't get much lift. Fred grumbled, but he could walk.

The pounding at the door had silenced. Wesley had learned to fear the silence. He knew the tenacity of the Federal Police. They hadn't given up. They were looking for another way. He half expected a torro to crash through the wall at any moment. They couldn't wait around for that to happen.

Wesley tried to help Fred pick up the pace. They walked left, right, and through the crisscross maze of the catacombs. He tried to put as much distance between them and the Federal Police as possible. He had found a pipe and was following it. It was the only way he could think of to keep from getting lost. The sound of running water began to echo against the cinderblock walls. Up ahead led to a spillway for sewage overflow. The smell of it was nauseating to Wesley.

The spillway was a deep ravine filled with thick, black bile. A large grated pipe jutted from the wall opposite of the door, steadily pouring more into that chasm. Inside the door was a ladder, which appeared to lead to the surface.

"Think you can make it up?" Wesley asked.

Fred shrugged but conceded to give it a try. He walked gingerly through the doorway, out onto the metal balcony. He kept his nose buried in his shirt, as the smell was much worse directly above the spillway. Slowly, he hugged the wall, keeping his back to the railing. He stretched his hand out wide until his fingertips could touch the ladder. With a sigh of relief, he inched his way over to it. He lifted one leg on the first rung. So far so good. Now was the moment of truth. If he could lift his other leg without aggravating his side, they may have found a way out.

Fred lifted his leg, squawking loudly. The sound echoed seemingly throughout the tunnel system.

This isn't going to work, Wesley thought, but to his amazement, Fred was already up onto the third rung. He was giving it all he had.

"You're doing good, Fred."

Fred turned his head to look at Wesley and gave him a brief smile, followed by the same look of sheer terror Wesley had seen at the train. Wesley spun around on his heels, his fists raised in the air. He was preparing himself to fight the Federal Police, but they weren't there. Only shadows.

"What was it?" Wesley asked, turning back to Fred. He hadn't moved. He had both arms clutched against the rungs of the ladder like a vice. He was sweating bullets, and his face was pale.

"I- I don't like…heights."

"You're only on the third step."

259

Fred looked down at the balcony and then over into the ravine. He tried to readjust his grip on the ladder when the pain in his side caused his foot to slip. He fell back from the ladder onto the railing. Tears welled in his eyes as he curled up on the balcony.

"Alright, we'll find another way," Wesley said, looking back down the tunnel.

"No," Fred managed, urging him to go on ahead. "At least go check it out and see where we are. I'll be fine here."

"I'm not leaving you behind."

"I'll be okay. Just try to make it back before the Federal Police, will ya."

Wesley hated leaving him there defenseless, but this was also a chance for him to scout out the area faster than before. His hope was that he could find a direct route out so that he could get them both to safety. He also wasn't sure how much more he could stand of the smell. He climbed to the top of the ladder. Unlike Fred, he didn't have a fear of heights, but looking down from the top into the ravine did give him a sense of urgency.

Fred would have probably fainted if he would have looked down from here, he thought as he glanced down at Fred. He stayed curled up on the balcony, but Wesley could see that he was watching him. He went to turn the handle on the hatch, but it was stiff and heavy. It was evident that it hadn't been used for quite a while, and rust had gotten to it. Wesley tried again, but it wouldn't budge.

"I can't open it," he said.

"Put your back into it," Fred called back.

That was much easier said than done. Fred had had a panic attack at the bottom. He was much braver from a safe distance. Wesley looped his legs through the rungs of the ladder to give himself more leverage. Using his legs pressed firmly against the backside of the ladder, he twisted the handle with all his might. The sudden break of the seal caused him to be overbalanced. He fell backward, catching himself with his legs.

"Careful," Fred yelled as Wesley hung upside down from the ladder. Wesley pursed his lips and swung his body back upright. To his dismay, the hatch didn't lead to the surface, but it wasn't the sewer either.

"I'll be right back."

***

Fred watched as Wesley disappeared into the hatch. He hated that he couldn't go with him. His fear of heights had been with him since he was a boy. He didn't know why, but looking over into the ravine, it felt as if it were pulling him in. He could feel himself falling to the bottom with a mere glance. Still, even now, he was peering at the bottom, through the grated floor of the balcony, as if it were calling to him.

He closed his eyes and crawled his way back to the solid concrete floor where his imagination couldn't run wild. All he could think about on the balcony was it giving way, sending him tumbling down into the abyss. It was then that he remembered the origin of his fears.

When he was a boy, his family were cattle ranchers. His dad had let him help to give birth to a newborn calf. From that day, he had felt a connection with the calf. When it was only a few months old, it had managed to wander away from its mother and slipped through the fencing. Fred found it grazing on a steep cliff on the riverbank. The water had carved its way beneath the soil and thrashed mightily beneath the cliff.

Fred walked carefully through the thistles along its edge. The steepness made him afraid, but with the briars, there was little room to maneuver. He reached and placed his hand gently on the calf's back when without warning, the earth gave way beneath their feet. Boy and bovine plummeted to the raging waters below. If it weren't for his father, Fred was sure he would have drowned in its clutches. Unfortunately, his calf did. The waters had taken him away into the unknown.

Fred felt a tear stroll down his face. It had been a long time since he had thought about that day. It had been a long time since he had thought about his family. When the family ranch financially collapsed, his family had all but abandoned him. He was nearing adulthood, and his younger siblings needed the attention. He was left to fend for himself.

Fred sat there thinking of his life — his time at the ranch, when the Federal Police saved him from living in the landfill, when he met Maud. He missed her. She was one of the few people that he felt actually cared about him. She didn't see him as useless or dead weight. Most people he came across tended to look down on him. Everyone else was smart or strong or at least tough. Fred was none of those things. He wasn't even brave enough to climb a ladder. He never truly knew what she saw in him, but she would never leave his side. Neither would Wesley. With everything they had been through, Wesley could have ditched him, but he had stuck around leading Fred with him. Wesley had always seemed so fearless, so ready for action. While Fred had been content with his captivity, Wesley wasted no time in getting them to freedom. That made him wonder what was taking him so long to return.

Fred leaned over onto the balcony. The hatch still laid resting on its seal. No sign of him yet. Dismayed, Fred sat back down on the concrete floor. The pain in his side had finally begun to ease. It was still sensitive to the touch, but he had a much easier time breathing than he had had before. He lifted his shirt to reveal his side to be almost completely black with only a slight hue of blue. Gently poking at it, and wincing all the while, he pressed on his ribs. None of them seemed to be broken. For that he was thankful. He wouldn't be any good to anyone if they were. Still, he wouldn't blame Wesley if he had left him. All he had done was slow him down.

A gentle rustle resonated through the catacombs, followed by a loud crack. It was as if someone had blown air into a paper bag and proceeded to pop it. Fred checked himself to make sure his injuries weren't worse than he expected. Finding himself okay, he looked back at the hatch. Nothing. He squinted his eyes trying to see through the dim light of the tunnel. Was it a flash of light? A move of a shadow? Or were his eyes playing tricks on him? The clickety-clack of footsteps on the concrete floor answered his question. He felt a cold chill shiver up his spine. He steadied himself for whatever was lurking in the shadows. Propped up on the floor alone, there wasn't much he could do if it was the Federal Police.

Well, Maud, looks like I'm coming home, he thought as the figure emerged from the dark corridor.

In the dim light, the figure looked like a giant to Fred's bleary eyes. It walked hurried but unfocused. It was searching. Fred tucked himself tightly against the wall. There was nowhere for him to hide other than out on the balcony. He squeezed his eyes shut tight.

Just don't look. Just don't look, he kept telling himself. He wriggled out onto the balcony and latched onto the ladder. He could only hope the figure behind him didn't see him.

Patiently he waited, never opening his eyes. If the Federal Police did see him, he would rather not know about it. If he didn't have to see them coming, he didn't have to feel the dread of it. Footsteps grew louder and louder, matching the rhythm of Fred's heart in his ears. Then they stopped. Fred gripped the ladder a little tighter.

This is it, he thought. He felt a hand touch his leg. He kicked, aggravating his side.

"Easy, Fred. I found us a way."

Fred opened one eye, peeking at the person in front of him. He recognized the face instantly. Wesley had come back.

"Wesley," another voice shouted from the passageway before Fred could even form the words. Wesley spun around at the voice. Fred saw the tension in him. Fists clenched, teeth gritted. He was ready for a fight. Then, he saw it. The black tactical uniform. The Federal Police insignia emblazoned on it. The friendly, familiar face, smiling at them. Smiling?

"Tobias?"

27

MICHAEL WAS STUNNED. It was because of Myers that the virus was even used in the first place. Why now did he have the change of heart to want to stop it? Was it part of a game he was playing, trying to get in Michael's head? That had to be it. But, there was no point in trying to manipulate him. He had already agreed to help Myers for his family.

"I don't understand," Michael stammered. "Defiant told me you were attempting to make a better virus. One that could change the way people remembered certain things. A better way of mind control."

Michael hated laying all his cards on the table, but he wanted answers. He was tired of being led around by half-truths. If Defiant was lying and Myers was lying, then maybe he could begin to discern some truth from between their lies.

"Defiant truly is a clever name for the rebels," Myers began. "But see, Michael, that is what they are—rebels. They don't have truth."

"Whose truth? I've been lied to by everyone I've come across. Truth is apparently relative."

"Michael, I've told you, I'm a man of my word. The rebels are working on outdated information. We're not trying to create the virus. It already exists. Your partner took care of that. That's not why I need you. I need you to fix it."

Michael began thinking it over. For once, things were becoming clear. That was why they went for Cade first. They forced him to make the delivery system of his virus better. That still didn't explain why they had killed him, or how he was supposed to help. The drug was created by accident, through miscalculations. Michael wasn't sure that he was even smart enough to modify it, much less reverse it.

"Why? Why did you create this monstrosity, only to hunt me down to undo it?" he asked.

"There are things far beyond your understanding at work here. The virus mutates, making vaccines next to useless. The safety precautions those of us who know about the virus took to protect our own memories are failing. And just like any virus, it's spreading."

Michael's heart felt as if it rose up into his throat. His life's work had fallen into hands that didn't know how to control the power they had. Like a match being used to start a wildfire, destruction was spreading. It was his fault. If only he would have gotten it right the first time.

"Are you telling me it's becoming an epidemic?" Michael asked, still trying to take it all in.

"So far no, but nature has taken control of it. Before, the virus was programmed to target the most recent memories. It was crude but effective. Most importantly, it was only contractible when injected directly into the bloodstream. The new strand is targeted and very specific. In its concept, those that administered it would be able to control which memories to select. As the virus mutates, it replicates whatever code was imprinted on it. Therefore, in another host, it would attach itself differently. To make things worse, this virus has found a way to transfer itself through bodily fluids—blood, sweat, saliva."

"If it can do that, how is it not an epidemic?"

"As of yet, only the virus replicates, not the drug it administers. Most people only end up with a mild to severe headache that lasts a few days. But, those that contract a carrier, those have unexpected results. Do you remember asking me about your wife?"

Of course Michael remembered. It was the only reason he agreed to help Myers in the first place so that he could undo what they had done to her. Michael didn't even have to answer to know where he was going.

"Are you saying Rebecca has this virus?" Michael shouted, shoving Myers into the wall behind him. "She was fine before you took her. You arrogant… I've already lost my father to this type of disease. I will not lose my wife too."

"Michael, please. I know you're upset, but it was not my intention." Myers' face fell as his body loosened. "She's not the only one. Come. There is something else I need to show you. Trust me, you'll understand."

Michael scoffed at the idea that he could understand. All he understood was that Myers and the Federal Police were bent on control, forgoing any of the consequences to get it. Something in Myers' eyes pulled at him, though. It was as if, for the first time, he was able to see the real Myers. It was the same look he had given Natalie in the observation room. It was like he, too, knew the hurt that was in Michael's heart.

Myers began walking back down the corridor as soon as Michael released him. His steps were slow as if he was begrudgingly pacing himself to his doom. He stopped short of the room covered in daisies and unicorns.

"Here," Myers said, lifting his hand toward the room without so much as glancing at it. "I haven't been here in quite some time. I can't bring myself to anymore."

Michael walked up to the door and uncovered the window. Inside was a teenage girl lying motionless on a bed. If it weren't for the monitors showing signs of life, he wouldn't have believed there to be any. A nurse wearing a full hazmat suit was tending to her.

"You're not the only one who has lost family, Michael," Myers said softly as a tear rolled down his cheek. "We first noticed the symptoms just over five years ago. Not long after the new virus was put into use. She was twelve when we had to confine her to this room to keep the virus from spreading."

"Is that why you wanted to adopt Allie?" Michael asked harshly. "Since you were losing your own daughter, you wanted to take mine?"

"Calm down, Michael. That was merely a ruse to help bring you here. I have no interest in taking any of your family. However, I do have some very bad news that I hate to have to deliver. Unfortunately, Michael, we will have to keep Rebecca here for now, now that we know that she's contracted it. We have to maintain control of this virus."

Michael instantly turned to face Myers. Myers dropped his shoulders, tilting his head down slightly. It was as if he was giving up, expecting Michael to hit him. Michael wanted to, but he couldn't bring himself to it. He understood the desperate measures a father would go through for his child. He had taken plenty himself. Knowing that Rebecca would be sealed inside one of those rooms spurred him on to finally get started on finding a cure. If he could find a cure for her, maybe it could work for everyone. Maybe his dream wouldn't be lost after all.

"If it's been five years, what have you gotten done in the way of a cure?" Michael asked.

"We've made progress but not nearly enough. Dr. Enri LeFleur and I have been working with researchers and biomedical engineers. They're the best and the brightest minds of the USF, but a cure is still out of reach. We've developed a localized version of the strand that's non-mutative, so it's safe. We've formed an experiment with it to test our creations. A person is injected with the benign version of the virus and shown a series of six color palettes. Basically, the color spectrum—red, orange, yellow, green, blue, and purple. In a successful trial, the patient would be able to recite back all six. So far, none have been successful."

"What about the Resilients? Are they affected by it?"

"The virus was initially designed as a countermeasure to the growing number of Resilients, therefore they are no less affected than you or me."

It was still foreign to Michael to talk about such things as countermeasures to the Resilients. That was a world he was not a part of, nor would he ever be. For the moment, the two could agree that a cure had to be found.

28

WATCH WAS FRANTIC as she typed into her computer, pulling screen after screen up on the wall. Damien no longer had his little yellow pencil stuck behind his ear. Rather, it laid among balls of crumpled paper. Vasher stood over them, watching solemnly.

"Something's going on, Jake, and I don't know what," Watch said, strumming the table as if she was still typing.

"Just breathe, Watch. I know we still haven't been able to resume communications with Maps, but I thought you two were making progress," Vasher said, trying to comfort the highly agitated Watch.

"We were," Damien said. "We had full access to the fortress, but then..."

"Everything's gone," Watch said, resuming her keystrokes. "All the files are gone. Our camera feed is gone. Our connection is gone."

Damien placed his hand gently on Watch's shoulder. She appreciated the gesture, but it was of no comfort. She had never left anyone behind, and now she had three behind enemy lines and three more heading in. No matter how hard she tried, it was no use. She was completely locked out of the system. Mission after mission she had coordinated for Defiant. Often times multiple missions at once. Always alone. Now she was at a loss.

This was it. It had finally happened. She was admitting defeat. She had given up. Quietly, she stopped typing and slid her keyboard away. She removed her earpiece and laid it on the desk. Standing up, she took a breath and proceeded to walk out the front door of the Defiant hideout.

She walked alone through the dark tunnel and listened to the silence. The smell of dust filled the air, but it was peaceful. It was the first time she had been outside in as long as she remembered. Defiant kept her so busy looking out for everyone, many nights she slept at her desk. She thought it was nice to finally unplug for a moment, even if it wasn't of her own choosing.

Aimlessly, she walked to the end of the tunnel and stared at the sky through the hole in the ceiling. The stars had almost completely faded in the morning light. Sunlight flooded the little platform between the two tracks. She laid herself down on the platform, watching the sky. There was nothing else she could do.

She wasn't strong like Natalie. She didn't have the photographic memory of Maps. She wasn't a leader like Vasher. She was a hacker and a really good one. But what was a hacker without a computer? She cursed at the air for not being good enough to help them.

As she lied there daydreaming, Damien rolled up next to the platform beside her. He had followed her out there, and she was sure he had heard her outbursts. The thought embarrassed her. Cautiously, Damien placed his hands on the platform to help lift himself out of his chair. His arms trembled as he leaned on the edge. Watch sat up to try to help him, but he brushed her off as he pulled himself up on the platform beside her.

"I know how you feel, Watch," Damien said, joining her in looking at the sky. She chuckled to herself. How could he possibly know how she felt? She had let her team down. She had never failed before. She didn't know how to. There was no way he could understand that.

"I know you mean well, but…" Watch began.

"It really is a pretty sight, isn't it?" he asked, still looking at the sky.

"I suppose."

"It's been a long time since I've seen a sunrise. I'm not even sure how long they kept me in that cell."

The words struck a chord with Watch. Although she felt like everything was falling apart because she couldn't help her friends, at least she hadn't been forced to live in a prison cell.

"Do you ever wish we could be free?" she asked.

"I thought that's what Defiant was working toward."

"No, I mean, free. Free from the struggle. Free from trying to live up to other people's standards. Whether it be the Federal Police or Defiant or the government—just free. The clouds are free. The wind is free. No one expects anything from the birds. They all just do what they do. I hope that one day we can be free."

"When I was stuck in that cell, freedom was what I wished for. I knew there was more I needed to do but didn't have a way to do it. I had carried the weight of everything on my shoulders, but looking back, it wasn't a weight I had to carry on my own. When Wesley came in, he saved me. Maybe it's time someone saved you." Damien leaned in close to Watch, taking her hand in his.

For a brief moment, she felt her heart flutter. A joy spread over her. Damien was right. It was as if the weight of the world had fallen off her shoulders. She looked deep into his pale blue eyes. He was stroking her hand softly as he leaned in a little closer.

She snatched her hand back from him. Now was not the time. There was too much at stake for her to have a crush. She apologized to Damien, who looked as if his spirit had been broken, as she dropped down from the platform. It wasn't that she didn't admire him, but what right did she have to feel that joy when her friends' lives were in danger?

The thought reinvigorated her. She helped Damien back into his wheelchair and sprinted back toward the hideout. She had an idea, and there was no time to lose. Vasher watched her as she flew through the door and straight to her computer. In a flash, all her screens were aglow.

"Did I miss something?" Vasher asked at her sudden reemergence.

"Cleared my head. Had an idea," she said, never turning her eyes from her computer. Damien eased his way back in, awkwardly approaching Watch. She barely noticed him. She was focused. "Pull up a grid of Clerica," she barked at him as he was returning to his computer. Quickly, she began filling his grid with the information she had been gathering. "Look. There's a complete network blackout from the center of Clerica north. The fortress and the train station are both completely offline. It's like someone cut the hardlines."

"Do I need to send a team out there to investigate?" Vasher asked.

"No. I don't need anyone else out there for me to worry about. I've got a better idea," she said, turning on the television. Immediately, she programmed it to receive the feed from Clerica.

"The news? You know that's filled with nothing but propaganda and stories skewed for ratings."

"Yes, but if someone cut the hardlines, that means there's going to be a lot of upset people without an internet connection. And with it including the distribution center, that's going to affect all of Metropolian. There will definitely be something about it. Watch the background. That could give us eyes in Clerica."

Vasher called everyone over to the viewing screen. Watch populated it with every news feed from Clerica. Every eye was watching for even the slightest detail. With the sheer size of Clerica and the blackout affecting over half of it, Watch knew it was a shot in the dark, but it was their best shot. Any information gained was more than what they had.

"Boss, a Fed PD attack helicopter just bobbled into frame, before the news crew caught it," one of them said.

"Run it back, and zoom in," Vasher ordered Watch. Barely visible, an AF-15 flew just in sight of the camera before vanishing. Watch began using the buildings in the background to determine where the helicopter was flying. With only a brief flash, it was impossible to tell if the craft was stationary or flying somewhere else. She mapped out both.

"It's the train station," Watch said. "It has to be. Based off my calculations, it was flying above the historic part of Clerica. Nothing's out there, other than the distribution center and the train station."

"Do you think they're onto Tobias?" Vasher asked, ordering his men to go gear up.

"I don't know how, but it's possible."

Vasher gathered his men and left out. Watch and Damien stayed behind to reattempt getting the communications back up. Damien sat quietly to himself, working. It was as if he wouldn't even look at Watch. That was until she threw one of his paper balls at him. She looked over at him smiling, while he gave her the strangest of looks.

She felt terrible for the way she had acted. He was only trying to be nice to her, and she pushed him away. In truth, she was afraid. There was a lot about her that he didn't know. No one knew her darkest secrets. She thought it better that no one did. It didn't change who she was, but she was afraid to ever truly get close to anyone. She was afraid if they ever discovered her secret, she would only be left hurt. She couldn't take any more hurt in her life. She had a good thing with Defiant. Those were the best years of her life, and she didn't want to risk losing that. It was better this way.

That, at least, was what she kept telling herself.

***

While Wesley wasn't surprised that Defiant had sent Tobias to accompany them, he was upset that he had wasted valuable time being chased by him. Wesley felt foolish for running when they were at the train. If he would have stood up to him then, the whole mess could have been avoided.

"Defiant thinks I need a babysitter?" Wesley snapped at Tobias.

"Wesley, I-"

"Don't," Wesley cut him off. "Follow me."

The room above the hatch had led Wesley to a secret level between the water and sewage and the street. The level was lined with wires and cables. Every street camera, phone line, and ethernet cable ran through there. It was how the Federal Police gathered information. Each line fed into a locked room made entirely out of a copper mesh.

Through the mesh, Wesley could see the flashing lights of the servers the cables were connected to. He didn't know much about computers, but he knew disabling those servers would interrupt the Federal Police's efforts.

Wesley snatched a heavy gauge wire free of its connection and used it to pick the lock of the room. He began smashing and kicking the servers, yanking wires free from the backs of them. He was determined to at least slow them down from whatever assault they were preparing for at the train station. Maybe he could buy a little time for Michael.

When he was satisfied that they were fully out of commission, he began to look for a way to get himself and Fred out of there. The room was secure, except for the floor hatch. Every door was sealed with heavy locks. Fortunately for Wesley, the locks were designed to keep people out of the server room, not in. He eased the door open and found a stairwell connecting the service tunnels to the surface. All he had to do was get Fred there.

That stairwell was where he was leading Fred and Tobias. It was their best chance to escape without alerting the Federal Police at the train station. They had to hurry, though, before they traced the information blackout to those servers.

"I only wanted to help," Tobias said as they approached the stairs. "Maps is in there too, and believe it or not, many of us in Defiant really do care about Michael. Vasher may not show it, but he doesn't show much about anything. Cade used to talk about him all the time."

"You all talk of Cade a lot. How did you know him so well?"

Before Tobias could answer him, the low rumble of an engine filled the stairwell. Wesley stood against the wall, staying just high enough on the steps that he could see it pass. A lone torro was slowly making its way by. It didn't seem to be actively pursuing anything, but just driving casually down the street as if such a sight was an everyday occurrence.

"I don't like this," Wesley said, crouching down to Tobias and Fred.

"Agreed," Tobias said. "Torroes don't normally just drive up and down the streets. The Federal Police tend to be a little more covert than that."

"Something big is going on. I know Michael needs our help, but do you think we should go to the train station and at least check it out?"

"No. I'm sure Watch knows, so Vasher is probably sending in a team. Let's figure out how we're going to help Michael and Maps. Here, I brought you this." Tobias handed Wesley a rifle from his back. In the commotion, he hadn't noticed that Tobias was carrying two.

Wesley climbed up the steps, peeking out of the stairwell. The torro was off in the distance, making a turn before disappearing from sight. To his right, he could see the helicopters still circling above the train station. The torro had been driving away from the train station, which Wesley thought was odd. The trio ran cautiously from the stairwell to the other side of the street, making sure there were no more Federal Police approaching.

"Where are we?" Wesley asked once they were safely hidden from view of passersby.

"We're in the residential area. See all these high-rises? They're apartment buildings," Tobias said.

"What's that delicious smell?" Fred asked, shuffling forward so he could see more of the street.

"Bottom floor's always a restaurant. People's got to eat."

Wesley could see the drool already forming in the corners of Fred's anxious lips. He stepped forward slightly to block Fred's path, should he decide to make a break for it.

"There'll be plenty of time for food once we've rescued the others," Wesley said. "How far are we from Myers' fortress?"

"It's just a few streets over," Tobias said.

The three walked together in a tight group through alleyways between the buildings, trying to avoid the main road as much as possible. Torroes would still periodically pass by as they were patrolling the street. Every corner they turned posed a threat of danger. At times, even the citizens would stop them since their behavior was unusual. Tobias would use his authority as a Federal Police officer to tell them to simply mind their own business.

"Myers is just on the other side of this building," Tobias told them as they approached a skyscraper. "Any idea yet how you want to try to get in?"

Wesley shook his head. He had been going through it over and over again in his mind. The fortress was impenetrable from the outside. He hoped to have a plan once he actually laid eyes on the building physically.

"How about a bird's eye view of the place?" Tobias asked, pointing up to the top of the building in front of them. "Watch this."

Two doors laid before them. One door led to a restaurant. The other led to the stairwell of the apartment complex. The door was securely locked, requiring a key card to enter. A small intercom was affixed to the wall beneath a security camera.

"Federal Police. Open up," Tobias shouted into the intercom, in a very serious tone. Within moments, the door buzzed, and Tobias swung it open. The stairs led to a room with elevators that they rode to the top floor.

The floor stood still as Tobias exited the elevator. Children playing in the halls clung to their parents. Adults cohered to the walls. A symphony of slamming doors broke the otherwise impermeable silence. Tobias strolled through without hesitation. Wesley and Fred kept right on his heels. Tobias walked to the end of the hallway and began rapping loudly on the door.

"This is the Federal Police."

The door opened a crack, and a small, middle-aged woman peeked through. Tears streaked her eyes as terror had overtaken her. Tobias was unrelenting.

"Federal Police business. We are confiscating this apartment." Tobias barged into the room and pulled the woman out. He motioned for Wesley and Fred to follow behind without tending to her.

"A little harsh, wasn't you?" Fred asked.

"The Federal Police are ruthless in their missions," Tobias said once he had shut the door. "If you're not, they can see right through you."

Wesley understood. He walked to the window overlooking the fortress. From the views he had seen from the ground, he had thought the fortress was relatively square, but from above, he saw that it was built more like an iron cross. The outer walls were connected to shafts which then led to a circular center. A domed skylight adorned the center like a jewel. An iron fence surrounded it on all sides, with only a single gate to enter in through. Wesley's hopes fell. The vantage point didn't help him to find a way in but rather reaffirmed his fears that it was impossible.

"Unless we fly over the top, and then somehow manage to drop in without getting shot, I don't know how to get in there," Wesley said, still staring at it through the window.

"I overheard Maps tell Watch that he had found a way out," Tobias said, walking up beside him. "If that's the case, we should be able to find some way in."

Tobias and Wesley huddled next to the window, looking it over. Fred joined them too but at a distance from the edge. Tobias watched the positions of the Federal Police, Wesley observed their defensive weapons, and Fred scanned the grounds for any possible entry point. Wesley was determined to find a way in. If Maps had found a way, then so could they.

29

"INVALID EQUATION," the calculation board kept repeating. The shrill, robotic voice continuously reminded Michael of his failures. So much so, he would mouth the words.

Here we go again, Michael thought.

It had been so long since he had worked on formulas, he wasn't sure if he even remembered how. He knew somewhere locked away deep in his mind, there was the answer. He searched his memories, but the thought was still foreign to him. The Federal Police had stripped him of his memories, leaving him handicapped to try to fix it. Alas, he continued to remind himself that if he was able to do it once, he could do it again. Maybe since he was starting with a clean slate, he could figure out where he went wrong.

"Invalid equation."

If he could get started, he may be able to figure out where he went wrong. Every time the board warned him of his invalidity, hope was replaced by frustration. His frustration grew until it finally boiled over. He threw his stylus across the room and sat against the wall pouting.

Rebecca used to get mad at him for working late. Now, he was working for her. He wasn't going to lose her. He had lost her too many times. He wasn't sure how much more his heart could take.

Michael picked himself up off the floor and looked at the stack of books on his work table. Myers had brought him every textbook, journal, and research report they had on the subject. Michael had foregone reading them in the interest of saving time. It was evident to him that that was a mistake. Not only that, dawn had swiftly come. He had gone straight to work. He couldn't remember the last time he had slept for any decent amount of time.

Michael switched off the screens and the lights, picking up the books on his way. He walked out his lab and down the hall. It felt strange to him to be able to wander around Myers' fortress unattended. Myers had put a lot of faith and trust in him. Michael didn't share the same with him, but for now, they were on equal terms. He walked through to the central room. He glanced up at the morning light pouring in through the glass skylight. The officers guarding the room looked at him and then returned back to their business as he walked to the living quarters.

"Look, Allie. Here comes your daddy," Myers said as Michael walked through the door. Allie ran to the door and hugged Michael with the same tight embrace she had given him in the hallway. He felt bad for not getting to spend more time with her than he had. Myers stood up from the couch and excused himself from the room.

"Myers, I agreed to work with you on this virus, but don't ever come around my family again," Michael mumbled underneath his breath, out of earshot of Allie.

"Where have you been, Daddy?" Allie asked once Myers left.

"It's a long story, but I've been trying to get to you."

"Please tell me we don't have to go back to that place again."

"What place? Our home?"

"No. The place where Janie was. They put me and Mommy in this room with her and a lot of other people. It smelled really bad there, and the people weren't very nice. Janie called me her Allie-Cat."

"No, sweetie. I hope we never have to see that place again. I'm so sorry they took you there," Michael said, hugging Allie tightly. Tears filled his eyes, thinking of the little girl called Janie. Michael knew she wouldn't last long in a place like that. It had been all his fault. He was just thankful for Allie to not be in that place anymore.

"Where did they take Mommy?"

"Mommy's sick right now. Daddy's got to make her better."

"Is that why she's been acting funny?"

"What do you mean?"

"She keeps forgetting things. She forgot about our house. She forgot about what happened to Grammy Nelda," Allie said, before becoming quiet. "Did they hurt Grams? She ran into the house when all the scary men showed up. She was helping us. She was grabbing Mommy's bible when the fire started. I couldn't see her through the smoke."

Michael sat there silently. He should have been there. He couldn't imagine how they felt. He was sure Allie felt like he had abandoned her. Michael reached into his shirt and handed her Rebecca's bible.

"Keep it safe for me," Michael said. "Grams went on to heaven, so they can't hurt her anymore."

"I promise. Daddy, I know it's morning, but can I go to sleep now? I'm tired."

Michael nodded and kissed her on her forehead as she ran off to a bedroom carrying the bible. Michael knew he needed to sleep too, but there was too much on his mind. His family had been through so much. He had been through so much. His entire world had been changed in an instant.

He got up from the couch and walked to the kitchen. Every cabinet was full of food. There were meats, and vegetables, and chocolates in the refrigerator. There was food he hadn't seen in years. He grabbed a canister of coffee from the cabinet; an indulgence he hadn't gotten to enjoy since the war. Pouring it into the coffee pot, he admired its simplicity in its ability to use electricity to make coffee. He watched as each drop of black gold dripped into the glass pot below. There was a time in his life he had taken these things for granted. Now, they were a luxury.

As much as he needed sleep, he assured himself there wasn't time. He grabbed his cup of coffee and the stacks of books and began to read. He started with the textbooks to remind himself of the basic fundamentals, then moved on to the journals. He felt as if he was having to relearn everything again. He got up and rummaged through a desk against the wall until he found himself a notebook. He began taking notes of things that he read and highlighted passages that seemed important. As a student, he never cared much for studying. He preferred to rely on his knowledge and reasoning skills. There was much more at stake this time than just a mark on a page. Rebecca was still counting on him.

***

Maps had sat in the supply closet, listening to the doctors and nurses work. He hoped they could make Natalie well and cringed whenever the monitors would sound an alert. He wished he could see what was happening, but he wouldn't allow himself to watch. He was afraid that a nurse may see him and be spooked. These people needed to concentrate on saving Natalie. She couldn't afford any distractions.

The minutes turned into hours, yet he waited. He began to feel cramped in the supply closet. He didn't really care to know what was in the cabinet with him. He had hoped bandages and such, but he was never brave enough to turn and look. With Myers watching from above, he had to hide somewhere quickly. He had eased the door open and backed into the tight space, squeezing in as best he could. He had never been so glad as to hear the hum and creaking metal as the observation room slid back into the wall from whence it came.

The room had gone silent. Maps assumed they must have finished, which meant, for now, Natalie was alright. There had been no bells or sirens to tell him otherwise. He decided he would wait in the closet a little longer to make sure the rest of the staff had cleared out. He didn't want to alert anyone to his presence so that he could have free reign to search for what room they had taken her to.

Maps' intent was laid in vain when the cabinet door abruptly opened before him. A nurse stared blankly at him crammed in the small closet.

"I'm sorry. I seem to have made a wrong turn," Maps said, stepping out of the closet to an otherwise empty room. The nurse's only response was to scream as she pushed him back into the cabinet and ran. Maps didn't bother with chasing after her. Instead, he took his opportunity to begin his search for Natalie.

He started searching in the rooms at the far end of the medical center. In case the nurse returned, he wanted to put as much distance between him and the operating theater as possible. His search proved fruitless, and he began a search in a new block of rooms. After his third block with no luck, he decided to take a much faster approach.

He walked up to the nurses' station and, carrying the full weight of the uniform he was wearing, demanded to know where Natalie was.

"Where is the patient that was just taken from the operating theater?" Maps asked in a gruff voice, slamming his hand down on the counter for effect. "Myers wants to see her."

"Myers is just going to have to wait," the nurse said unfazed.

"Listen, lady."

"No, you listen. She was just taken back for conditioning."

"I don't care if she was taken back for the shampoo to go with it. I need to see her."

"No. Only medical staff is allowed through those doors, so I'd suggest you go and have a nice day."

"Through here?" Maps said, already pushing against the swinging door.

"You can't go in there."

"Too late. Looks like I'm already in," he said as the door swung shut behind him.

He sprinted down the hallway, looking in the windows of the rooms as he passed. A few rooms down, he saw her. She was asleep on the bed. They had cleaned her up and changed her clothes. There was no more harrowing bloodstain. The gown she wore even hid the bandages underneath. Maps searched the hallway for a wheelchair and brought it into the room with her. They had her connected to a large machine, pumping fluids into her. While he knew those fluids were important, he had to get her out of there.

Carefully, he removed the needle she had in her arm, which connected her to the machine. He gently lifted her and sat her in the wheelchair, covering her over with the blanket from the bed. He had never seen Natalie so still and quiet. There was a sweetness about her that she kept hidden from the world. Only Maps even knew of its existence. He kissed her softly on the cheek, grateful that she wasn't aware of it. She would have disapproved.

Maps rolled her farther down the hallway, looking for another exit to avoid going back by the nurses' station. Using his back, he pushed open a door at the very end of the hall and rolled her through. The door had no handle on its other side, sealing them from returning.

That's okay. I didn't want to go back that way anyway, Maps thought.

He looked around the area. They were once again in the general hallways of the medical wing. *Almost to freedom.* A few nurses emerged from one of the rooms. Maps confidently nodded at the nurses, acknowledging them. Never breaking stride, he rolled Natalie down the hallway. All was going well until Natalie began to stir. Her groans caused the nurses to pause and look at them.

"She's okay. She's just a little out of it," Maps told them with a smile. That seemed to appease them. He bent down beside her to try to tend to her. Her eyes shot wide open as she studied Maps' face thoroughly. As if he had been attempting to murder her, she let out the shrillest howl that was only amplified by the hard surfaces in the hallway.

"Natalie. Natalie. It's okay. Look at me," Maps said as she began to swing and claw wildly at him. "Natalie, it's me, Maps."

She calmed for a moment as she traced the lines of his face with her eyes. But like the calm before a storm, she let out another violent howl. The nurses were running to them. There was no talking his way out of it. He couldn't stop the nurses from getting to Natalie. They took her and began rolling her away.

She was breathing heavy. Her eyes were fiercely locked onto his. She wasn't fighting the nurses. Her outburst seemed to be directed at him personally.

"I hate you!" she screamed at Maps before disappearing around a corner.

30

THE FEDERAL POLICE moved like clockwork, guarding the fortress. Four guards walked in a figure-eight pattern on every rooftop, making sure that no particular area was ever in the blind at any moment. Two guards paced in circles around the two watch towers at the entrance gate. Wesley and Tobias had been watching them for over an hour, studying them, learning their movements. Fred had given up long ago and was sitting on the couch, doodling.

"Is there no way for you to just walk up to it, Tobias? I mean, you are an officer," Fred had asked.

"Unfortunately, no. Myers hand-picks those that guard his palace. They work there, they live there, they sleep there. Most of the guards all know each other, even if the palace staff don't. No one can go in unless they're invited. Otherwise, me and Vasher would already have."

That had been twenty minutes ago. Nothing else had been spoken since. Wesley was out of ideas, and it seemed so was Tobias. Fred jumped from the couch, rushing over to them, ignoring his fears. He was waving around his doodles.

"I think I have it," he said, sounding very sure of himself. Wesley and Tobias looked at him intrigued. "People live there, right? What is it that all houses have? Toilets. They're guarding the top as if they were about to go to war, but how many people do you think they have watching the crapper?"

Wesley rubbed the bridge of his nose with his forefinger. While he admired Fred for thinking outside the box, he wasn't sure that would work. For one, the actual pipes that ran inside were nowhere big enough for a person to fit through.

"I don't know about that, Fred," Wesley said.

"Look, I've been thinking it through," Fred said, lifting his doodles. "We know we can access the sewers because I can still smell it on me. All we have to do is go back down there and stop up the lines to the house. They're going to call a plumber, and then presto, we go in disguised as plumbers."

Wesley did have to admit Fred had given it a lot of thought, but he wasn't sure about it. There was no way for them to pose as plumbers. They had no equipment, no suits, and most importantly, no identification to show at the door. Nevertheless, the idea fascinated him, and so he tried thinking it through further.

He thought he had almost come up with a solution when he saw Tobias walk to the door silently. He pressed his ear to the door and gestured for them to be quiet. As soon as Wesley tried to inquire, he began motioning for them to hide. Fred ducked into the bathroom, while Wesley dove behind the couch. As soon as he did, the door came crashing down as a Federal Police officer walked into the room.

"Tobias?" the officer asked as Tobias was brushing off the splinters from his uniform.

"Ever heard of knocking, Matthys? You should try it some time," Tobias said.

"What are you doing here?"

"I heard a report that there were some intruders held up in this apartment, so I came to investigate."

"Yeah, and I heard one of them was dressed like a cop."

"Someone's going around pretending to be us? Who would be that stupid?"

"Hmm. Mind if I look around?" Matthys asked, pushing his way past Tobias.

"Be my guest," Tobias said. "Wasn't anything here. I was just on my way out until you tried to hit me with a door."

Matthys wasn't amused and began pilfering through the apartment. Wesley kept his eye on him while staying out of his sight behind the couch. Wesley stayed squatted, encircling the couch to keep it between him and Matthys as he searched the living room.

"Later, Matthys," Tobias called, stepping into the hallway as Matthys went into the bathroom.

"Get back here, Tobias," Matthys said, giving chase. "We've got to get back to the train station. Hempton's calling in everybody. Apparently, he's found the rebels. We've probably already missed the first wave, but I want to make sure the colonel knows we didn't defy a direct order."

Tobias froze. "Which rebels?"

"What do you mean 'which rebels?' The rebels. The ones that keep interfering in everything we do."

"You mean we've caught another cell of them? I didn't figure they would try something again after we blasted that village in the Forbidden Zone."

"You think Hempton would be worried about just another cell? He found their headquarters. Now come on. I can't afford another ding on my file. Six years later and he's still got me on grunt duty."

Wesley watched as Tobias continued to stand in the doorway attempting to talk Matthys into going alone. The talks did not seem to be going in the way Tobias wanted. If he left with Matthys, Wesley and Fred were on their own. To make it worse, he knew exactly which rebels he meant—they had found Defiant.

***

Gunfire exploded, ringing out like fireworks trapped in a steel drum. The sound took everyone by surprise. Watch hastily pulled up the security cameras along both tracks outside of their hideout. Hempton's face was emblazoned across the screen. He was followed by a massive army, making their way through the still active train tunnel. A hundred officers marched behind a line of torroes that made their way on the tracks. Vasher's group was pinned down in the rubble at the platform.

Panic flooded the room. Everyone scrambled to different places. Vasher had already left with most of their fighters. Those that remained began grabbing weapons, while others were shredding documents.

Damien laid a rifle across his lap and began rolling himself to the door. Watch stopped him immediately.

"Where do you think you're going?" she asked him, spinning his chair around.

"I was…I've got to help."

"You can. You're going to help me. Start giving these out," she said as she ran and grabbed a dusty box from off a shelf. Inside the box were large, clunky blocks of plastic.

They looked like they hadn't been used in decades. "They're two-way radios. If our main comms are down, they're going to need a way to communicate."

Damien obliged, handing off his rifle. He began to pass out as many radios as he could. Considering the age, he told Watch he thought it prudent to check the batteries before handing them out. Their comrades were appreciative. They each wore fear on their faces, hid behind a mask of solemnness.

"What's your security like?" Damien asked Watch once he had handed out the radios.

"We're not prepared for that."

While Defiant had lived in fear of this day, they knew should it come, they would be outmatched. Their guns were only what could be bought off the black market or stolen from the Federal Police themselves. The largest weapons they had as a defense were rocket launchers, which were of little consequence compared to the torroes. Their hope was that their hideout would remain a secret. The only way in and out was aboard the train, which was automated. If anyone was to ever see them board it, they wouldn't know which stop they had gotten off at, especially since the last stop didn't exist. Watch's predecessor had reprogrammed the train to travel to the collapsing station. She continuously made sure that doing such couldn't be traced. They were isolated. They felt safe.

The lights dimmed as the room shook. The fighting was getting closer. Watch did the only thing she knew to do—she went to her computer. She filled every screen in the room with cameras from both tunnels. Vasher and his team were using the rubble at the platform for cover. The rest of Defiant were running down the empty tunnel to join them. Rockets and grenades were being lobbed by both sides. The torroes kept the foot soldiers of the Federal

Police protected, but the rubble was proving adequate for Defiant. They had reached a stalemate. The torroes, however, were slowly inching their way forward.

"Guys, the torroes are moving," Watch called out over the radio. "If you don't do something fast to stop them, they're going to be on our guys in just a minute."

The call-out worked. Those that were carrying rocket launchers began sprinting double time. They crawled up on the platform and, using the dividing wall as cover, began to unleash a direct assault on the torroes. When one would fire, another would fall in right behind to fire again. For the moment, Defiant was winning. Watch feared what would happen when they ran out of rockets. She could only hope the torroes would be disabled.

"Watch, look," Damien yelled to her. A fourth torro had come into view at the back of the Federal Police's army. It was pushing its way through the dividing wall of the tunnel. The black beast of the torro tore into the soft concrete wall. Dust and debris filled the air as black uniforms lined the hole in its wake.

"Guys, turn around. Torro coming up from the rear."

Watch felt the percussive force as a rocket had been launched at the new torro. Damien began pulling on her to move. She had been so glued to monitoring the action, she failed to realize the emerging torro was just outside the door to their hideout. She threw her radio at Damien and grabbed hold of his wheelchair. She pushed him around the desks and into a back room. She sealed a large steel door behind them, before pushing him through a series of more rooms. She stopped at a narrow door among a line of others. Momentarily frozen, she stared at the metal door before her. She fidgeted with her hands for a moment before opening the door and easing Damien inside.

A small cot lined the far wall. A few t-shirts laid on top of the blankets. Charcoal drawings adorned the stone walls. Little trinkets and souvenirs rested on top of the dresser Watch was rummaging through. She had never had anyone in her room before. It was her private place of peace. It was her haven to retreat from the stress her job put on her. It was her place to go where she felt as if she could be her true self. She wasn't sure how she felt about having Damien in there taking it all in.

"Is this...me?" Damien asked, taking down one of her charcoal drawings.

"It's...nothing," she blushed. Who did he think he was? It was bad enough that she had to bring him in there for him to start going through her things. She had drawn it when he first arrived at Defiant. It was more of a memory than a keepsake.

"It's nice," Damien said as she took the picture from him.

"As soon as I find it, we can go," she said, still rummaging through her dresser.

"What?"

"I know it's in here."

She pulled up a heart-shaped locket with the letter *V* engraved on the front. She gripped it tight in her fist, clutching it to her chest.

"What is that?"

"It's nothing. Let's go," she said as she put it around her neck, dropping it inside her collar. "There's a bunker just up ahead. We'll be safe there."

She pushed Damien through the doorway, thankful to get him out of her room, though she was sure she would never see it again. She wished she knew what was going on outside. The radio had been silent of chatter. That deep into their hideout, the onslaught had been muffled into nonexistence. She grabbed the radio and turned the volume up, hoping to hear some news.

Screams broke the radio silence.

"Retreat," Vasher cried, followed by more silence.

"Vasher, what's going on out there?" she asked into the radio. She couldn't take any more of the suspense.

"Watch, if you can hear this, get to the bunker," Vasher panted. Pain was evident in his voice. "They're coming."

Watch buried her face in her hands as she slumped to the floor of the bunker. Defiant had become her family, and the Federal Police had stripped her of that. Tears flooded her eyes as sobs turned into cries on the cold stone floor of the bunker. Damien eased himself down from his chair. He wrapped her up in his arms, pressing her head to his chest. No words were spoken. He just held her as she cried. Watch put her arms around him, squeezing him tightly. She had given him such a hard time, but at that moment, she was exactly where she needed to be.

"Listen, Damien," she said, still fighting back tears, "I'm sorry about before. I just wanted to tell you…"

"Not right now," he said as he brushed back the few stray hairs that had escaped from her ponytail.

Watch closed her eyes with her head resting on Damien's chest. She had found a true friend in him. He would never know how much she appreciated him in that moment. She could feel her body trembling, both from the cold damp air of the bunker and the fear of what was happening to the ones she cared about. Damien must have felt it too. He squeezed her a little tighter.

The radio silence was interrupted again by Hempton's slow, raspy voice.

"Mr. Vasher, I'm disappointed in you. You seem to have chosen the wrong side."

"How did you find us?" Vasher groaned.

"We've been watching you and your organization for some time now. It had come to our attention that you were collecting Resilients."

"I don't know what you're talking about."

A loud pop was sent through the speakers of the radio. The sound startled Watch, causing her to jolt. She could only assume someone had struck him.

"Don't be coy with me, Mr. Vasher. I actually commend you for your efforts. Your band of rebels has defied our plans on multiple occasions. I'm sure of which was no easy feat. So far, we have tolerated this behavior to a certain extent, because you were taking care of the Resilient problem for us. Those that could not be affected by our serums tended to find their way to your organization. Thus, it kept them from corrupting the law-abiding citizens. However, we have deemed your organization is no longer required, as the Resilient problem has been eradicated."

"Stop trying to control people's minds, and there won't be a problem."

"Defiant to the end. Your organization was truly aptly named. You see, Mr. Vasher, in your own personal life, the world before may have been optimistic. Hopeful. I dare say even joyful. However, your life is small compared to all the lives of the Federation. If you were to look beyond the borders and boundaries of your own life, the world outside was riddled with chaos and destruction. We have brought peace, and a peace everlasting. There are those like you that fail to see that."

"You murder innocent people and you call that peace?"

"Again, Mr. Vasher, look at the bigger picture. An individual's life is minuscule by comparison. A person dies, but a person dies every single day. Sometimes a little sacrifice is necessary for the good of all mankind."

"You're wrong. People do matter."

"Yes, people do matter. It is the person that is the problem. Human nature is the very essence of chaos. Wars have been fought for centuries over human nature's desire for something better that is yet to come. A hope."

"A better day is coming. I'll die to find it."

"My point exactly. That hope is a false promise. If such hope were attainable, the cycle would have been broken. You see, Mr. Vasher, that is our desire. To break the cycle. The repetitive ebb and flow of violence. Our serums are not meant to destroy but to shape the world. To show the people that the best days are not yet to come but are here upon us. They are now."

"These are not my best days, Hempton. This is your nightmare."

"I can see there is no use. Take him. Bury the survivors."

31

MAPS WAS HEARTBROKEN. Those were not the words he wanted to hear from Natalie. The look she gave him, the deathly glare, the horror in her eyes, it made him feel like a monster.

Pull yourself together, he thought to himself. He knew it was the Federal Police's doing. They had done more than just healed her body, they had affected her mind. He wasn't sure how, though. She was a Resilient like him. The virus shouldn't affect her.

Maps steadied himself. There was nothing more he could do for her if she didn't recognize him. Nothing short of sedating her would calm her down enough to sneak her out of the palace. He would have to be patient. Michael still needed his help. The last he saw of him was with Myers in the observation room. After seeing Natalie, Maps had forgotten the plan. He was sure Michael felt like he had left him behind. Maps forced himself to focus. He had to start acting like a true member of Defiant, not one who had been pretending for the last two years. That's why Natalie couldn't see him the way he had hoped she would.

He left out of the Center for Wellness, willing himself to leave Natalie and return to the mission. He wasn't sure where Michael was, and without Watch to assist, he had to find him on his own. He reasoned the best place to start was to return to the woman. He was sure the little girl was Michael's daughter. Wherever she was, Michael wouldn't be far behind.

He eased himself behind the pillars of the central room, stealthily walking back to the east wing. He hadn't yet figured out how to get the girl away from the woman, but he was planning as he went. When he had met her, he had broken into her home, and she held a knife to his throat. He didn't want to repeat the same situation. This time, he chose to knock. To his surprise, Michael answered the door.

"Michael?" Maps was stunned. Michael looked awful. His eyes were bloodshot. His hands were twitching. He looked exhausted.

"Maps," Michael began, pulling the door tight against his body. "Why are you here?"

"I'm here to save you and help get your daughter out of here."

"Allie is asleep. You're a little late. We're not going anywhere."

"I'm sorry, Michael. I was sidetracked. You saw what happened to Natalie."

"Natalie tried to kill me. I'm better off on my own, without Defiant. You helped me get Allie back, that's all I had asked of you."

Michael slammed the door in his face. Maps had to step back to keep from being hit by it. Whatever the Federal Police had done had seriously affected Natalie and apparently Michael as well. For a man so spurred on to save his daughter, he was very reluctant to leave. Maps had to know why. He had to know what game the Federal Police were playing.

"The job's not done, Michael," Maps said, rapping loudly on the door. "I'm supposed to help you get your daughter out of the building. This is very much still in the building."

His knocks were met with no reply. He was being ignored. Maps was determined he was not going to leave the palace empty-handed. He came in with Michael and Natalie. He was going to leave with at least one of them, regardless the cost. Maps jiggled the handle. Michael had locked it tight. That was not a problem. He knew another way.

He strode across the hall and kicked out the air vent. He crawled in and shimmied his way back into the network of ducts. At least this time, he only had to cross a hall and wasn't being chased by officers.

"I told you, the job's not done," Maps said as he pulled himself through the air vent into Michael's room. Michael was sitting at a table. Mounds of books were stacked beside him. Papers were strewn about over the table's wooden surface and all across the marble floor.

"Are you here to kill me too, Maps?" Michael asked, dropping the pencil from his hand.

"Kill you? Why would I want to...No. I'm here to save you."

"Just like Natalie?"

"Look, Michael. I don't know what happened, but something's different with Natalie. They did something to her. She doesn't even recognize me anymore."

"The virus..." Michael said, filling Maps in on the details of both the new strand of the virus as well as what it had done to Rebecca. "So, you see, Maps, I can't leave. Not yet. I've got to find a cure." Michael motioned to the books he had laid on the table.

"Michael, why don't you get some sleep? I've got a photographic memory. While I may not understand what I'm reading, I can at least recite to you what I've read. Besides, I think the coffee has made you a little jittery." Maps took the cup from Michael's shaking hand. He doubted if Michael's penmanship was readable with the fierceness of those tremors.

"You haven't had any more sleep than I have."

"No, but I also haven't been reading textbooks for who knows how long. Those things could bore anyone to sleep. At least go take a nap. I'm sure this would make a lot more sense to someone with a fresh mind."

Michael once again argued but was finally persuaded, leaving Maps alone with the books. He looked over the heap before him. None of them seemed to be any real page turners. He could barely understand the titles of most of them.

"Molecular Aversion to Systemic Contagions," Maps read aloud. "Sounds exciting."

After skimming through his fourth textbook, he was beginning to severely regret his decision to help. He felt as if he was reading a Greek manuscript of the exciting adventures of drying wet paint.

Join Defiant to get out of Clerica and all of its mind-numbing paperwork. Work some missions. Infiltrate the Federal Police. Get shot at a few times. Find my way to a palace in the middle of Clerica doing mind-numbing paperwork, Maps thought as he slumped back into his chair.

"How's your reading coming?" Michael asked as he emerged from the backroom. Maps wasn't aware that he had been reading long enough for Michael to have gotten a nap.

"Well I know that the polyhedral structure of a protein is a capsid, which is then often coated with a lipid," Maps said, sounding very sure of himself.

"And that means what?" Michael asked, hiding a faint smile.

"I have absolutely no idea."

"Cade would have told you that you have the basic workings of a virus," Michael said, walking over to him. "Don't worry, I didn't know either until a few hours ago."

"Do you really think you can make a cure?" Maps asked. He hated to admit it, but while he cared for people like Rebecca, he was more so thinking of Natalie.

"I have to."

***

Michael peered through his microscope. After he and Maps had studied the textbooks, he was anxious to get back to work. Maps stood behind him, helping in any way that he could. Michael heard him yelp as the door to the lab swung violently open. Myers had come to check on them.

"Who is he, and what is he doing in here?" Myers asked when he saw Maps in the laboratory. "Guards! Guards!"

"He's okay," Michael said without lifting his head from his microscope. "He's with me."

"I do not allow any Federal Police officer I do not know into my facility."

"You act like you don't trust your own people," Michael chuckled. "Besides, he's not Federal Police. He's Defiant."

Myers snarled and demanded a progress report. Michael filled him in, saying that there had been some progress but nothing substantial. Between the books he and Maps had read, they were advancing much faster than he had before.

"Gee, thanks for calling me out like that to Myers," Maps said as soon as Myers had left.

"You know, he isn't as bad as he seems. I mean, he's Satan in a purple bathrobe, but not that bad."

"He's gotten to you, hasn't he? They've gotten inside your head."

"Only once, a long time ago. I just finally understand him. He and I aren't that much different. He's doing what he has to do to protect his family, the same as I am. I don't agree with his methods, but I do see his intent."

"I can't believe you would even say something like that. After all he put your family through. Your friends," Maps said, shaking his head.

"I know, Maps. And I know the awful things the Federal Police do. It's just, sometimes it's hard for me to see him as the head of such an organization after seeing the pain in his eyes over his daughter. And over Natalie."

Maps stared at him. "What do you mean 'over Natalie?'"

"When we were in the observation room, I saw him just standing there with the most heartfelt look on his face. Even after she had tried to kill both of us, he was the one who ordered them to save her life."

Maps walked away silently. Michael knew it was a lot for him to take in. Even so, Michael was becoming less and less concerned for Myers and more so on finding a cure. If he could find the cure, not only could he save Rebecca but also inoculate the Federal Police's primary weapon. He could end the nightmare. He wished he had his notes from when he created the drug.

"What happened to your old notes?" Maps asked as if reading his mind. Michael pondered for a moment if he had actually spoken his thoughts out loud.

"They were destroyed," Michael said with a sigh.

"How do you know?"

"Because I destroyed them."

"What? Why?"

"It's a long story that I would rather not talk about. That day was, without a doubt, the worst day of my life."

Michael was glad Maps didn't press the issue further. His was a secret that was better left untold. No one knew other than the members of his unit. Often times, the memory would still jar him awake at night. He would lie to Rebecca, telling her it was just a bad dream. There was no way he could ever tell her. She would never forgive him.

To push the thoughts from his mind, he moved on from his microscope and back to the calculations board. Within a few moments, it was back to singing its typical anthem. Michael turned off the sound. The word "invalid" had already lost all meaning to him. He was determined not to let it frustrate him like it had so many times in the past.

"That's wrong," Maps said, walking over to the board.

"Thank you, Maps, but the screen has let me know that multiple times."

"No, I mean…that," he said, pointing to an equation on the board. "Physiological Studies, Albert Leoschvitz, page fifty-seven. That should be a negative."

Michael stared at him in amazement. There was no possible way Maps could retain that much information in his mind. Michael didn't argue. He walked to the board and changed the sign. There was no shrill call of invalidity. The screen didn't flash red. For the first time, he had an answer. He could have kicked himself for missing something so simple.

"Does that mean we have a cure?" Maps asked.

"No, unfortunately. But with it, we can stop it from spreading. That means we're almost there."

Michael began working on creating the compound in the real world. He slowly began measuring and mixing beakers together. Maps watched him closely. He wasn't as apprehensive as Cade had been. That made Michael feel slightly more confident. As the last chemical broke the surface of the mixture, there was a slight change in the color. That was it. There was no smoke. No intense heat. No adverse reactions.

He told Maps to inform Myers, to which he reluctantly agreed. Michael wanted to test his new compound on an actual patient. While it wasn't a cure, it could be the breakthrough they were hoping for. As Maps reached for the door to leave, Myers came barging in.

"Myers, your timing is impeccable," Michael said, looking him over. Myers was disheveled. His purple robe was gone. His sleeves were rolled up to his elbows, and he was sweating profusely.

"Michael, listen," Myers panted. "They're coming."

"Who's coming?"

"The Federal Police."

32

WESLEY AND TOBIAS both knew they had to get back and warn the others. Wesley was more concerned with Damien and Watch. In his eyes, neither of them was old enough to be taking part in such an organization, much less be attacked for it. Matthys was going to be a problem. He was still standing in the doorway talking to Tobias.

He was relentless in trying to get Tobias to come with him. Tobias' counterarguments were useless. Matthys forced him to come along. Wesley and Fred were on their own.

"Fred, you still there?" Wesley called as soon as Tobias and Matthys were clear of the room.

"Yeah, I'm still here. That was a close one," he said as he pulled back the shower curtain.

"I need your opinion. Matthys just took Tobias. We know Michael and Rebecca are with Myers, and the Federal Police are leading an attack on Defiant. Where do you think we need to be?"

"Well, you know Myers' fortress is locked down, and you called my sewage idea a long shot. I say we go help Defiant."

Wesley agreed. Both situations were impossible missions. Matthys had already said that they were missing the first wave. That meant that Defiant was already under attack. He feared the worst if that was the attack they had been gearing up for at the train station. There was no way he and Fred could stand up to such firepower. All they had was a rifle.

"Hey, Fred, you up for round two with a torro?" Wesley asked.

"What do you mean?" Fred puzzled.

"I'm going to go steal one."

Wesley had grown tired of being outmatched by the Federal Police. If he was going to fight them, he was going to with their own firepower. He had already learned the controls from the last time he had commandeered one. With torroes patrolling the streets, all he had to do was wait and strike.

Wesley left the room and went to the bottom floor of the apartment complex. There was no sign of Tobias or Matthys anywhere. He told Fred to wait upstairs. He would signal him when he had control of the torro. He tucked himself underneath the stairwell next to a garbage can. There, he waited with a clear view of the street.

Only moments went by before the torro made its way through on patrol. Wesley continued to wait. Once it had passed him by, he emerged from his hiding place. He ran behind the torro, making sure to stay in its blind spot. With the solid back-end, Wesley knew he was hidden from their view.

He placed a hand on the hardened steel, his fingers gripping an indention in the metal. He pulled himself up, resting his feet on a tiny ledge at the bottom. Taking his time for safety, he crawled up the torro until he was directly above it. He fired his rifle at the building in front of them, creating a small cloud of dust.

The torro stopped and fired at the dust cloud. Wesley repeated, firing somewhere else. He had to make the torro think they were under attack so that they would keep firing. He knew sooner or later they would have to reload. He just had to make sure they ran out of bullets before he did. The top hatch opened like Wesley had intended. Using the butt of his rifle, he incapacitated the unsuspecting officer. He then took out the other officers within.

"You people don't deserve to even wear a uniform," Wesley said as he dropped in through the hatch. "We officers wore it with pride and honor. We were protecting our fellow man. Not tyrannizing them."

Wesley opened the door of the torro and pushed the officers out. Once it was secure, he drove around to the opposite side of the building and flashed his lights, giving Fred the signal.

"Now what?" Fred asked once he was inside the torro.

"The train station," Wesley said.

"You mean the place where the Federal Police have been gathering the last few hours?"

"Chances are they were only gathering there to orchestrate their attack against Defiant. They are probably long gone by now. Even if they're not, it's the only way we're going to be able to get this thing there to help them."

Wesley could see the train station in the distance as they approached. Helicopters were still circling from above. Torroes still lined its exterior, though it didn't seem to be as many as there were before. Wesley was nervous, but they had no choice. If there was anything left of Defiant, the only way to get there was to go through. Fred wore his fear on his face as he sat there gripping his harness tight enough for his knuckles to go white.

Wesley neared the torroes and fell in line with them, trying not to be noticed. The station had been completely shut down. All the passengers had been replaced with foot soldiers. More were offloading from the train. Some were bloodied and injured. Wesley was too late. They had missed the battle. He checked the control panel to make sure he was in high-speed operation mode.

"Get ready, Fred. We're going in."

The torro bolted forward as Wesley jammed the accelerator to the floor. He made a straight line toward the train. The force of the collision crushed the side of the train before toppling it over. Wesley was trying to stop them from disembarking the train, cutting down the opposition's forces. The torroes behind him began firing, bullets bouncing off the rear panel. Fred returned fire. With the train derailed, the tunnel was wide open for them to travel down. Rockets began to rain in on them from the ground troops. They were surrounded. Wesley charged for the tunnel, but another torro quickly blocked his way.

"I'm out," Fred said, still trying to fire the machine gun.

Knowing how easy it was to ambush someone reloading the gun, Wesley took his rifle and began to provide covering fire as Fred reloaded the gun. While Wesley was firing, he hadn't noticed another torro had driven in front of him. This one was pushing the first one out of the way.

Wesley looked closely at it. Tobias had commandeered his own and was trying to even the score. Being just one man, he was struggling to both drive and operate the machine gun, but he was managing. Wesley pulled alongside him, firing against the black wave of troops.

Tobias stopped firing. Wesley looked over and saw that he was sustaining heavy rocket fire. One had completely blown out the windshield, while another had made contact with the machine gun. Shards of blasted metal peppered Wesley's own torro. Fred tried to provide him some covering fire, but they were coming at them from all directions.

"Take out those rocket launchers," Wesley screamed. Officers were crawling on top of both torroes like ants on a defenseless insect. Tobias was firing his rifle through the windshield, trying to fend them off. Wesley opened his door, spraying bullets through the opening, as Tobias opened his just enough that Wesley could pull him across.

"What are you doing here?" Tobias asked.

"Right now, I'm trying to save your life."

The torroes had them boxed in. They were trapped. While Fred continued to fire, Wesley took control of the steering. Tobias switched the control panel to ramming mode as they pushed their way through officers and torroes. Wesley created an opening just big enough for them to fit through. Once they were through, Tobias switched them back to driving mode.

"Why aren't they chasing us?" Fred questioned, watching his screen.

Tobias pulled up the rear-view camera to see what Fred was looking at.

"Crap. Brace yourselves," he yelled as the ceiling seemed to disintegrate above them. Missiles rained down around them from helicopters above. Fred tried to aim the machine gun at it, but the angle was too steep. The gun couldn't reach that high up.

"They're going to kill us," Wesley said, pushing his way through the fallen concrete rubble.

"No, they're not," Fred said. "Get me over there next to the train. There's a rocket launcher over there. One of the Feds must've dropped it when you tipped the train."

Wesley pushed through the rubble, bobbing and weaving from the missiles. When they were alongside the train, Fred jumped from the torro. This time, he tucked his arms and legs in, rolling along a concrete slab. Wesley tried to maneuver the torro to shield him from the helicopter's guns.

"This is it, Maud. I'm about to make you proud," Fred yelled as he fired the rocket. Wesley's eyes followed the rocket as it lit up the helicopter in a blaze of glory.

"Fred," Tobias shouted. Wesley jerked his head around back toward Fred. A second helicopter was approaching from the distance. Fred's shirt was riddled with red dots as he laid motionless on the ground.

"No, Fred! No," Wesley cried.

"Wesley, we have to go," Tobias said, pulling Wesley back from the window. "We're defenseless if we get in range of the second 'copter's missiles. Don't let Fred's sacrifice be in vain."

Wesley apologized to Fred as he pushed the torro through the debris and into the tunnel. The tunnel shook violently as the helicopter began dropping its missiles. Tobias guided Wesley through the series of tunnels, giving him directions back to Defiant. The tremors soon stopped as the helicopter gave up its assault.

As they got close, thick smoke filled the tunnel. They were unable to see through the blackness. The torro came to an abrupt stop, pressing Wesley and Tobias tightly in their harness. The mound of concrete and ash had come swiftly out of the void. It was too much for the torro to move. Its wheels dug deep into the earth as Wesley tried.

"Looks like we're walking," Wesley said, exiting the torro.

Concrete and twisted steel lined the ground. Glowing red embers radiated eerily through the heavy smoke. The combination of smoke, dust, and ash made it difficult to breathe. Wesley bit down on his shirt, sucking air through the fabric. He and Tobias made their way over the devastation. The smoke began to dissipate as the sunlight shown from above. There were no signs of survivors. No signs of life.

"We have to find the bunker," Tobias said as they trudged through. "It's where they would go in case of an air strike."

After an intense search, Wesley finally found the corner of a large steel door, covered over in debris. As they lifted it away, they were shouting and rapping against the door, listening for survivors. Only silence. Together, they unlatched and lifted the door with the remaining debris. The room inside was dark and still. Dust filled the air.

"Vasher, Damien, Watch, anybody?" Wesley called down the steps of the bunker. The silence was broken by a cough.

"Wesley? Is that you?" Damien called from the darkness.

"I'm so glad to hear your voice. How many of you are down there?"

"Just me and Watch." Damien emerged from the darkness, slowly being pushed up the steps with Watch's assistance.

"Where are the others?" Tobias asked. "Where's Vasher."

"I think Hempton took Vasher. The others..." Watch's voice trailed off.

"We have to get back to the torro," Wesley said, grabbing Damien from Watch. "Maybe we can at least help the others."

As they walked carefully through the smoke and rubble, Watch and Damien told them about the attack on Defiant. All Wesley could think about was Hempton. All he could see in his mind was his smug smile as he marched his army toward his friends.

"Hempton has to be stopped," Wesley said. "All he brings is death and destruction with him. We have to push back. Defiant failed to act against him and look what happened. This will be everything if we don't end this."

33

"WHAT DO YOU MEAN, they're coming? Isn't this the headquarters of the Federal Police?" Michael asked. Myers leaned against the counter, still trying to collect himself.

"You don't understand, Michael. Hempton has staged a coup. He's taken over the Federal Police. It seems my superiors don't appreciate my efforts in finding a cure for their weapon. There are many that still believe Serum V is viable and not dangerous. I tried to show the senators my work, but they refused to see the potential. We must hurry. Michael, I have your daughter standing by on our evacuation route."

"What about the officers outside?" Maps asked.

"There's a reason I only allow certain officers within my gates. Those that are with me are loyal to me. You'll be safe."

Michael quickly grabbed printouts of his work and placed the vial of compound in his pocket. The last time he had seen Myers so frightened was when Natalie made her attempt with the bomb. Michael knew that whatever was coming was deathly serious. Five armed officers stood outside the laboratory as an escort to their evacuation. They ran down the corridor, but Michael stopped short.

"You said Allie was waiting, but what about Rebecca?" he asked.

"I'm sorry, Michael. She's a carrier. There's nothing we can do for her," Myers said.

"You can't, but I can. Maps, go to Allie. I'm right behind you."

A few officers were about to give chase, but Myers stopped them. It seemed that Myers had finally given up on Michael's usefulness in favor of his own safety. Michael was actually glad. He didn't want the officers to slow him down in reaching her. If Myers was right, there wouldn't be much time.

Michael looked through windows as he sprinted past rooms. There were so many patients. He wished he would have been able to help them. So many were left to have their minds slowly drift away. Their realities distorted by chemicals in their brain. He wouldn't let that happen to Rebecca. He wouldn't let her slip away into oblivion.

Michael skidded on his heels, trying to bring himself to a stop. Rebecca was sitting on her bed with her knees tucked under her chin. Michael tried to open the door, but it was locked. A key card was needed to open it, and he hadn't passed a nurse in a long time. They, too, were fleeing for their lives.

"I'm coming right back," he told Rebecca through the small window on her door. She sat on her bed, watching him.

Michael took note of her room number so that he could find his way back much faster. He ran back down the hall to the nurses' station. The hallways were vacant. There was no running, no screaming, no sound whatsoever. Then there was a ding. Someone was getting off the elevator. A short man in a white coat was lackadaisically stepping out, reading over a clipboard. With his pencil line mustache, Michael recognized him immediately.

"Dr. LeFleur," Michael shouted, breaking into an all-out sprint. The startled doctor threw his clipboard down and began running away from him. Michael ran as hard and as fast as he could, but with so much distance between them, he was barely making any ground. The doctor slowed ever so slightly to turn a corner, and Michael tackled him to the floor.

"I need this," he said, snatching the key card from his neck.

"No, you can't do that."

LeFleur latched on to Michael's leg, struggling to retrieve the lanyard. Michael pushed him off, but again he clawed his way. To free himself, Michael backhanded the doctor across his jaw bone. The doctor loosened his grip, and Michael ran back to Rebecca.

Nerves were beginning to get the better of him, as it took him a few tries to get the key card to work. As he opened the door, Rebecca ran to him, embracing him tightly and kissing him deeply. In that moment, all the world faded. He wrapped his arms around her, holding her close against him. In all the time he had spent trying to save her, he forgot to do the most important thing—love her. He placed his hand on her cheek, rubbing it gently with his thumb, before running it through her long, auburn hair. His fingers glided gently through her curls.

"Where have you been, Michael?" she asked, burying her head in his chest. Tears filled her eyes. Michael could feel them soaking through his shirt.

"In the wrong place trying to make it right, when I should have been here with you." He kissed her once more. "I've been typical Michael. I've been working, trying to save a life. This time—yours." He pulled the compound from his pocket. "You've contracted a virus that affects your memories. Without this, you'll slowly fade away. I couldn't let that happen. It seems like all I ever do is lose you when all I've ever wanted to do was love you. You're my heart, Rebecca. You and Allie are everything to me. I'm sorry I haven't been there, but I promise you there's nowhere else I've wanted to be."

Michael stepped into the hallway and gathered an empty syringe from the supply cabinet on the wall. He filled it with the compound and pressed the needle to Rebecca's skin. He could only hope that the compound worked and that it was safe. He had never gotten a chance to test it, and he only had the one.

"This may hurt a little," he told her as he administered the compound.

Rebecca's face turned pale. Her body began to convulse as her eyes glazed over. She fell back against the bed. Michael scooped her up in his arms.

"What have I done? No, Rebecca. No. Stay with me."

The convulsions stopped as quickly as they had started. Michael held her tightly with his face buried in her shoulder. He was afraid to look. He couldn't live with himself if the thing he had worked so hard for had killed her instead. He felt a gentle touch on his cheek. He lifted his head up. Her brown eyes were staring back into his.

"Michael," she said softly.

"Becca. You're okay." Michael breathed a sigh of relief. He had never felt such terror, even with all that the Federal Police had put him through. "Rebecca, we have to hurry. The Federal Police are coming. I have a friend who's taking care of Allie, but we have to get to them."

Rebecca lifted herself up from the bed, surprisingly strong after her episode. The two ran as fast as they could from the Center for Wellness to the connecting room.

"My name is Michael Anderton. Where is Myers' evacuation route?" Michael asked the guard watching over the room.

"Down there. That door. West wing. Security code is one zero one nine. Go, Michael. We're all counting on you."

Michael and Rebecca ran down the stairs and through the door the guard had guided them to. As Michael entered the doorway, Myers came barging in from the entrance way.

"Thomas, they're coming. They've stormed the gate. Michael, what are you doing here? Go. Get to safety," Myers yelled, running toward Michael. Gunfire echoed as Thomas began firing on Myers' pursuers. After only a few shots, Thomas fell from his perch.

"Hello, Mr. Secretary," Hempton said as he entered the room. Michael hid in the doorway. "It seems you have forgotten what your position has entitled to you."

"Listen, Hempton. What they're telling you is wrong. Serum V is dangerous."

"While that may be your opinion, my job is to fulfill the duties of our organization. It seems somewhere along the way you've begun to ignore those duties."

"I was doing my job. As secretary of security, I was to look out for the good of the people."

"No, Mr. Secretary. I'm afraid you're mistaken. We have the good of the people at the forefront of everything we do. Your efforts have undermined us. You have let rebel groups form under your watch that has taken many resources to put an end to. You have exposed our secrets to those not privy to such information, all the while attempting to counteract our strength. You have failed in your duties, Mr. Secretary, so I have come to relieve you of them."

"No, Hempton. Don't."

"Don't beg, Mr. Secretary. It's not becoming of you. For your crimes of treason and conspiracy, you have been sentenced to death by execution. Goodbye, Mr. Secretary."

"No," Michael shouted, darting from the door. His shoulder collided with Myers as the sound of the shot pierced his ears. Michael fell to the floor, clutching Myers in his arms. The crimson stain pooled underneath him. Michael was too slow.

"Michael…" Myers wheezed as blood dripped from the corners of his lips. "You must go. Go west to the mountains. Get away from the Fed…" His eyes faded.

"Mr. Anderton, what a surprise it is to see you," Hempton said.

Michael stared at Hempton in horror. An army of black uniforms stood behind him. Myers and his body-guard laid dead on the floor.

"It's been a long time, Mr. Anderton. I suppose you owe a great deal of thanks to your rebel allies for helping you escape our clutches the last time we met. Few people get to return home after time spent in the Void. If it weren't for that little incident, none of this may have even been necessary. However, Mr. Anderton, your services are no longer required either. As such, I also sentence you to death by execution."

Michael looked down the barrel of Hempton's pistol. His heart stopped. All time stood still. The bullet pierced the air swiftly. The sound was deafening. He felt the breath slipping from his lungs. His body was jerked backward. And yet, he was alive. A hand was pulling him back by the collar of his shirt. A door slammed shut in front of him.

"Get up, Michael. We have to run," Rebecca shouted.

She ran to the large vault door and punched in the code. Michael saw the wooden door before him open as Hempton stepped through. He pushed Rebecca forward into the vault as a bullet ricocheted off the door. He grabbed the big door and pulled with all his might. Sparks flew as a second bullet collided with metal just in front of his face. Rebecca grabbed onto him, pulling him and the door. Michael collapsed to his knees at the clunk of the seal. He waited for Hempton to open the vault at any moment.

Rebecca urged him on. The vault led to a dimly lit stairwell leading deep underground. Michael kissed Rebecca, and the two ran hard down the steps. If this truly was Myers' evacuation route, Allie and Maps would be waiting for them at the end.

34

THE TUNNEL WAS LONG, dark, and musty. Myers must have had it built in case of such an emergency. Judging by the amount of dust, it had never been used. Although the tunnel was quiet behind them, Rebecca had become worried. The footprints on the ground showed signs of a struggle. Michael saw them too. They both feared for Allie's safety, but Myers had assured him that she would be there. If Hempton and his men couldn't get through the vault, she had to be safe, Michael had assured himself.

The tunnel led to a second vault door. This one had been left cracked open. Michael rushed to push it open. Empty caverns stood on the other side. There was still no sign of Allie or Maps.

"Look," Rebecca said, pointing up at the top of a pillar. Etched in the stone, barely visible, were tiny arrows. "That has to be the way."

Miles of vacant, abandoned caverns sprawled out beneath the city. It seemed as if they stretched throughout all Metropolian. Evidence of the war shown on some of the walls and pillars. Large metal beams ran from the floor up to the ceiling. Michael surmised that part of Metropolian had been built on top of the ruins of an older city destroyed in the war. The desolation grew worse the farther they went. Rebecca continued to guide them, searching high and low for arrows scratched in the bricks.

"Tell me we're going to find her," she said. "Tell me we didn't leave our daughter behind in the hands of that lunatic."

"We're going to find her, Becca. I promise. Myers said that…"

"And where was Myers? Why would he protect her and not himself?"

It was evident that Rebecca's fears were beginning to get the better of her. The truth was, Michael didn't want to ask himself that question. He had expected her to be right on the other side of the door. They had walked for miles, and yet there was nothing.

"Just have a little faith, Becca. She's alright. I know it," Michael said, taking Rebecca in his arms. Somehow, deep within him, he knew she was safe. No matter how much his fears pulled at him, something kept urging him forward. It was as if a tiny voice kept telling him to take one more step. It was the same feeling he had felt before. She was safe in Myers' fortress then. He knew she would be safely waiting for him now.

Sunlight broke through the dusty haze of the caverns as fresh air hit them like a refreshing wave. Birds sang their songs in the distance, among the shrubbery that waited for them outside. Michael crawled through the hole first and then helped Rebecca out. Metropolian was far in the distance. Black helicopters buzzed around it like gnats.

"Daddy," the little voice said, spinning Michael around on his heels.

"Allie," Michael and Rebecca cried at once. She ran to them, and the three embraced each other tightly.

"I'm never letting either of you go, ever again," Michael said as he kissed them both.

"No kisses for me, thanks," Maps said, walking up to their huddle.

"Maps, I'm glad to see you made it," Michael said. "Thank you for taking care of Allie."

"She's a spirited one, I'll give her that," he chuckled. "I think we fought all the way here. I pretty much had to drag her along, because all she wanted was to get back to you. I think I know who she takes after."

"What about the others? Any more of Myers' officers make it out?"

"No, just me and her. They gave me instructions to follow the arrows and then left us. They went back for Myers."

"It was no use. Hempton's in charge now. Myers is..." Michael chose his words wisely to avoid scaring Allie. Maps nodded in understanding. "What now?" Michael asked, looking at the greenery surrounding him.

"I say we get back to Defiant. Maybe they can make something of all this. I need them to help form a plan to get back to the fortress for Natalie."

"I'm sorry, Maps. I used all of the compound I had on Rebecca."

"You can make more, can't you?"

"If Defiant can make me a lab." Michael reached into his pocket, touching the corner of the folded paper. His formula had survived the escape, he just had to find the chemicals to recreate the compound. "But, how are we supposed to get to Defiant? The way they're circling over Metropolian, there's no way we can get to the train station."

"Don't worry, I can get us there."

"Of course you can, Maps," Michael retorted. "I suppose you are fitting of your name, just like Watch."

"Actually, it's just short for Mapson. James Mapson. It sort of stuck with me."

Michael threw Allie up onto his shoulders and took Rebecca by the hand. For the moment, they were free. They had evaded Hempton and the Federal Police. They weren't actively being chased. Michael felt like for the first time in what seemed like a long time, he could breathe.

The smell of the earth and plants reminded him of home. He missed their shack. He missed the simplicity, but he knew he had a job to do. He was anxious to get back to Defiant and back to Wesley. He knew Wesley would be happy to see that they had succeeded. It seemed that their adventure was far from over, though. If Myers was right, he had to come up with a cure for the virus before it was too late. Michael had a hand in its creation, so he felt it was his responsibility to make it right.

Maps led them through the barren terrain. The vegetation had still yet to fully return from the winter. It crunched beneath their feet as they walked. It seemed like they had left civilization behind.

Amidst the still, dead grass, Michael found an unlikely sight. A little purple flower sprung up among it. Michael lightly plucked it and gave it to Allie. He tucked it gently into her hair while she smiled at him. It warmed his heart to see her smile. Her world had been completely shattered. She had seen so much that Michael had tried to shield her from, and yet she was still able to smile. That gave Michael the hope for the future that he had lacked for some time.

Those hopes faded when off in the distance rose a plume of black smoke from the center of a fallen city. Michael had never gotten to see the outside of Defiant's headquarters, but he knew it had been underneath a collapsing train station. That station must have been at the center of the city. Maps was running hard for it. With Allie on his shoulders, Michael couldn't keep up. If the Federal Police had found Defiant's headquarters, all hope was lost. There was no one left to resist against Hempton's tyranny. There was no way for him to create a cure to save the people.

He watched as Maps continued to run. Just beyond the hill, the big black behemoth broke over the edge. The metal plating radiated in the sunlight. The machine gun moved left and right, searching for a target. The torro was headed straight for them. Maps dropped to his knees, hiding in the tall grass. Michael told Rebecca and Allie to do the same. They had to stay out of sight.

Move, Maps. Move, Michael thought.

Maps had ducked his head down, trying to conceal himself. He couldn't see that he was directly in the path of the torro. Michael ran for it, telling Rebecca and Allie to stay. He had to either get Maps to move or change the course of the torro.

He ran, waving his arms and shouting at Maps. Maps saw him but so did the torro. The machine gun aimed itself at him. Michael dropped to the dirt. The torro was coming for him. He crouched low and ran behind the grass. Buried within it was a fallen brick pillar. He tripped, rolling end over end through the field. As he regained his composure, the torro stood before him as a black wall.

This is it, he thought.

The torro rolled to a stop before him. Michael took a deep breath. The top hatch opened.

"Michael," Wesley shouted. "You're alive."

Michael's heart was still racing. It was more than a pleasant surprise to see Wesley in the torro.

"What happened to Defiant?" Michael asked.

"Hempton destroyed it. Only the four of us are left," Wesley said as the others emerged from the torro. "What about Myers?"

"Hempton. He's taken over the Federal Police. He killed Myers."

"That man," Wesley said through gritted teeth. "Someone has to stop him."

"I agree, but there's nothing we can do. Defiant's gone, and there's only eight of us. Before he died, Myers told me to go to the mountains. Something's coming, Wesley, and it's up to me to stop it."

"I can't go with you. I have to stop Hempton."

"Wesley, listen to yourself. He's ruthless, and now he's the head of the Federal Police! Come with us."

"I once knew a man who was willing to risk everything to save his daughter. He was brave enough to stand up to the head of the Federal Police without question. He inspired me. I have to do this, Michael. I have to do this for Joanna. I have to do this for Fred. I have to do this for me."

"Don't worry, Michael. He won't be going alone," Tobias said. "Defiant were my people. Because of Hempton, I lost them, and Vasher, and Cade. It's what we have to do."

Wesley climbed down from the torro. He stuck out his hand toward Michael. Michael looked down at it, then embraced him tightly.

"You've been my best friend, Wesley. If there was any way I could talk you out of it, I would. I'll see you again after all of this is over."

"When this is over, my friend," Wesley said, returning the gesture. He watched as Rebecca and Allie were walking toward the hill. "Take the torro. Get Rebecca and Allie as far away as you can. Tell Allie her Uncle Wesley loves her."

Wesley and Tobias began their trek toward Metropolian, the way Michael had come from. Wesley hugged Allie and Rebecca as he walked by, before fading into the distance. Michael and Maps boarded the torro, where Damien and Watch were already at work getting the systems running. Maps drove the torro over to pick up Rebecca and Allie.

It was a tight squeeze for the six of them in the four seated torro. Allie sat on her mother's lap, while Damien propped himself up on the boxes of ammo. He was out of his wheelchair, but he was still on the road to recovery. He kept it folded neatly in the corner. Watch argued with him, trying to give up her seat, but he wouldn't have it. Michael watched as the terrain made its transition from grass flatlands to the rocky mountainside.

"There's a settlement just over these mountains," Watch said, reading off information from the torro. "We're outside of the USF, so we're no longer in Federal Police jurisdiction."

This is it, Michael thought as he nestled into his seat. They were safe.

The Story Continues…

The Resilient

Into the Forgotten

Available

December 2018

Adam K. Ogden

A quick word from the author...

"Thank you for reading my first novel. No story, no matter how thought out or well written, is worth anything without those that take the time to read it. You are greatly appreciated, and I hope you are as excited as I am to continue this fantastic journey!"

-Adam K. Ogden

Please leave me a review through whichever retailer you've purchased this book from. More reviews mean this story can reach more people.

Also, follow me to keep up with updates and more stories that have yet to be released!

Like my Facebook Page:
Adam K. Ogden

Or visit
www.adamkogden.com

Thank you!

Adam K. Ogden

Adam Ogden is a writer, musician, business owner, and engineering graduate. He has been a long-time reader of action adventure stories, following along with multiple well-known series. Those stories were, in part, an inspiration for this story.

The story of *The Resilient* came to him one night in a dream. As he began putting the dream into words on a page, the story took on a life of its own. It carried, even the author, on an unexpected journey.

This is his first novel, which was carried to completion. This novel has sparked a new adventure, as such novel could not be contained in one book. It has spawned a series to follow the daring crooks and turns it leads down. Other titles have also been planned outside of The Resilient series and will be released shortly.